SEAL TEAM SEVEN
DIRECT ACTION

KEITH DOUGLASS

SEAL TEAM SEVEN: DIRECT ACTION

A Berkley Book / published by arrangement with the author

PRINTING HISTORY
Berkley edition / January 1997

The Putnam Berkley World Wide Web site address is
http://www.berkley.com/berkley

ISBN: 0-425-15605-2

BERKLEY®
Berkley Books are published by The Berkley Publishing Group,
200 Madison Avenue, New York, New York 10016.
BERKLEY and the "B" design
are trademarks belonging to Berkley Publishing Corporation.

PRINTED IN THE UNITED STATES OF AMERICA

10 9 8 7 6 5 4 3 2

HUNDREDS OF HOURS AND THOUSANDS OF ROUNDS . . .

. . . expended in training saved Blake Murdock's life. He didn't think about it; he just fired until his man went down and then shifted to another target. First everyone with a weapon, then everyone standing, then everyone moving. The M-4 magazine ran out just as a screaming face loomed in front of him. The M-16 took a magazine change faster than any other weapon in the world, but there wasn't enough time. Murdock's left finger was on the trigger of the M203 grenade launcher, and he yanked it. The recoil banged against his shoulder and the figure in front of him went down with twenty buckshot in his chest from the 40mm M576 multipurpose round. So close was the range that the shot group was the size of a fist, and the plastic pellet cup and cap were blown right into the wound.

Murdock stood panting, smoke curling from the end of his suppressor, the room reeking of burnt gunpowder, dead bodies all over the place.

SEAL TEAM SEVEN
Direct Action

Don't miss these other explosive *SEAL TEAM SEVEN* missions:

SEAL TEAM SEVEN,
SPECTER and
NUCFLASH

By Keith Douglass

CARRIER
VIPER STRIKE
ARMAGEDDON MODE
FLAME-OUT
MAELSTROM
COUNTDOWN

THE SEAL TEAM SEVEN SERIES:

SEAL TEAM SEVEN
SPECTER
NUCFLASH
DIRECT ACTION

"I don't think they play at all fairly," Alice began in a rather complaining tone, "and they don't seem to have any rules in particular; at least, if there are, nobody attends to them—and you've no idea how confusing it is. . . ."

Lewis Carroll
Alice in Wonderland

1

Friday, August 18

0205 hours
The Red Sea harbor of Port Sudan
Islamic Republic of the Sudan

When Lieutenant Blake Murdock made up his mind to be a Navy SEAL, back when he was a midshipman at the U.S. Naval Academy, he knew he'd be spending a lot of time in the ocean. But it never occurred to him that he'd ever have to swim through raw sewage. Unfortunately, the cold hard reality was that the world's ports and harbors were prime SEAL hunting grounds, and in most of them waste was treated by flushing it into the ocean.

Swimming toward the entrance to the harbor of Port Sudan, Murdock put the thought of whatever he might be sharing the water with right out of his mind. It was the only way; you just made sure all your immunizations were up to date. And with each kick of his fins Murdock was keenly aware of the gamma globulin shot that felt like a golf ball wedged in his right ass cheek.

Being a SEAL was living proof that you could get used to anything. If you couldn't, you never made it out of the Basic Underwater Demolition/SEAL course, or BUD/S for short. If you looked like the fastidious type, the instructors found a nice big pile of dog shit for you to roll around in during morning PT, and allowed you to wear it on your fatigues for the rest of the day. You didn't have to like it, they would explain, never kindly; you just had to do it. If not, you could always quit.

Yes, BUD/S was a sure cure for whatever fears had a hold of you. Like anyone with a fair imagination, it would have been understandable for Murdock to be a little nervous about the fact that the reefs of the Red Sea teemed with large numbers of some of the most aggressive shark species in the world, and that they liked to feed at night. But during BUD/S, one leg of a five-mile night surface swim had taken him right through a barking and splashing rookery of *real* seals—the buffet table of the great white shark. After that he didn't waste any more time thinking about sharks, especially ones he couldn't see.

And Murdock had his hands full just doing his job. He was swimming fifteen feet below the surface of the water, concentrating on the attack board he held before him. The attack board was how SEALs found their way through the seas: a piece of molded plastic with two hand grips, mounting a large bubble compass in the center with a digital combination depth gauge/watch above it. Although all the instruments were luminous, sometimes the nighttime darkness of the sea swallowed their faint light, so the board also had a tubular plastic holder for a Cyalume chemical light stick. Twisting a knob opened a lengthwise slit in the holder, allowing Murdock to regulate the amount of light that was cast onto the board.

Murdock had been following a compass bearing and keeping the time, since he knew exactly how long it took him to swim a hundred meters. Tied to him by a six-foot-long buddy line was Electrician's Mate Second Class William Higgins, the squad radio operator, known as the Professor to the rest of the 3rd Platoon, SEAL Team Seven, because he enjoyed reading the kinds of books that had been rammed down their throats in school. Lightly grasping Murdock's elbow as he swam beside him, Higgins was counting each kick of his fins as a backup to Murdock's navigation, knowing exactly how many kicks it took them to travel a hundred meters.

Murdock and Higgins were each wearing the Enhanced Draeger LAR-V underwater breathing apparatus. It was a pure oxygen rebreather that recycled exhaled air and left no telltale trail of bubbles. The LAR-V had been in the SEAL inventory for years, but the new enhanced model had a larger oxygen bottle with thirty percent greater capacity for long swims. The Draegers were worn on their chests; their weapons were strapped across their backs.

Since the SEALs were planning on leaving the water, they swam in the new three-color desert camouflage uniform, tan and pale green with streaks of pink. Sage-green fire-resistant Nomex flight gloves protected their hands. Their swim fins were strapped over regular-issue jungle boots.

Nearing the end of one compass leg, Murdock paused to employ his last and most accurate navigation aid. It was a plastic box the size of a cellular phone: a MUGR, or Miniature Underwater GPS Receiver, known to the SEALs as Mugger. He unreeled the tiny floating wire antenna and sent it off to the surface. When it got there, the set picked up signals from the closest four Global Positioning Satellites and told him within ten feet exactly where he was on the earth. The Mugger could also be programmed to navigate an entire route. All you had to do was follow the arrow on the screen. A lot of SEALs liked to use it exclusively, but Murdock only allowed 3rd Platoon to use theirs to back up their navigation. He hated the idea of trailing the antenna on the surface, even though it was nearly invisible. Besides, something might go wrong with the set. Satellites might not be in line, the batteries might go dead, anything. The Mugger provided peace of mind, and saved him from having to periodically surface and stick his face mask out of the water to check his bearings, what SEALs called making a peek.

Murdock was right where he was supposed to be, so he went back to the attack board, took up a new compass heading, gave Higgins a squeeze on the arm, and resumed the swim.

The water was pitch black. Murdock couldn't see a thing except the dim glow of the attack board. Without the steady pressure on his elbow he'd never have known Higgins was right beside him. The other fourteen SEALs of 3rd platoon, seven other swim pairs, were also in the water, but Murdock and Higgins wouldn't see any of them until they reached the target.

Murdock knew they were now inside the harbor, though there were no propeller sounds or any other indications of that. The docks and cargo handling facilities were on the coastal spit of land to his right. The harbor channel ran both left and right from the Red Sea entrance, curving around a central peninsula that was the city of Port Sudan. And that was where Murdock, Higgins, and the rest of 3rd Platoon were headed. The waterfront.

Since the military coup of June 1989, the Sudan had been ruled by a radical Islamic regime that opened its arms to every terrorist group in the region: the fundamentalists trying to overthrow the Egyptian government, the Islamic militants who had learned their trade fighting the Russians in Afghanistan and now worked against their home countries, Palestinian extremists opposed to any peace with Israel. Even the bombers of the World Trade Center in New York City had Sudanese links.

At Erkowit, sixty miles south of Port Sudan in the picturesque Red Sea hills, the Sudanese Government had taken over a luxury resort hotel and converted it to a terrorist training camp/rest center.

Israeli intelligence had picked up word that a four-man terrorist cell had finished training and was on its way to a bombing campaign against American targets in Europe. The cell was staying at a safe house on the Port Sudan waterfront, waiting for the merchant ship that would take it out of the country. The Israeli Mossad had passed the information on to the CIA through normal liaison.

As he started to run up against the rocky bottom of the Port Sudan waterfront, Murdock took another GPS shot with the Mugger. He and Higgins were right on the button. Murdock headed for the surface, very slowly, since the microorganisms found in all tropical waters became phosphorescent when agitated. Not that any microorganisms could have survived the Port Sudan harbor muck anyway.

Murdock broke the surface, just for an instant. The nighttime air temperature was around ninety degrees. The water *smelled* like shit too. The target was directly in front of him, a two-story waterfront villa that dated back to the colonial period, when the British established Port Sudan to export cotton, sorghum, and sesame. The Sudan now had friendly relations only with the other outlaw states of the world, and even though the port was the country's only import and export window to the world, international political isolation and economic mismanagement had slowed trade to a trickle.

The villa, once the showcase home of a managing director, was crumbling along with the rest of the city. It had once been white, and was now gray and peeling. The villa's address was the Sharia Kabhashi Eissa, the waterfront road. The harbor was a perfect avenue of approach for Navy SEALs, but Murdock guessed that the terrorists weren't very concerned. The West had always been reactive, moving only after a terrorist outrage occurred. Having the chance to finally do something proactive was making Murdock's palms itch.

From the water, the rocky shore of the harbor swept up to a ten-foot-high seawall and the lawn of the villa behind it. A simple stone stairway provided access from the shore to the lawn. It met an ornate stone balustrade, about three feet high, which acted like a fence between the lawn and the seawall. The balustrade tied into a seven-foot-high solid stone wall which boxed in the other three sides of the grounds.

The Israeli Mossad had prepared a target folder on the house in case their SEAL-equivalent Ha'Kommando Ha'Yami, or Naval Commandos, ever needed to make a nighttime visit. Just as well, from Murdock's point of view, since the Israelis excelled in Special Operations intelligence, and the CIA did not.

According to the folder the stone stairway from the shore to the lawn was both alarmed and booby-trapped. A Kalashnikov-armed guard patrolled the lawn and balustrade, and another guard was stationed on a second-floor balcony that overlooked the lawn. The only way to enter the house from the lawn was through an inch-thick cast-iron door, always locked. The windows were covered with iron security grates and shut tight, except for the old and overworked air conditioners that rattled away in a few of them. The grounds were well lighted. The guards were not equipped with night-vision equipment, and if they had once been good, they were now casual and sloppy after endless days of unchanging routine.

Murdock had taken all that into account in his planning. Also the fact that in the tropics people did their living in the relative cool of the evening and their sleeping during the hot times of the day. The terrorists were no exception.

"They practically never sleep," the CIA briefer had told him. "There's always a couple of them up shooting the shit or screwing around."

Murdock obviously couldn't attack in the daytime. But he could during those golden hours between 1:00 and 5:00 AM when the human brain was always at its worst.

He was going to go in fast and hard, and had picked his weapons accordingly. Normally in an enclosed-house and close-quarters battle situation such as this, the weapon of choice would be the German Heckler & Koch MP-5 9mm submachine gun—in this case the MP-5SD4 with an integral sound suppressor. The model was customized for the Navy SEALs, with special stock, handgrip, safety, and tritium dots on the sights for night and low-light shooting. But the problem with the MP-5 was that the sound suppressor took a lot of velocity off the round. The effective range was less than fifty meters, and sometimes the rounds would even bounce off a car windshield. Even the non-suppressed MP-5 wasn't much good past 150 meters.

In a house that wasn't a problem, and the low-powered 9mm pistol round was ideal since it wouldn't be punching through any walls and hitting any good guys. But if things went sour, you were at a disadvantage. The SEALs of Team Six discovered this while assaulting the Governor General's mansion during the invasion of Grenada. They were quickly surrounded by enemy troops who had a great time shooting up the mansion with assault rifles and heavy machine guns. The majority of the SEALs, who were armed with MP-5's, couldn't shoot back because the enemy was too far away for their submachine guns to reach. Only continuous fire support from Air Force AC-130 Spectre gunships kept them from being overrun.

Murdock didn't have a Spectre or any other support available, so he wasn't going to make that mistake. The now-standard sixteen-man SEAL platoon could be broken down into two eight-man squads, First and Second. Each squad could be further broken down into two four-man fire teams. Murdock had armed his First Squad and one fire team of the Second, the assault element, with the short, sliding-stock carbine version of the M-16A2, the M-4A1. An older version had been called the CAR-15 in Vietnam. And each weapon had an M203 40mm grenade launcher mounted beneath the barrel. Because he still wanted to keep things quiet, Murdock added the Knight's Armament Company M-16 sound suppressor, made expressly for the SEALs. It was a stainless-steel tube that screwed onto the flash-hider threads of all M-16-series rifles. It was just eight inches long and one and three-quarter inches in diameter, self-draining after immersion in water, and unlike other suppressors, capable of handling full automatic fire without any damage or impairment in the noise reduction. The final accessory was the AN/PAQ-4 laser aiming light, which screwed underneath the M-16 carrying handle and projected a fine beam of laser light visible only through night-vision goggles.

What remained of Second Squad, commanded by Lieutenant j.g. Ed DeWitt, was the security and support element. Since they would have to weigh in with heavy firepower in the event of trouble, DeWitt and Chief Petty Officer "Kos" Kosciuszko were armed with the Heckler & Koch HK-21A1 machine gun in 7.62mm NATO. Murdock had taken advantage of his attachment to the CIA to dump his SEAL-standard M-60E3 machine guns. The latest M-60's were flimsy, and needed to be almost completely rebuilt every ten thousand rounds to maintain their reliability. The HK-21, on the other hand, in use by SEAL Team Six since Grenada, was just as light as the SEAL chopped-barrel M-60. It was the Mercedes-Benz of machine guns. AT-4 antitank rockets and claymore antipersonnel mines completed their armament. The two snipers, Quartermaster 1st Class Martin "Magic" Brown, and Torpedoman's Mate 2nd Class Red Nicholson, were packing some very special toys.

Each SEAL carried his equipment in a nylon mesh American Body Armor special operations vest. There were six two-magazine pouches across the chest for those armed with M-4's, and large pouches for the drum-fed belts of the machine gunners. A radio pouch in back held an encrypted Motorola MX-300 walkie-talkie in a waterproof bag, and grenade pouches were on the web belt that secured the bottom part of the vest. Everyone's backup weapon, the SIG-Sauer P-226 9mm pistol, rested in a strap-down nylon thigh holster.

They wore no body armor, no matter how much anyone would have liked it. You can't swim in body armor.

Murdock and Higgins moved closer to the shore, and soon the water around them was filled with SEAL swim pairs, brought to that exact point by their Mugger GPS sets. They linked up with Murdock and then spread out in a line facing the villa.

Finally the last pair checked in, and Murdock's gut relaxed slightly. Any pair that couldn't make it to the target by the designated cutoff time was supposed to head back out to sea for pickup. Murdock was glad it hadn't been necessary. It was a complication his central nervous system didn't need.

Murdock gave a signal down the line. While still breathing from the Draeger, he and everyone else unstrapped their units, weight belts, and swim fins. If things didn't go right from the start, they'd have to move very quickly. He checked his dive watch. Murdock had a firm rule against attacking on the hour. A few more minutes and they'd go.

2

Friday, August 18

0308 hours
Port Sudan

Murdock signaled the man next to him. Magic Brown, the platoon's best sniper, crabbed forward until he was almost out of the water. Brown slowly and carefully opened the bolt of his McMillan M89 sniper rifle to allow the water to drain from the barrel and chamber. The M89 was a purpose-built silent sniping rifle, 7.62mm NATO, with a shortened barrel and a fixed, factory-mounted sound suppressor. Firing subsonic ammunition, it was good for a head shot at 150 yards, which was the state of the art for a suppressed sniping rifle. It was about as loud as a Daisy BB gun.

Brown brought the weapon up into a good sitting position, with his elbows braced against his knees. He peered through the Litton M921 3-power starlight scope mounted on the weapon. Another good SEAL piece of gear. With a body made of hard Teflon, it was the only electronic night-vision sight in the world designed to be completely immersible in seawater to a depth of fifty meters.

Murdock was watching through his own Litton waterproof single-tube night-vision goggle. The small single eyepiece covering only his right eye solved the main problem of night-vision goggles. If you were wearing NVGs and had to take them off for any reason, your night vision was gone for up to half an hour. And if a flare or light went off in front of you while wearing them, you were temporarily blinded by the flash of magnified light. But with one NVG tube on your shooting eye and the other eye clear, you were good to go in any situation.

Through the lime-green scene in Murdock's NVG, he could see the lawn guard moving toward the balustrade. The guard was looking out at the harbor, though not down below the seawall. Murdock felt as much as heard the muffled pop beside him, and the guard on the second-floor balcony dropped with the spastic twitching that comes from a brain shot.

At the clattering sound of the body and rifle hitting the balcony, the lawn guard spun around to look. There was another pop farther off to Murdock's right. Red Nicholson had fired his McMillan M89, putting a 7.62mm hollowpoint in the back of the guard's head. The guard slumped to the grass without a sound. Magic Brown had already worked his bolt and was ready for a follow-up shot. It wasn't needed. Not that SEALs were overly concerned about such things, but the hollowpoint bullets were perfectly legal. Contrary to popular belief, terrorists, guerrillas, and irregulars were not protected by the Geneva Conventions.

Several more pops came from Nicholson's vicinity. Red was right in line with the gap between the villa and its neighbor. An electrical transformer stood in full view on a light pole, and Nicholson was quietly shooting the transformer casing full of holes with his McMillan. As the cooling oil leaked out of the transformer, the unit blew with a sizzling crack and haloed flash of blue light. All the lights in the neighborhood went out, everyone hopefully thinking that it was just another Port Sudan power outage.

Even though all the SEALs by now had their walkie-talkies,

earpieces, and microphones on, Murdock hadn't needed to give any orders. Chief Petty Officer "Kos" Kosciuszko and Lieutenant j.g. Ed DeWitt swept out of the water, dropped their diving rigs on the shore, and began boosting the assault element over the seawall.

First over was Chief Petty Officer Tom Roselli, "Razor" to his friends. No one in the villa fell under that heading. Right behind him was Machinist's Mate 2nd Class David "Jaybird" Sterling. They sprinted across the lawn directly toward the cast-iron door to the villa. It took them only seconds to apply a cutting charge of lead sheath explosive over each of the hinges of the door. This was a triangular strip of high-velocity explosive sheathed in metal. The point of the triangle focused a shape-charge effect. The sheath blew a linear cut only as wide as a pencil, but deep enough to slice a steel building girder in half. Once the sheaths were on, the SEALs hung air-mattress tubes that they'd filled with seawater over them. These would drastically muffle the sound of the explosions. The final touch was a tiny charge to the bottom of the door to flip it backward out of the way.

Murdock went over the wall right behind Razor and Jaybird. Chief Kosciuszko, who had the same approximate build as a mountain gorilla, almost threw him right over the balustrade. Following up after him were the rest of 1st Squad: Professor Higgins, Hospital Corpsman 2nd Class "Doc" Ellsworth, Minemen 2nd Class Scotty Frazier and Greg Johnson, and Gunner's Mate 3rd Class Al Adams. Gunner's Mate First Class Miguel Fernandez, Radioman 1st Class Ron Holt, and Seamen Joe Lampedusa and Ross Lincoln from 2nd Squad were also part of the assault element. There was no confusion or hesitation. After days and nights of intensive rehearsals on a mock-up, with every move choreographed like a Broadway musical, there had better not be.

Ed DeWitt, Chief Kosciuszko, and the two snipers would hang back to cover the water, the grounds, and the exits from the villa. When during the planning DeWitt had complained about being left out of the assault assignment, Murdock had just grinned and told him it was his military fate. The lieutenant was always going to choose to be the bride, and the j.g. would always be the bridesmaid.

By the time everyone was over the wall the charge was ready, the assault element crouched next to the side of the villa in a formation called the "train." One man directly behind the other, right hand on his weapon and the left clasped to the shoulder of the man in front. Higgins squeezed Murdock's shoulder, a signal passed up the line letting him know that everyone behind was ready. Murdock squeezed Sterling's shoulder, and Jaybird signaled Roselli to fire the charge.

The chief was holding a flash-tube firing device, a hand grenade-type fuse attached to twenty feet of thin hollow plastic tube with a blasting cap on the other end. When you pulled the pin and let the spoon fly free, a powder flare shot down the tube and detonated the charge instantaneously, but with you a safe distance away. Just the thing for a dynamic entry, and a lot better than standing around tapping your toes waiting for a time fuse to go off.

Razor Roselli fired the charge. The ground rocked, but there was just a heavy *whomp* instead of the usual deafening crack. The air filled with rain from the water tamping.

Murdock followed Sterling through the mist and smoke into the door opening. The house was completely dark. The butt of his M-4 was locked into his shoulder, and the laser aiming dot looked like a searchlight in the green field of the NVG.

Designed for the tropics, the villa was open and airy, with high ceilings and open doorways. Roselli and Sterling disappeared into the nearest room. Everyone's microphone was voice-activated. As he sped down the hallway, Murdock heard Roselli's voice. "Room one, clear; moving."

The next room down the hall, the large living room, belonged to Murdock and Higgins. Doc Ellsworth and his fire team went pounding up the stairs to the second floor. Fernandez and his fire team split off and headed for the kitchen and front of the house.

Murdock ran toward the doorway, as he'd done a hundred times in rehearsal. He'd go through diagonally, take a step to the right, and slam his back against the wall. His sector of fire started at the right-hand corner of the room and swept to the center. Higgins would do the same on the left side of the doorway. The firing would be single-shot, unlike the movies where everyone blows off whole magazines on full auto. With an assault rifle fired on automatic, the first round goes into the target but then the upward force of the recoil sends all the other rounds high. A trained shooter could put out almost the same rate of fire on single-shot, one after the other, as fast as the sights could be centered and the trigger squeezed, except that all the rounds would be going into the target.

It all went according to plan, but when Murdock began scanning for targets, the pitch-dark room viewed through his goggles turned into a fucking convention center. It was full of shouting people who knew something was going on and were trying, with little success, to get organized in the darkness. Murdock was glad he was the only one who could see. He shot the first man on his right, the suppressor only giving off a quick muffled snap.

Then a flashlight came on. Murdock closed his goggled eye, opened the other, and took down the man with the light. Unbelievably, he heard Higgins both shooting and calmly reporting on the radio, "Contact, room two."

A better man than I, thought Murdock, because even though the guy he'd shot was dead, his flashlight wasn't. It lay on the floor casting a nightmare's worth of illumination over the room. Now everyone could see him instead of the other way around. Not only that, it seemed as if most of them had started shooting. Muzzle flashes exploded in front of him. Murdock tossed his head back to flip the NVG up out of the way, and kept shooting.

Hundreds of hours and thousands of rounds expended in training saved Blake Murdock's life. He didn't think about it; he just fired until his man went down and then shifted to another target. First everyone with a weapon, then everyone standing, then everyone moving. The M-4 magazine ran out just as a screaming face loomed in front of him. M-16's took a magazine change faster than any other weapon in the world, but there wasn't enough time. Murdock's left finger was on the trigger of the M203 grenade launcher, and he yanked the trigger. The recoil banged against his shoulder and the figure in front of him went down with twenty buckshot in his chest from the 40mm M576 multipurpose round. So close was the range that the shot group was the size of a fist, and the plastic pellet cup and cap were blown right into the wound.

Murdock stood panting, smoke curling from the end of his suppressor, the room reeking of burnt gunpowder, dead bodies all over the place.

0310 hours
Port Sudan villa

Lieutenant Murdock might have wanted things kept quiet, but Razor Roselli had trouble with orders that conflicted with his personal survival. He wasn't about to enter the locked downstairs bedroom door without some preparation. Besides, after all the unsuppressed gunfire he'd been hearing, he figured he was absolved.

He nodded to Jaybird Sterling, who reached behind his back and drew out a Remington 870 12-gauge pump shotgun with the barrel cut down to the magazine tube and no stock, just a pistol grip. Sterling shot the hinges off the door with two solid slugs.

Roselli kicked his side of the door down and whipped in an

M-67 fragmentation grenade whose fuse he'd let cook off for a couple of seconds. The grenade blew, and they went in.

Blinded by the grenade smoke, Roselli sensed something thrashing on the floor and fired.

Jaybird, on the other side of the doorway, was sweeping the room with his laser, trying to punch through the haze. A figure sprang up from the floor and rushed across his field of view. Jaybird settled the laser on his target and fired. The figure went down with a hideous high-pitched screaming. Sterling kept shooting until the noise stopped. Nothing else was moving in the room, so he moved forward to take a look. In the laser light the figure turned into a woman with a child in her arms.

"What do you got?" Roselli called over. When he didn't get an answer, he walked over and punched Sterling's shoulder. "Whatcha got?" he repeated.

Jaybird was still staring down at the bodies. "Two," he said flatly.

"I got one, and the frag got another," Roselli said conversationally. "Room six clear, four tangos down," he radioed. He pushed the microphone down and yelled at Sterling, "C'mon, let's get going." When Jaybird didn't move, Roselli grabbed an arm and slung him out the door.

0310 hours
Port Sudan villa

Murdock rammed in a new magazine and threw the empty into his vest. Then a new buckshot round into the M203. Nothing was moving in the room. He heard Higgins fire twice, then nothing. "You okay, Prof?" he called to Higgins.

"Yes, sir," Higgins replied calmly.

The first thing Murdock did was stamp on the flashlight and return the room to darkness. Then he and Higgins toured the room, firing a round into the head of each figure on the floor. Better than a wooden stake through the heart.

"Room two, nine tangos down," Higgins reported over the radio, doggedly following SOP to the last.

"Save some for us," came Doc Ellsworth's voice over the net. "Upstairs secure, two tangos down."

Damn, thought Murdock, there were a hell of a lot more terrorists in the villa than the CIA had thought. Though the fact that they'd got it wrong wasn't exactly a surprise.

Beside him Higgins gave voice to his thoughts. "If it wasn't for all the guns, I'd say we fucked up and hit a Chamber of Commerce meeting or something."

"Sound off," Murdock ordered over the radio, and each member of the assault element reported in, alive and unwounded. "Clear and search," said Murdock. "Let's make it quick." The SEALs would now make a hasty search of the villa for documents and intelligence. "Victor Two, any movement?"

"Clear," reported Ed DeWitt.

Evidently the neighbors knew who lived there, and if a bunch of terrorists wanted to have a spat with firearms that was their own business.

Just as they'd rehearsed, Higgins held open a waterproof dry bag while Murdock shoveled in the contents of the terrorist's pockets, along with all the papers that had been scattered around the room. Then Higgins used a miniature video camera with a night vision attachment to record the faces of the dead.

Each assault pair reported over the radio that they were done.

"Charges ready?" Murdock demanded.

"Victor 1–2 ready," said Doc Ellsworth.

"1–1 ready," said Razor Roselli.

"2–1 ready," said Miguel Fernandez.

"2–2 ready," said Ron Holt.

"Pull fuse," said Murdock. "Everybody out. Victor 2, copy?"

"Victor 2, copies," said Ed DeWitt, letting everyone know that the security element wouldn't blow them away as they came out the door.

The charges were 1-quart issue plastic canteens filled with a napalm mixture, a blasting cap, a two-minute safety fuse, and a fuse igniter. The fire would consume the villa within minutes, removing most of the evidence of what had happened.

Murdock stationed himself by the blown door and counted everyone out of the house. He was the last man to sprint across the lawn to the balustrade, where Ed DeWitt and Kos Kosciuszko were laying in the grass behind their HK-21's, smiling big old smiles and hoping some trouble would pop up so they could lay waste to it at the cyclic rate of 900 rounds per minute.

Murdock went over the seawall and they followed right after him. The snipers covered while everyone strapped on their Draegers. While he worked, Murdock sucked on the plastic drinking tube of the CamelBak water bag attached to the back of his vest. It held seventy ounces and didn't make any sloshing sounds when you moved. After all the heat and exertion he needed to get rehydrated before the swim out.

When they were ready, each swim team gave Murdock a thumbs-up that their equipment was working and slid into the water. Murdock checked them all off like a worried mother hen. He looked at his watch. They'd been in and out of the villa in less than six minutes. It had seemed like an hour.

Then Murdock and Higgins donned their mouthpieces and disappeared beneath the waters of Port Sudan harbor, just as the flames began to light up the villa's windows.

3

Friday, August 18

0436 hours
The Red Sea, 1.5 miles off Port Sudan

Murdock had already used his Mugger to confirm that the fishing boat bobbing directly above him was in the same spot *his* fishing boat was supposed to be. The second confirmation was the orange chem light tied to the bottom of the boat. Even so, he and Higgins broke the surface with their weapons ready. A Sudanese crewman was peering cautiously over the stern.

"X-Ray," Murdock challenged, his index finger resting against the trigger guard of his M-4.

"Bravo," the Sudanese replied.

Murdock and Higgins went up the ladder, and were quickly ushered into the interior of the boat. It was a nondescript commercial fishing boat, controlled by the CIA and manned by an Arab and Sudanese contract crew that did assorted covert jobs in the Red Sea region. Just the thing for an unobtrusive extraction. But since good SEAL operations didn't leave anything to chance, and always required an alternate means of getting out of town when the job was done, the Special Operations submarine *U.S.S. King Kamehameha,* a converted ballistic-missile job, was cruising beneath the Red Sea awaiting an emergency beacon signal.

In the fishing boat's galley Murdock found Razor Roselli and the CIA maritime operations paramilitary officer sitting at a table drinking coffee. The Razor had already showered and changed into a green flight suit. He pretended not to notice while Murdock stood there dripping on the deck. Then he pretended to notice. "Oh, Jeez, sir, didn't see you come in," the Razor said innocently, though his grin gave him away. He tossed Murdock and Higgins liter bottles of mineral water that they both drained dry.

"Hot work," Razor said.

"Have we got everyone?" Murdock demanded.

"You're next to last," said Roselli. "Everybody but Doc and Scotty are back."

Murdock didn't like that one bit. Ellsworth and Frazier had left before Higgins and himself, and were even stronger swimmers.

The CIA man was up and pumping his hand. "Fantastic job, Lieutenant Murdock. Chief Roselli gave me a quick preliminary debrief. Sounds as if it went like clockwork."

"Thanks," said Murdock, "but the chief's been known to lay it on thick. We killed a lot of bad guys, and damn near all of them fit the descriptions, but we still don't know if we killed the right ones."

That didn't faze the CIA man one bit. He continued to gush, obviously thrilled to have his name attached to a winning effort. "Once we look at the video and the documents, I'm sure everything's going to shake out just fine."

"Better rinse the salt water off you, Skipper," Roselli said pointedly, meaning that standing around worrying about Doc and Frazier wasn't going to do a damn bit of good.

Murdock sent Higgins off to the single-stall shower. The boat crew had laid on extra fresh water to accommodate sixteen SEALs. Ed DeWitt and the rest of the platoon were cleaning their equipment, which every SEAL did automatically before even thinking about eating or sleeping. They were understandably wired, and not just from the adrenaline. It had been the kind of real-world op that every SEAL dreamed about pulling off.

"Hey, Skipper!" "You finally made it." "Fucking-A, sir!" "You didn't lose the Professor, did you?" "Of course he didn't, that would be careless." So went the chorus that greeted Murdock's entrance.

Murdock let them run on. "Beautiful op, guys," he told them. "A first-class job by everyone. Really professional." Then: "Thanks for bringing me along."

The platoon got a laugh out of that and shrugged off the praise. Murdock knew that in their secret heart of hearts, most SEALs felt that officers were a fairly useless bunch of dicks whom the Navy forced them to carry along on missions. So he humored them about it, which you could do while still remaining the boss, especially since in his experience the officer was the first guy everyone looked to when the shit hit the fan. Murdock also knew the boys were secretly pleased when the lieutenant gave them an attaboy, which was why he did it.

By then Higgins had finished in the head, so Murdock rinsed off first his equipment with fresh water, then himself. A dry flight suit and boots were waiting for him when he got out. Then he sat down with the platoon and turned to his weapons and equipment, all the time worrying about Ellsworth and Frazier.

Fifteen minutes later Razor stuck his head into the compartment. "They're back," he announced, ushering in a soaking-wet Ellsworth and Frazier.

Murdock let out a sigh of relief at getting all his boys back unhurt. The difference between the SEALs and nearly every other military unit was that SEALs expected *not* to lose people. This was the very reason their selection and training were so brutal. Only thirty-three SEALs had been killed by enemy action during the entire Vietnam War. During the Gulf War no

SEALs were lost despite missions that included taking down oil platforms and inserting agents directly into occupied Kuwait City. SEALs felt that if one of their own was killed, it was because someone had screwed up. That always weighed heavily on Blake Murdock's mind.

The rest of the platoon gave Ellsworth and Frazier a warm and friendly welcome along the lines of: "About fucking time." "Now we can get out of here." "Any day, there, you two."

"Fuck you all," Doc Ellsworth replied.

When the din died down, Razor Roselli stepped to the fore. The crowd hushed, waiting for his thoughts. "What took you so long, Doc?" Razor asked with deep but utterly insincere concern. "You get a cramp?"

The platoon cackled. The Doc popped the shoulder straps of his dry bag and dumped it onto the deck. It was bulged out to the size of a filled Navy seabag. "This pig was weighing me down," he said. "You'll shit yourselves when you see what's in it." He opened up the dry bag, took out a nylon duffel, and unzipped it. The duffel was filled to the brim with U.S. currency, all apparently one-hundred-dollar bills.

The platoon whooped in exultation. The general consensus was that there sat the makings of a platoon party that would go down in Naval Special Warfare history, with enough left over for a new car for everyone.

Before Murdock or DeWitt could find their tongues, Chiefs Roselli and Kosciuszko took charge, the human equivalents of a bucket of ice water to the nuts.

"Razor and me," Kos Kosciuszko announced, while Roselli zipped up the bag, "and Mister Murdock and Mister DeWitt are going to count all this. Then we will fucking seal it."

"You sure you don't want to reconsider that, Chief?" said a voice from the back of the mob.

"Yeah, Chief," said someone else. "Think it over. This could be one of those once-in-a-lifetime shots you come to regret when it's time to retire."

Unlike most SEALs, who only took their work seriously, Kos Kosciuszko took life too seriously to accept a ribbing in the proper spirit. And, of course, the platoon knew it. "My reputation isn't worth ten times that money," he informed them with a murderous look on his face.

"Don't make me blow the head off anyone who just wants to sneak in and have another little look in the bag," Razor Roselli added with his usual evil smile. He knew most of them were joking about copping the money, but it was a lot of temptation to be sitting there at close quarters. All it would take was for one guy to get a stupid attack and do something he'd regret.

Thank God for the chiefs, Murdock thought. Then he chuckled. Otherwise he might have been tempted himself.

As it turned out, there was three million dollars in the duffel, all hundreds, all crisp and brand-new.

"You keep doing that, sir, and you're going to give yourself a hard-on," Razor Roselli cautioned Ed DeWitt, who was unconsciously fondling a large stack of bills.

DeWitt whipped his hand away as though it was on fire, and everyone laughed. Then he recovered nicely. "Just practicing in case the lieutenant makes me sleep with it."

There was more laughter. Murdock good-naturedly declined the CIA man's joking offer to take the money off his hands.

The fishing boat headed south, and the *Kamehameha,* unneeded, drifted away. After a leisurely journey of several days and a confinement below deck that drove the platoon of active SEALs crazy, the boat emerged into the Gulf of Aden and then the Indian Ocean. One night two U.S. Navy SH-60F Seahawk helicopters plucked 3rd Platoon and all their gear from the fishing boat and carried them to the aircraft carrier *U.S.S. Nimitz.* A C-2A Carrier Onboard Delivery aircraft flew them to the British/American naval base at Diego Garcia in the Indian Ocean. At Diego the platoon boarded a C-141 jet transport for a very, very long flight back to the U.S.

4

Monday, September 4

0645 hours
Naval Amphibious Base
Coronado, California

Blake Murdock hated garrison life with a burning passion. Even the sound of the BUD/S tadpoles singing as they ran by his window was no compensation. The field was where you dove, fired weapons, and blew things up. Garrison was where there were always mounds of paperwork waiting whenever you returned from the field. And there was way, way too much command supervision here at Coronado.

Team Seven had originally been stationed at Little Creek Amphibious Base near Norfolk, Virginia, the home of the East Coast SEALs. But then someone up in the chain of command became offended by the aesthetics of having an odd-numbered team in the midst of all the East Coast "evens": Teams 2, 4, 6, 8, and SEAL Delivery Vehicle Team 2. Murdock also suspected that all the action Team Seven had been seeing was beginning to grate on the "Jedi Knights," the high-speed-low-drag hostage-rescue specialists of Team Six up at Dam Neck, Virginia. A turf war was inevitable.

And with Team Six firmly established as Delta Force's

counterpart in the elite Joint Special Operations Command, it was more than clear who was going to win. So after the typical bureaucratic power games at command level, Team Seven was shipped off to Coronado and Naval Special Warfare Group One, the West Coast home of the "odd" SEAL Teams: 1, 3, 5 and SDV-1, not to mention the Special Warfare Center and the Basic Underwater Demolition/SEAL course.

Since Team Seven still didn't publicly exist in the SEAL order of battle, and carried only four platoons instead of the official (but almost never fully manned) ten, it had been redesignated a "black" team. The mission was now primary support for the intelligence community, with special classified intelligence missions known only by their code words, dirty little jobs that didn't officially happen, the kind of ops that the platoon referred to as "weren't there, didn't do that." Like Port Sudan.

The headquarters was located in the fenced-off Special Warfare area of the base, but the building wasn't marked—even though all SEALs knew what it was. The important thing was that no one other than SEALs knew.

For Murdock Coronado had two main disadvantages. The first was operational: they were now five hours further away by air from Europe, and therefore less likely to be employed. Exactly what Team Six must have had in mind. But then again, they'd gotten the Sudan op, so maybe there were some advantages to playing with the CIA. That is, as long as you remembered to sit with your back to the wall when you were around those boys.

The second disadvantage was more personal. There were far, far more opportunities for his wild young SEALs to get into trouble. San Diego was just across the bay. L.A. was a short drive north. And the Mexican border and the sinful pleasures of Tijuana were just a stone's throw to the south.

Murdock dearly loved his job, but it was getting to the point where he was afraid to step over the quarterdeck each morning and hear what new atrocities 3rd Platoon had committed the night before. Granted, the boys were expected to blow off some steam after an op, but they'd been back two weeks and weren't showing any signs of slowing down. The weekends were even worse: more time to get into mischief.

But of course Murdock did step over the quarterdeck in the morning, and of course SEAL Team Seven's Command Master Chief was hovering nearby, checking on the uniform, haircut, and shave of everyone, officer and enlisted, as they showed up for work. And officer or enlisted, if you weren't squared away, you were going to hear about it in a hurry.

A smart officer always took the pulse of the Command Master Chief for early warning of impending disasters, and Murdock was a smart officer. It also helped if the Command Master Chief was George MacKenzie, who had previously been the platoon chief of 3rd Platoon and had kept Murdock out of more trouble than he could say.

"Morning, Master Chief," said Murdock. "Got time for a cup of coffee?"

"Good morning, sir," the chief replied. The formality was for public consumption; now Mac took care of all the platoons in the team, not just one. "I'd love to, but *you* don't have time this morning."

And it had been a pleasant morning, up until now. "Okay, Mac, give it to me straight."

"Well, sir, Jaybird and Doc sort of ran amuck last night."

"Does the Captain know?" were the first words Murdock got out, even before inquiring as to the nature of the crime. Jaybird and Doc running amuck wasn't exactly what you'd call a news flash.

The Captain, as every naval commanding officer is called, regardless of rank, was Commander Dean Masciarelli, known in the teams as the Masher, the newly arrived C.O. of Team Seven. Another result of the move to Coronado was that the team was now led by a standard-issue commander instead of a captain. Murdock didn't want be the first one to test the new skipper with any major liberty incidents. From all indications, the man didn't have much of a sense of humor.

In the old days all that SEAL officers aspired to was command of a team and retirement as a commander. If by some stroke of luck you made captain, that was just pure gravy. Now the SEAL community regularly produced a couple of admirals, and the no-mistakes-on-my-watch mentality and political gamesmanship had gotten almost as bad as the rest of the Navy.

"No, sir, he doesn't," Chief MacKenzie said calmly. "And with any luck he won't. Razor's kept the lid on."

Murdock resumed breathing regularly. If the Command Master Chief was going to acquiesce in keeping the lid on the incident, it had to be something less serious than murder, armed robbery, or consensual sodomy. "You going to tell me what happened, Master Chief, or are you going to leave me hanging a while longer?"

MacKenzie's eyes gleamed mischievously. "Oh, no, sir, I wouldn't deprive Razor of the pleasure of telling you himself. He's waiting in your office."

"You want to come along?"

"I'd love to, sir, but Mister DeWitt hasn't arrived for work yet. On Friday his belt buckle looked like he'd polished it with snot, so we're going to have a little talk this morning about how many quarterdeck watches he owes me."

"Enjoy, Master Chief." Old Mac had taken to Command Master Chief like, well, like a SEAL to water.

As advertised, Doc Ellsworth and Jaybird Sterling were waiting outside his office. To Murdock's utter shock, they both came smartly to attention and chorused, "Good morning, sir!"

"Morning," Murdock grumbled on his way through the door. Fuck, he thought; it had to be serious if those two bastards were resorting to textbook military courtesy.

Also as advertised, Razor Roselli was waiting in the office with the kind of expression on his face that, as the platoon liked to say, came from having to eat shit donuts first thing in the morning. Murdock collapsed into his chair and said, "Okay, Chief, let's have it."

The Razor nodded and stuck his head out the door. "In!" he commanded.

Ellsworth and Sterling marched into the office and centered themselves in front of Murdock's desk, remaining at attention.

"They've both been informed of their rights under Article 32," said the Razor.

"That right?" Murdock asked them.

"Yes, sir," they both said.

Roselli began. "Sir, these . . . these two little diddy-boppers got in the firewater last night and danced their way into a real hairball."

Murdock got a real kick out of his chief's tone of righteous outrage. In his years with the teams Razor Roselli had destroyed more bars, worldwide, than insurance arson. But that was how SEAL chief petty officers were made. When Razor was a troop and fucked up, the platoon chief had hammered him. Now that he was a platoon chief, it was his turn to be Dad. On another level, though, it made Murdock uneasy. If the Razor was going to make the two of them stand at attention while he told the tale, it had to be a real beaut.

The Razor continued. "You're aware of the carnival that's been on base the past week, sir?"

It wasn't fitting together, but Murdock had hopes. "The one for the kids, right? Rides and games and all that?" What did they do, he wondered, fuck someone's daughter on top of the Ferris wheel?

"Yes, sir," Razor said crisply. "They also had some animals. It seems that a camel went missing last night."

"A camel?" Murdock asked in disbelief, shooting up straight in his chair and staring at Doc and Jaybird. They were giving him the innocent puppy-dog look. "You mean a full-size, Mark-1 camel? Hump and all?"

"That's right, sir," the Razor went on, straight-faced. "This camel disappeared from the carnival, and then turned up again in the process of being inserted into the garage of the Special Warfare Group commanding officer."

"Not Commodore Harkins," Murdock pleaded with Doc and Jaybird. "Not his fucking personal quarters."

"Oh, yes, sir," the Razor assured him, while beads of sweat began to break out on Jaybird and Doc's upper lips. "These two were interrupted in the act by Chief Master at Arms Marlowe, who was on patrol at the time."

"You got caught?" Murdock bellowed. Doing the crime was one thing, but a SEAL getting caught in the act was unforgivable.

"We thought about killing him," Jaybird blurted out. "But we figured you'd be even more pissed." He caught the chief's fiery look, and added, way too late, "Sir."

"Chief Marlowe is an old buddy of mine, sir," said the Razor. "He brought the incident to my attention, and we handled it chief-to-chief."

Murdock had to strain to keep from letting out an audible groan of relief. Chief-to-chief was the only thing that kept the Navy running, not to mention officers like himself out of courts-martial. "Is the camel okay?"

"Operational, sir, and returned to its rightful owners."

"They don't want to press charges?"

"No, sir. They were a little steamed about what was on the camel, but I managed to smooth things over."

Murdock knew he was going to be sorry, but he had to know. "Okay, what was on the camel?"

"The number seven, sir."

"A seven?" Murdock flashed a massively pissed-off look at his two miscreants; they both wilted. "Oh, that's good. That's very fucking good. You two should instruct operational security. And of course while the commodore was standing in a pile of camel shit in his garage this morning, he'd never look at that number and make any connection with Team Seven. No, noooo, not ever. Brilliant, just fucking brilliant."

The two looked like they were trying to dissolve into the deck.

"Was it painted on?" Murdock asked no one in particular.

"What's that, sir?" asked the Razor.

"The number, was it painted on?"

"No, sir."

"Well?" Murdock demanded.

"It was shaved on," the chief said finally.

"*Shaved* on? Where?"

"On its ass, sir."

Doc and Jaybird dissolved into giggles, which only ended when the chief gave Jaybird a mild open-handed slap across the back of the head.

Murdock stared at his framed commission on the wall for inspiration. He was no expert on camels, but from what he'd heard about their general temperament, it was hard to imagine one standing still for having its ass shaved by a couple of drunken SEALs. Then again, he wouldn't put it past Doc Ellsworth to whip up some kind of camel tranquilizer . . . no, no, it was best not to even *think* about things like that. What you didn't know you couldn't testify to.

"Let me sum this up," he said. "You drank enough alcohol to turn the higher function areas of your brains into Vaseline. Then, when you had become just stupid enough, you stole a camel, which I assume costs enough to knock this gig into the major felony class. Then you were going to tether this live camel, marked with everything except my name, rank, and social security number, in the garage of the quarters, the *home,* of the commodore who personally commands all the teams, special boat squadrons, detachments, and units in the West Coast and Pacific theater of operations. The man who writes our commanding officer's fitness report and reviews mine. Does that about cover it?"

Ellsworth and Sterling merely shrugged, as if it had all seemed like a much better idea the night before.

Murdock let them sweat for a while longer. "Okay," he said to the two. "Your choice. Captain's mast or platoon punishment."

"Platoon punishment, sir," they both blurted out. The Razor would take it out of their ass a lot worse than the commander, but they'd keep their rates, and their record books would stay clean.

"Is that all, sir?" the Razor requested.

Murdock nodded.

"Out!" the chief hissed at Jaybird and Doc.

As soon as the door closed behind them, Murdock and Roselli stared at each other. Then they both burst into laughter.

"A fucking camel," the Razor wheezed, holding onto a chair for support.

"The fucking commodore," Murdock moaned.

"A seven on its ass," the Razor said weakly. "We can only give thanks that they got caught. Fuck, I know alcohol affects the judgment, but come on!"

"Nice save on that, Razor."

"We were lucky, Boss." The chief started laughing again. " 'Standing in camel shit.' I thought I was really gonna lose it when you said that." He shook his head. "And this commodore? You know what a tight-ass he is? It would have been a shit-storm around here. If they decided not to shoot us, we'd all be assigned to the cold-weather detachment in Kodiak for the rest of our careers."

"The only thing I don't know is how Master Chief Mac kept a straight face on the quarterdeck," Murdock mused.

"The word is going to get around," said the Razor. "This is a minor SEAL legend in the making."

"Just as long as the Skipper doesn't hear about it until after I get orders out," said Murdock. "And just as long as no one else in the platoon gets the idea to one-up this little stunt."

"They won't," the chief said confidently. "Not after they see the pound of flesh I'm gonna take out of Jaybird's and Doc's asses."

Just then Lieutenant j.g. DeWitt stomped into the office, his face crimson. "Man," he announced. "The Master Chief really ripped me a new asshole this morning. He never got so hung up on my fucking belt buckle when he was in the platoon."

Murdock and Razor looked at each other, and exploded into laughter again.

"It's not that fucking funny," DeWitt said huffily.

"Oh, yes, it is," said Razor Roselli.

"We've got to get these boys out of town," Murdock said to his chief.

"The trucks are scheduled for 0730," said the Razor. "Which means they'll probably show up sometime after 0900."

"A week in the desert is just what the doctor ordered," said Murdock.

"Besides, sir," Roselli said, "if we don't get Mister DeWitt either squared away or out of the Command Master Chief's sight, he'll be standing watches until he's a lieutenant commander."

"Or until Master Chief Mac retires," said Murdock, chuckling along with him.

"That's not funny," said DeWitt.

"Oh, yes, sir, it is," said Razor Roselli.

5

Monday, September 4

1345 hours
Chocolate Mountain Gunnery Range
Niland, California

The training ground of the West Coast SEALs was the Chocolate Mountain Gunnery Range, a former aircraft bombing area now set aside for ground-war use. It was a three-hour drive east from San Diego into the southern California desert, near the town of Niland. The SEALs had been using Chocolate Mountain since the Vietnam War, when the canals of the nearby inland Salton Sea stood in for the canals of the Mekong Delta during cadre and platoon predeployment training. It was big, anonymous, and secluded; you could make a lot of noise without disturbing the neighbors.

Unlike almost every other service, SEAL field training was traditionally run by the man in the platoon who had the most experience in the skill to be taught. Rank had nothing to do with it, and neither did rate.

Like all enlisted men in the Navy, SEALs carried a rating, like Mineman or Machinist's Mate, which they'd picked up after boot camp. But for SEALs the ratings were meaningless, having been discarded on the Silver Strand at Coronado when they'd graduated from BUD/S. Unfortunately the Navy, in its infinite wisdom, still took them seriously. So a SEAL master free-fall parachutist and dive supervisor who also happened to carry a hull technician's rating still had to study welding manuals twice a year for the written test required for promotion. And an aviation ordnanceman who'd gotten tired of loading sonobuoys on P-3 Orion sub hunters and gone to BUD/S was still competing for promotion, not with other SEALs, but with everyone currently loading bombs on aircraft. Stupid, yes, but as SEALs liked to say, that was the fucking Navy for you. Only SEAL hospital corpsmen utilized the same skills as their counterparts in the black-shoe Navy, though they learned to inflict more casualties than they treated.

And in addition to the complex skills required of each member of the SEAL community, individual SEALs also gravitated toward more specific areas of expertise: weapons, communications, intelligence, parachute rigging, etc. These also broke down into more detailed talents. One SEAL might be an absolute master in the use of the Stinger antiaircraft missile down to the repair of its complex electronics; another in all aspects of intelligence photography; yet another in the esoterics and employment of laser target markers.

For the 3rd platoon, the first day's training at Chocolate Mountain was handled by Radioman 1st Class Ron Holt, the pistol expert. For there was a new weapon in the inventory that they were getting their hands on for the very first time: the Mark 23 Mod O Special Operations Forces Offensive Handgun System. The name was a mouthful, but it was a brand-new pistol, the product of some history that deserved re-telling.

In the early days, the weapon of choice in the Underwater Demolition Teams had been the Smith & Wesson revolver .38 Special. Just in time for Vietnam, the SEAL teams received a stainless-steel Smith & Wesson 9mm automatic pistol with a screw-on sound suppressor. This was the Mark 22 Mod O. During Vietnam it picked up the name Hush Puppy, since it was used more often to silence barking dogs and honking ducks than human sentries. Contrary to popular legend, there never were very many, only enough to issue a couple per platoon. And these were passed on to the next platoon when they arrived in-country. The rest of the SEALs in a platoon carried the Smith & Wesson revolver or issue Colt .45 automatics. Pistols were just backup weapons, and SEALs felt that your shit was pretty weak if you got yourself into a tactical situation where you had to use one.

This continued into the 1970's, with the model of pistol being a SEAL's personal choice. As the Hush Puppys fell apart from overuse, they were replaced by the Heckler and Koch P9S 9mm automatic fitted with a Qualatec suppressor. Again, very few of these were procured.

In the late 1970's hostage rescue became a growth industry and pistols gained importance as primary assault weapons. Delta Force armed itself with a modified M1911A1 Colt .45 automatic. SEAL Team Six chose the stainless-steel Smith & Wesson .357 Magnum revolver and 9mm Beretta automatic. The FBI Hostage Rescue Team, having been trained by the British SAS, adopted the SAS-standard Browning Hi-Power 9mm automatic.

Hostage rescue shooting, which the British termed Close Quarters Battle or CQB, was of a standard totally alien to the U.S. military. It required entering a room filled with screaming people, distinguishing friend from foe, and shooting the foes in the head in a span of time measured in tenths of seconds. Mistakes and misses were not allowed.

CQB shooting demanded as many as five hundred rounds per man per *day* to gain proficiency, and a minimum of three hundred to four hundred rounds per week to maintain that proficiency.

SEAL Team Six soon discovered that the strain of that many rounds caused the slides of their Berettas, otherwise fine weapons, to weaken. When one blew up during firing and took out a SEAL's front teeth, Team Six moved to the SIG-Sauer P-226 9mm automatic, as had the British SAS.

Meanwhile, the Beretta had gone into U.S. general issue as the M-9, including a Special Operations version with a slide lock and barrel extension for a Knight's Armament Company snap-on sound suppressor. This was in service with all SEAL teams at the end of 1987. But by then all the teams were doing CQB shooting. They ran into the same trouble with the Beretta and gradually moved over to the P-226.

Things came to a head when the Special Operations forces of all the services were placed under U.S. Special Operations Command, which had its own budget authority. Someone at USSOCOM happened to check the numbers and freaked out at the multitude of different pistol models everyone was carrying, each requiring its own unique and very expensive spare-parts package and armorer training.

So USSOCOM put out a design competition for a new handgun. In case Congress might wonder at the need for yet another pistol, it was called the Offensive Handgun to distinguish it from the self-defense weapons carried by truck drivers and gate guards in the conventional military. The weapon had to be .45-caliber, with a magazine capacity greater than the seven rounds of the old Colt .45, with a sound suppressor and a laser aiming module. And it had to be able to shoot at least thirty thousand rounds without any parts failure.

The winner of the competition was Germany's Heckler & Koch, with a weapon based on their USP Universal Self-Loading Pistol. It was double action, with a twelve-round magazine, a decocking lever to silently lower a fully cocked hammer, and ambidextrous safety and magazine release catches. The screw-on sound suppressor was by Knight's Armament Company, whose products SEALs knew and trusted. The laser sights that snapped under the barrel hadn't arrived from the factory yet.

Ron Holt began the late morning training session by giving an introductory class on the weapon. It didn't take long. Whereas other members of the U.S. military would only have summoned up some interest if the weapon dispensed iced beer, SEALs couldn't wait to play with a new toy. And since their lives would probably depend on the thing, they damn well were going to get it down cold.

When the class was over, the platoon spent an hour taking the pistol apart and putting it back together, until they were comfortable with it. Blake Murdock had some initial reservations about the weapon, which from the comments around him his platoon seemed to share. The pistol was a big son of a bitch, over two and a half pounds unloaded and just over four pounds with a full magazine. That was a lot of weight to pack on your hip during the course of a mission. And it looked like they were going to have to visit the sewing machines in the parachute loft to modify their holsters. The pistol was over nine and a half inches long and the suppressor seven and a half inches, sixteen and a half inches screwed together. Unless their holsters rode higher up on their hips, the suppressor would be cracking on their kneecaps every time they moved.

But the proof was in the pudding, so after lunch they headed out to the range to give the weapons a workout.

Each SEAL Team was budgeted for 300,000 rounds of pistol ammunition per platoon, per year. So it took a little time to unload the ammo cans from the back of the platoon Hummvee and break it down.

And with five twelve-round magazines per weapon, the shooting benches were soon littered with piles of the empty cardboard boxes that had held the .45 hardball, full-metal-jacketed ammo.

"Israeli Military Industries?" Scotty Frazier wondered aloud, reading off one of the boxes. "What the fuck are we doing buying .45 ammo off the Israelis? They don't even use anything in .45."

"It's one of those foreign military sales deals," explained Miguel Fernandez, who had pulled some military training group time overseas. "They buy F-15 fighters with the aid money we dole out, and we buy .45 ammo and shit like that from them to even out the bookkeeping, make it look like we're getting something back, not spending so much."

Eric Nicholson tried to work that out, but it didn't happen for him. "What the fuck?"

"Look," said Razor Roselli. "The U.S. picks up everyone's check, the manufacturers get paid for the weapons, and the taxpayer gets fucked. That's all you gotta know."

The platoon snickered. "International Relations 101 by Chief Roselli," said Ed DeWitt.

"Well, am I wrong, sir?" the Razor demanded.

"No, you aren't," DeWitt admitted. "But we give Israel the aid because of the Camp David agreements, and the fact that they're under the gun."

"Yes, sir," said Roselli. "But the Russians aren't supplying the other side anymore, so who's going to take the Israelis on? No one. But we're still dishing out over three billion a year."

Any regular Navy officer walking by would have been astounded to overhear the learned discussion of Middle Eastern politics this provoked among the enlisted swine, but SEALs liked to keep up on where their services might be required.

It only ended when an exasperated Ron Holt asked if anyone would like to shoot some fucking rounds.

They started off on a classic pistol range with paper bull's-eye targets. Murdock soon had to admit that the weapon was fantastically accurate. The pistol had a special O-ring that locked the slide to the barrel when it came into battery. It made it more accurate than most SEALs could shoot, though Holt won all the beer that was bet that day with a cloverleaf group—all rounds in a single jagged silver-dollar-sized hole.

The platoon was used to the lighter-recoiling 9mm, so it took them a little while to get accustomed to the kick of the .45. Once everyone was shooting to his satisfaction, Holt let them add the suppressor to see what kind of difference it would make in the placement of their groups. The suppressor could be loosened and indexed to ten different positions, with the rounds grouping in a different spot at each position.

"When Holt thought they were good to go, he announced, "Okay, let's go to the CQB range."

That was to everyone's liking, but first they had to replace the targets and police up all the trash, ammo cans, and expended shell casings.

"No, no, no," Razor Roselli said kindly, holding up his palm to stop them. "I don't want you studs straining yourselves in this hot sun. Jaybird and Doc already volunteered for the detail. The rest of you head over to the shade and get some water."

The rest of the platoon snidely voiced their thanks to Sterling and Ellsworth, who were already bent down picking brass out of the sand and grumbling through only the beginning of Razor Roselli's platoon punishment.

When they were finished, the platoon went over to what had been the first CQB range at Chocolate Mountain. Old auto tires were stacked on top of each other and filled with sand to absorb bullets and prevent ricochets. The tires were laid out in the shape of rooms and hallways. It had been rendered obsolete by the new killing house with bullet-trap walls, but it suited Murdock's purposes. With all the SEAL platoons running around Chocolate Mountain, it was a lot easier to reserve.

The British SAS had been the first in the CQB business, and taught everyone the ropes. The initial shooting technique was theirs, developed from the Grant-Taylor method of instinctive firing perfected by the gentleman of the same name while he was the number-two man on the police force of pre-World War II Shanghai. He saw plenty of action, and later taught his technique to British and American intelligence operatives and commandos during World War II.

Instinctive firing was done with the shooter facing the target with both legs spread, both arms extended in front and locked, and the pistol held in both hands. The shooter didn't use the sights, but instead looked out over the top of the weapon, picked out a distinctive spot on the target, and fired.

Once they had become more established, Delta and SEAL

Team Six moved to the modified Weaver stance, where the shooter presents his body sideways so as to be less of a target. A two-handed grip is used, with the shooting arm straight and the support arm bent and locking the shooting arm across the chest.

The Americans also developed "rapid aim fire," where the weapon was brought up with the barrel slightly elevated. The shooter picked up the target on the front sight, centered it on the rear sight, and fired in a split second. Much more accurate than instinctive firing, and just as fast.

This was how the SEALs of 3rd Platoon shot. They set up good-guy and bad-guy targets throughout the CQB range and moved through in fire teams. They fired while moving, from the prone, rolling, and squatting.

Murdock had just finished a first run with his team when his pager went off. He looked around. "Anyone else?" All the SEALs checked theirs and shook their heads. "Fuck!" Murdock exclaimed. If it had just been some petty bullshit, the Chocolate Mountain duty would have radioed him from the headquarters building. It was obviously too confidential to put out over the radio, so now he'd have to drive up there. And he'd been looking forward to more shooting. "Fuck me," he repeated.

"We'll save you some rounds, Skipper," said Professor Higgins.

"We'll try not to have too much fun," added Ed DeWitt, enjoying one of the rare times it paid to be the j.g.

When Murdock stomped into the headquarters building, the warrant officer on duty forestalled any tirade by telling him, "You gotta get back to Coronado ASAP. There's an HH-60 turning on the pad right now."

When Murdock began to sputter, the warrant added, "It's come-as-you-are. You don't need any gear, and I'll get your Hummvee back along with word to your platoon. Have a nice trip, and no, I don't know any of the details."

Later, Murdock was embarrassed that his first thought had been, "Shit, what did the boys do this time?"

6

Monday, September 4

1500 hours
Naval Amphibious Base
Coronado, California

Murdock was met at the helo pad by Command Master Chief George MacKenzie and immediately whisked into a white U.S. Navy van.

"What did I do?" were Murdock's first words.

"Nothing this time," Mac replied. "Or at least nothing I know about. You've got a heartbeat to get a shower and into some khakis, then I have to run you over to Group. The Skipper's over there waiting for you, pissing up his toenails."

"And why is the Skipper pissing up his toenails?"

"Because he doesn't know what this is all about either."

"Great."

MacKenzie gunned the engine and pulled out. "Did you get a chance to shoot?" he asked.

Murdock nodded.

"What do you think of the Mark 23?"

"It shoots like a dream, but it's a heavy beast."

"A head shot is a head shot," MacKenzie said heatedly. "So why not stay with the 9-millimeter? And if you've just got to have a .45, why not buy the Glock 21 off the shelf? With the fluted firing pin, it's the only pistol in the world you can fire coming out of the water without having to break suction in the chamber. And for all the frigging money they're going to waste on it, how often do you use a pistol anyway?"

"How do you *really* feel about it, Mac?"

MacKenzie chuckled. "You mean I never told you that opinions are like assholes, everyone has one?"

"Maybe once or twice."

MacKenzie got Murdock showered and changed, and deposited him outside the headquarters of Naval Special Warfare Group One.

"You're not coming in?" said Murdock.

"Wasn't invited."

The Team Command Master Chief not invited? "What the hell?"

"Get in there," said MacKenzie. "And good luck." He drove off.

Murdock quickly found himself in the secure conference room, which was theoretically shielded from electronic surveillance.

Besides himself, there were only three other SEALs there. That might have been reassuring, except that one was Rear Admiral Raymond, the commander of Naval Special Warfare and the boss of all the SEALs. He was joined by Commodore Harkins, the boss of all the SEALs on the West Coast. The man Jaybird and Doc had attempted to introduce to the camel. And Commander Masciarelli, Murdock's boss.

There were four CIA officers, two of whom Murdock had worked with while planning the Port Sudan op. The other two looked very senior, very high up.

Finally there were two guys who just had to be cops of one variety or another. But Feds, because they dressed like IBM salesmen.

Admiral Raymond was regarded in the community as a

real-deal SEAL who still went out and did PT with his SEAL platoons. He'd picked up flag rank by accomplishing the missions during the Gulf War and not killing any SEALs in the process, something his predecessors hadn't managed to do in either Panama or Grenada. He greeted Murdock with a warm handshake. "A hell of a job in Port Sudan, Blake. And you make sure you tell all your boys I said so."

Murdock had never met the man before, but he immediately felt like going out and killing someone for him. "Thank you, sir, I'll be sure to."

Commodore Harkins, on the other hand, was widely regarded as just another staff pony. He gave Murdock a stiff handshake, and said, "Nice to meet you, Lieutenant."

"Good to meet you, sir," Murdock replied formally.

Commander Masciarelli, a little unhinged by the unusual circumstances and the presence of all the brass, shot Murdock a somewhat frantic look that said sit the fuck down and keep quiet.

The admiral gave the CIA men a nod that he was ready. Don Stroh, who had worked with Murdock on Port Sudan, stood up and moved to the podium at the front of the room.

"Gentlemen," he said, "I'm Don Stroh from the Central Intelligence Agency Covert Action Staff. This briefing is classified Top Secret Cable Crane. Need to know does not extend beyond this room without the personal authorization of the Director of Central Intelligence."

Jeez, Murdock thought. He knew the code word classification didn't mean anything in itself—some computer had vomited it up at random. What was important was that he was sitting in on it in the midst of all the brass.

Then Stroh froze him in place with his next words. "For the benefit of Lieutenant Murdock, who missed the preliminary meeting, I'll introduce everyone." He gestured to his CIA cohorts. "Mr. Hamilton Whitbread is the Director of Covert

Action Staff. Mr. Gene Berlinger is the Director of Special Activities Operations. You know Paul Kohler."

The first two were big boys, thought Murdock, almost deputy director level—Special Operations and Covert Action, the people he'd been working for lately. Kohler had worked with Stroh on Port Sudan.

"And from the Secret Service, Deputy Director Jim Capezzi and Special Agent Dennis Flaherty."

The Secret Service? Murdock couldn't figure it out. Unless maybe some bad guys were planning to kill the President and needed to be taken out. His palms started itching again.

Then Stroh said, "Since this briefing is directly related to Operation Granite Ghost, Lieutenant Murdock's raid on Port Sudan, I'd like to begin by extending him the Agency's congratulations on a job well done. Video and document analysis, along with communications intercepts, confirmed that the target four-man cell was accounted for in the villa, along with a number of significant high-level personnel of the group involved. The adversary has no idea what happened, or even if any non-Sudanese external force was responsible. From other documents recovered, preliminary indications are that the raid derailed at least five other future terrorist operations. Well done, Blake."

To Murdock's utter embarrassment, Stroh began clapping, and everyone else in the room must have felt they had to join in.

Stroh continued. "Since our main focus today is the money recovered by Lieutenant Murdock in the Sudan, I'll let Denny Flaherty give us the background."

Murdock knew it. He just knew that damned three million was going to come back and bite him in the ass one day. That was why he kept the receipt in his safety deposit box. Let them try what they wanted. He was covered. He'd tell the admiral that himself.

This small-scale internal emotional episode was cut off by

Special Agent Flaherty, a beefy Irishman with a pronounced Boston accent. Boston College, Boston College Law School, Murdock thought.

Flaherty wasn't much for bullshitting around. He clicked on a slide projector to display a blowup of a one-hundred-dollar bill. "Gentlemen," he stated, "the entire three million dollars discovered in Port Sudan was counterfeit."

That stunned Blake Murdock, since he'd personally counted the money at least three times and it had all seemed genuine to him.

"Are you familiar with the Supernote?" Flaherty asked.

Murdock looked around. Everyone else was looking at him, so he shook his head no.

"In 1992," said Flaherty, "two Lebanese-born drug traffickers got caught trying to bring three tons of hashish from the Bekaa Valley in Lebanon through Boston Harbor. They were looking at thirty years mandatory, so they asked the federal prosecutor if he'd be interested in high-quality hundred-dollar counterfeits being printed in Lebanon. He was. They turned the bills over, and the U.S. Attorney passed them on to Secret Service.

"These bills," said Flaherty, "were close to perfect. Our top technical analyst, who had examined every counterfeit ever produced, called them genuine. On a second viewing, he picked out three tiny imperfections which are now our only way of identifying this note, which we named the Supernote. It's also been called the Super 100."

Murdock checked around the room. Everyone else was just listening dispassionately.

Flaherty continued. "The Federal Reserve uses some extremely sensitive scanners to screen all the currency that comes through each of the twelve Fed Banks. The black ink on our notes is magnetic, and the scanners read the magnetic field down the center line of the portrait. The scanners are so precise that a thousand genuine hundred-dollar bills are rejected for every one that's later found to be a counterfeit. Gentlemen, the Supernote passes right through the scanners.

"The vast majority of counterfeits we run into are printed on offset presses, the same way books and magazines are produced. They feel flat, wrong. To get around the problem of the paper, counterfeiters bleach one-dollar bills and use them to print counterfeit hundreds. That's very big in Colombia and Thailand right now.

"But the Supernote is printed using the intaglio process, exactly the same way the U.S. Mint makes legitimate currency. An engraved plate is slammed onto paper, which gives the bills their distinctive feel. The Supernotes have sequential serial numbers, just like the real thing. The paper used in the Supernote is an almost exact duplicate of the paper produced for the U.S. Government."

Then Flaherty went on to answer the question that had just popped into Murdock's mind. "None of our paper is missing," he said. "Crane & Company have been making it for the government since 1879, and none of it has gotten away from them. The Supernote paper is a perfectly manufactured copy. And incidentally, we're not missing any printing plates either.

"We subsequently discovered that these bills had been circulating in Europe, the Far East, the Middle East, and Russia since the early 1990's, but with very few showing up here."

"I'll take it now," said a smoother voice from around the table.

Flaherty paused. "Gentlemen, Director Capezzi."

This was the first briefing that Murdock had ever been to where none of the higher-ups asked a bunch of dumb-ass questions just to show everyone how well informed they were. Then he realized, to his horror, that they had all heard this before. That the briefing was for *him*. Oh, shit, where was this heading?

Capezzi was a little smoother than Flaherty, but just as blunt.

"There are now nearly four hundred billion dollars worth of

U.S. paper money in existence," Capezzi told them. "Of that, around two hundred and fifty billion is in foreign hands. If their own currency is unstable or inflationary, people like to have dollars. And every hundred-dollar bill that a Russian sticks in his mattress is an interest-free loan to the U.S. Treasury, an amount of money that we would otherwise have to obtain by issuing interest-bearing bonds. It saves us twenty-five billion dollars a year in interest, based on what's out there right now. And if these loans in the form of currency stay in the mattress and are never called in, that's even more money in the bank for the U.S. Treasury.

"Ironically enough, in the past few years in which we've become aware of the Supernote, our main obstacle in combating it has been our superiors in the Treasury Department. While the total money supply consists of hundreds of billions of dollars in currency, the amount in wire, check, and credit card transactions runs into the tens of trillions. So Treasury doesn't bother itself much with cash. And the bottom line is that for the last five years Treasury has felt that any public acknowledgment of the problem of the Supernote would risk a loss of confidence in the dollar as a reserve currency overseas."

In his devious SEAL brain, Murdock was starting to figure out why there were no high-level officials from the Treasury in the room. Had the Secret Service gone over the heads of their bosses, or just around them to the CIA?

"Unfortunately," said Capezzi, "we are now beginning to see just such a loss of confidence. The Russian Central Bank estimates that Russians hold twenty billion dollars of U.S. currency, and that up to twenty percent of that may be Supernotes. In Germany banks will not accept one-hundred-dollar bills from Russian citizens. British, Irish, Greek, and Hong Kong banks are increasingly reluctant to exchange hundred-dollar bills from anyone, period.

"The Secret Service has always been aware that the hundred-dollar bill is most common under attack by counterfeiters. We also feel that the unchanging design of our currency has been advantageous to counterfeiters. On the other hand," Capezzi said wryly, "Treasury feels that the consistent appearance of the currency symbolizes its stability. In the 1980's Secret Service became concerned about the threat posed by color copying machines and laser printers. But by 1986, all we could get Treasury to agree to was the addition of a polymer thread in the paper and microprinting around the portrait of the hundred-dollar bill. It took Crane & Company until 1990 to master the polymer thread. By then the Supernote also contained the polymer thread and microprinting."

The implication blew Murdock away. Someone was better at counterfeiting U.S. currency than the U.S. Government was at producing it.

"I'm sure you're all aware of the recent decision to redesign the hundred-dollar bill," said Capezzi. "I can tell you that this was in direct response to the Supernote. Secret Service wanted holograms, chemical markers, and multiple colors. Australia has a note made of flexible plastic, which is both durable and counterfeit resistant. What we're getting is a larger portrait moved off from the center of the bill, a section of ink that changes color from green to black as the bill is moved, and a watermark. The colors will still be green and black. Our perspective is that this may buy us a little time. However, Treasury refuses to recall the old hundreds, feeling that market preference will cause rapid exchange of the old bills. We estimate that replacement will take years. During that time production of the Supernote will continue, and they will continue to be passed."

Capezzi sat down, and Don Stroh of the CIA replaced him at the podium.

"According to our information," said Stroh, "this counterfeiting operation began in Lebanon in the 1970's, during the civil war. The Christian Phalangists hired professional engravers to make hundred-dollar-bill plates. They printed them on bleached one-dollar bills. The notes weren't very good, but were successfully used to buy small arms in the Warsaw Pact countries. When Syria occupied Lebanon, which they continue to do to this day, they took over the counterfeiting operation. The Supernote plates have been continually refined and updated, year after year, until they have reached their present level of excellence. We have reports that expert engravers formerly employed by the East German Stasi were brought in to perform the work.

"After Syria allied itself with Iran during the Iran-Iraq war of the 1980's, we believe they invited the Iranians into the counterfeiting operation. With this the scale and sophistication increased, since Iran's oil money was able to buy a great deal more expertise.

"According to our information, Iranian industry has been responsible for reverse-engineering an almost exact duplicate of our currency paper.

"We believe that at one time the printing component of the operation was located within a secure building at the Iranian national mint complex in Teheran. They utilized two intaglio presses, functionally identical to the ones our own mint uses, purchased from a Swiss company.

"When this information came to light, the U.S. government approached the Iranian government through back channels and demanded that the counterfeiting operation cease. We informed the Iranians that we regarded it as an act of war.

"The Iranians publicly called the allegation, quote, wild hallucinations of the American extreme right, unquote. Our information now is that the entire counterfeiting operation has been consolidated within Lebanon. This allows both Iran and Syria to deny all responsibility for it.

"Our Secretary of State has brought the problem of the Supernote to the Syrian President directly." Stroh smirked. "As we might have expected, he knows nothing about it. We weren't too surprised, since the President's brother and Syrian

Air Force intelligence also run opium, heroin, and hashish production in the Bekaa Valley and use the money to finance their operations. The Supernote moves out of Lebanon along the drug routes.

"These counterfeits," said Stroh, "are not the result of a simple and limited criminal enterprise. Rather, they are our worst nightmare—the products of a large-scale, concerted industrial effort by hostile governments. We are convinced that Syria and Iran's long-term objective in producing the Supernote is economic terrorism—a direct attack on the monetary system of the United States.

"We believe the following are Syria and Iran's immediate but secondary objectives.

"To compensate for the cutoff of economic and military aid which followed the dissolution of the Soviet Union and Warsaw Pact.

"To compensate for the failings of the Syrian and Iranian national economies.

"As demonstrated by Port Sudan, to provide a source of funding for Islamic terrorist groups.

"But we believe that Iran and Syria's primary goal, as demonstrated by the huge numbers of Supernotes in the Russian Republic and former Soviet Republics, is to obtain nuclear weapons technology, nuclear materials, and most likely nuclear weapons themselves. In a development that we view as highly alarming, several North Korean intelligence operatives were recently apprehended in Hong Kong attempting to pass half a million dollars in Supernotes."

The room fell silent, and Murdock felt it was time for him to ask a question. "Do we have any idea how many Supernotes have been produced?"

"Perhaps two billion dollars a year," said Stroh. "Perhaps more."

If you couldn't buy a nuke with that, Murdock thought, you

couldn't buy a nuke. And the North Koreans and Iranians were among those known to be hard at work trying to make them.

Stroh clicked the slide projector. It displayed an aerial photograph, overhead imagery of a town. The detail was such that it had to have come from either a KH-11 or KH-12 spy satellite.

"Baalbek, Lebanon," said Stroh. He flicked out a high-speed laser pointer and threw a red dot on the screen. "This is the warehouse where the Supernote is now produced. It is right in the middle of town. As you know, gentlemen, Baalbek is the headquarters for the Iranian Revolutionary Guard presence in Lebanon. We estimate a minimum of four hundred combat-ready Revolutionary Guards and perhaps the same number of Hezbollah militia in Baalbek at any one time. The warehouse is also guarded by elements of a commando battalion from Syrian Army Special Forces Division Number 14."

Stroh paused. "We would like Lieutenant Murdock and his platoon to go in and take out that warehouse."

Just like the E.F. Hutton commercial, all eyes in the room were locked onto Blake Murdock. For his part, he had a quick mental picture of himself turning slowly on a spit over a cheery fire. With an apple in his mouth.

7

Monday, September 4

1550 hours
Naval Amphibious Base
Coronado, California

Everyone seemed to be waiting for him to say something, so Murdock decided to take the bull by the horns. "I appreciate your confidence in my platoon," he said. "But I think first of all I need to know just exactly what you want me to do."

"Fair enough," said Stroh. "That warehouse has to be completely destroyed. The presses, the chemicals, whatever stockpiles of paper and finished bills are there. And the plates for the Supernotes. The plates absolutely have to be destroyed."

"Then it seems to me," said Murdock, "that the easiest way to go about that would be with one or two F-117 Stealth fighters and several laser-guided bombs."

"That would be our first choice also," said Stroh. "But with every country in the Middle East currently engaged in peace talks, the U.S. can't precipitate an act of war with Syria. The Syrians know that perfectly well, of course, and have been using it to get away with murder for years. It's also why we have to hit them right now, because once they sign a peace treaty they'll be untouchable. And for all those reasons, the guidance we've received for this mission requires that it be entirely covert."

Murdock was well used to such typical governmental hypocrisy. When the Israelis had dumped the intelligence about the terrorist cell in Port Sudan into the CIA's lap, the Agency had had trouble deciding what to do.

There were no photos of the terrorists, just physical descriptions, and if the terrorists got out of the Sudan they could change identities and modes of transport a dozen times, and it would be only too easy for the intelligence community to lose track of them.

The solution was clear, but the sticking point was Executive Order 12333, signed by President Ronald Reagan on December 4th, 1981. It stated, "No person employed by or acting on behalf of the U.S. government shall engage in, or conspire to engage in, assassination."

As an example of classic American naivete, the executive order was unsurpassed. The assumption was that it was better to launch multimillion dollar air strikes against Libya, dropping thousands of tons of bombs and killing perhaps hundreds of innocent people, than it was to blow Colonel Khadaffi's head off his shoulders with one well-aimed round. The invasion of Panama and the post–Gulf War Tomahawk missile strikes against Iraq were further examples of the order's consequences.

The bottom line was that, like any good bureaucracy, the CIA kicked the problem upstairs. In this case to the White House. Violation of the law was grounds for impeachment. However, bombs going off in Europe during the election year of an incumbent American Government that could have done something to prevent it was something that struck right to the heart of politics itself.

The solution was also typically American: call in the lawyers. They drafted a tortuously reasoned finding that required Blake Murdock and 3rd Platoon, SEAL Team Seven, to "attempt" to "apprehend" the terrorists.

Surrounded by embarrassed CIA officers who did everything but wink and nudge him with their elbows to let him know what was expected, Murdock had merely shook his head in disgust and signed the required five copies of the form acknowledging that he understood the orders and took complete responsibility for carrying them out. But later, in private, he'd broken it down this way for his platoon: "We're going in to kill the motherfuckers." And that was exactly what they had done.

So, since they couldn't go to war with Syria even though they were going to war with Syria, all Murdock could say was, "I understand." Then he took a deep breath. "But I'm concerned that this mission seems to be outside NAVSPECWAR's parameters for SEAL operations."

First developed during the Gulf War, the criteria for the employment of SEALs had proven very effective. They included:

1. A high probability of mission success.
2. Operations in a maritime environment or within one day's patrol of the water.
3. Missions which required no more than a full platoon to undertake successfully.
4. Taskings which assured high survivability of the operators involved.

Murdock had been referring to criteria number two, though what he really had in mind was number four. These people seemed to be asking a SEAL platoon to bite off a lot more than it could chew.

"According to USSOCOM protocol this would normally fall under the heading of a Delta Force mission," said Stroh. "However, we would like to keep the number of people with knowledge of the operation as small as possible. You were already acquainted with the details and the money through the

Port Sudan operation, and frankly, in view of its success, we wanted you to take this on. Admiral Raymond concurs with us."

If the admiral was going to put his chop on it, Murdock knew that avenue was closed. "I don't have any other immediate concerns," he said, leaving himself a little room. "I'll start my planning immediately. Will I be working with you and Paul Kohler again?"

"We don't want to mess with success," Stroh said with a smile.

Then Gene Berlinger, the CIA Director of Special Operations, spoke his first words of the afternoon. "We have already assembled an operational plan for Lieutenant Murdock's platoon."

Probably something the CIA paramilitary guys had put together, Murdock thought. Some of them were former SEALs, but even so, they weren't out operating every day the way he and 3rd Platoon were. "I'll be glad to take a look at it, sir," Murdock replied. "But I would only be comfortable executing my own plan."

"Your comfort, Lieutenant, is not a consideration in the execution of this mission."

So now the games had begun. Murdock had had some experience with this sort of thing. Special Operations Command staff officers, generally Army types, thought you should sit in the corner sucking your thumb while they put together a plan worthy of Alexander the Great. Then they'd pat you on the ass, send you out to execute, and blame you when it fucked up.

Blake Murdock had been required to jump through his ass due to inadequate planning too many times in his career. He wasn't afraid of assholes in suits. He was a little afraid of a career-ending fitness report, because he really liked being a SEAL. But he was absolutely terrified of getting his whole platoon wiped out.

"With respect, sir," said Murdock. "If I'm the one who's

going into Lebanon, it'll have to be to execute *my* plan. Not the plan of anyone who isn't coming along. If that doesn't fit in with *your* plans, then you need to find someone else."

"You seem so reluctant," said Berlinger. "Perhaps we should."

Whitbread of Covert Action Staff, a separate department in the CIA, seemed amused by the whole scene. Commander Masciarelli looked utterly horrified. Commodore Harkins sat impassively, waiting to see which side of the net the ball would land on. But Admiral Raymond had a "that's my boy" expression on his face.

"I want him to be cautious," Admiral Raymond growled. "Especially with this mission. I don't want someone who's just going to buckle up his chin strap and go out and get a bunch of my SEALs killed. Lieutenant Murdock is absolutely right. He's more than proved that he can both plan and operate. And he's not going anywhere near Lebanon until he tells me he can get the job done. Since we've already decided that he will do the mission . . ." At this the admiral paused, and when no one in the room contradicted him, he went on. "Before anyone gets bent out of shape, let's allow him to put together a plan and brief it back to us."

No one objected to that, especially since the admiral, and by implication Murdock, had now assumed full responsibility for the operation. Everyone else's ass was fully covered.

"Blake," the admiral ordered, "get to work. Don Stroh will give you whatever you need to get started."

"Aye, aye, sir," said Murdock. "All I need right now is permission to bring my second in command and platoon chiefs in on this. And also the Team Command Master Chief."

"That's unacceptable," said Berlinger.

"Not counting staff jobs and a tour I did at BUD/S, I have about five years of Special Operations experience in the field," said Murdock. "My two chiefs have a combined total of thirty-one. The Master Chief has nearly that much himself."

That had always been Murdock's gripe. The chiefs were what made the teams, and compared to their experience officers were just a bunch of amateurs. Yet officers always thought they knew best.

Now Whitbread, the director of Covert Action staff, spoke *his* first word. "Granted."

The meeting broke up, and the admiral brought Murdock over to a quiet corner. "What do you *really* think about this, Blake?" he asked.

Sometimes when the brass did that, they were really asking you to tell them what they wanted to hear. But this wasn't one of those situations.

"I'll tell you the truth, sir. I don't have a good feeling about it. I know what I *can* do. I can go in and take out the key players if someone can target them for me. I *may* be able to blow the warehouse. But as far as guaranteeing what's going to be destroyed in it, you know I can't do that. At this stage of the game I don't even know if I can get all the way in to the target, do the job, and then get out."

"I hear what you're saying," the admiral replied, obviously hearkening back to his days in Vietnam. "If you had a couple of fighter squadrons putting close air behind you as you exfiltrated Baalbek, that would be one thing. But you won't have that, or fire support of any kind."

"Sir, if it can be done, I'll do it. I just don't know if it can be done without either an F-117 or an entire Ranger battalion."

"Blake, this is a hairy one, but it has to be done. And for a lot of reasons, *we* have to do it. And we can't fail. You do it *your* way, and if anyone screws with you or tries to force you into anything, I want you to sit right down on your ass and not move until you get on a secure phone with me. That's an order, you understand?"

Now Murdock really felt like killing someone for the man. "Yes, sir."

8

Tuesday, September 5

0800 hours
Naval Amphibious Base
Coronado, California

"I'm sorry, sir, but this sucks," Razor Roselli raged. "I mean, this really blows. It's going to take the whole platoon to pack the demo and do the shooting on this op. The fucking target is in the center of a town right smack in the middle of Indian Country where everyone and his fucking *dog* packs an AK or an RPG, and they all sleep with one eye open because the Israelis fly in and snatch Hezbollah chiefs whenever they can. Now maybe, just maybe, I can infiltrate a platoon through the fucking town and the checkpoints and the barking dogs and get them to the target. As far as getting them the fuck out and home in one piece, I have no fucking clue."

"Razor, shut up," Master Chief MacKenzie ordered. "You're making my ears hurt. Everyone gets your point. But since the reason we're here is to see if we *can* do the job, let's get on with it."

Unlike many officers, whose reaction would have been utter horror, Murdock liked what he was hearing. SEALs had died in Vietnam, Grenada, and Panama because they were so motivated and anxious to accomplish the missions that they ignored the fact that the missions were flawed and the op plans sucked. It had almost happened to him a couple of times, and it wasn't going to again. He was glad his chiefs had that mind-set too.

Murdock was also silently patting himself on the back for including George MacKenzie in the planning group. He, Mac, Roselli, Kos Kosciuszko, and Ed DeWitt were sitting in a secure planning room amid stacks of maps, papers, intelligence files, and satellite photographs. Some of it was on computer, such as all the SEAL mission planning checklists, and SOCRATES, the Special Operations Command Research, Analysis, and Threat Evaluation System. Unfortunately, SOPARS II, a computer system which would have automated the whole pre-mission planning process by combining digital maps, virtual-technology terrain models, building blueprints, all the planning checklists, and everything else you needed in a single desktop PC, had been cancelled due to funding constraints.

It wasn't that there was no money, just that all the services preferred to step back and let USSOCOM fund projects like that out of its own hide; then they'd swoop in and reap the benefits. USSOCOM was currently having to pay for very expensive helicopter programs, and feeling the pinch.

DeWitt chimed in. "Let's do this by the book. Start on actions at the objective and work backward from there to how we're going to get in and get out. Work from general to specific."

"Mister DeWitt is right," said Kos Kosciuszko. "The only way we'll knock the problem is by blocking it out piece by piece. If the planning's done right, there's no such thing as a target that can't be taken down."

Murdock thought they were on track. Surprisingly enough, SEALs frequently paid less attention to planning and rehearsal than they needed to. The culprits were usually officers, who thought that because they'd graduated from BUD/S, they were so big, so tough, and so bad that they could just strap on their six-shooters and take out anyone without even trying. But as a wise old chief had told an aggressive young Ensign Murdock years before, the SEAL Budweiser badge might be pretty but it didn't make you bulletproof.

And whenever time was short and he was tempted to half-ass some small detail of his planning, Murdock remembered the time he'd gotten tapped as a junior evaluator on a Marine Corps Expeditionary Unit Special Operations Exercise. The MEUs went out to sea on six-month deployments, and a SEAL platoon was always part of the amphibious squadron. This platoon had been led by two lieutenants, which sometimes happened. For the exercise they were going to conduct a HBVSS, or Helicopter Visit, Board, Search-and-Seizure, of a suspected hostile merchant ship, something that had been done every day during the Gulf War. The two lieutenants showed up at the planning conference without their chief, and in full view of all the Marines started arguing like a couple of little children over who was going to carry the SATCOM radio. It went on for a while, along the lines of: "I carried it last time." "No, you didn't, *I* carried it last time."

Murdock had been appalled. Then the Marines broke in and asked the SEALs how they wanted the Cobra helicopter gunships to deploy. What did they mean? the SEALs asked. Well, the Marines explained, after the SEALs fast-roped onto the deck, did they want the Cobras in a racetrack pattern around the ship, or hovering near the bow to cover the bridge with their 20mm cannon? Oh, came the response. After they'd gotten that straightened out, the Marines asked the SEALs what they planned to do. Head for the bridge, came the reply of the two John Waynes. Okay, said the Marines, but how are you going to get there? What ladderways will you use? What if they're blocked? Will you breach them or go around? All absolutely elementary stuff. Duh, responded the SEAL lieutenants.

Murdock had felt like slapping the shit out of them. It was

okay for SEALs to have a reputation as prima donnas. They were. But not as idiots and non-professionals. He'd never forgotten it, and after that he never went anywhere or did anything without first consulting a chief or a leading petty officer.

"Okay," said DeWitt. "What about a standoff attack with a couple of mortars?" It never made any sense to walk all the way up to the target if you could stand back and shoot it up from a distance.

"Not sure enough," said Razor Roselli. "We might damage the place, but we'd never know how well we really did. And no way could we come back and do it again if we didn't do it right the first time."

Murdock was measuring a Lebanon map with a ruler. "We'd need at least a 120mm mortar and a shitload of ammo, and that's a lot to be dragging around the Bekaa Valley at night."

"A few fast-attack vehicles and the mortars on trailers," DeWitt responded.

"There's no ground high enough in a ten-thousand-meter circle around Baalbek where we could observe and adjust the rounds on target," said Murdock. "We'd use up all the ammo and never hit the warehouse. And like Razor says, even if we hit it we wouldn't know how much damage we did."

"We've got to get all the way in to the objective," Roselli insisted. "Okay, we tiptoe in. Now, if we're not compromised on the way in and the guard force has its head up its ass and somehow we manage to get into the warehouse, we're not going to have a lot of free time to plant charges. And if we can't place the charges in the right spots, we've got to pack in a lot more explosives. Which is even more trouble."

"You know what this really looks like," said DeWitt. "A destruction raid mission for a whole Ranger battalion."

"I already brought that up," said Murdock. "It didn't fly."

At that point Murdock called a lunch break, which for one

and all meant throwing on shorts and a T-shirt and trying to get rid of their frustrations with a solid hour-and-a-half workout.

When they got back to the planning room, Murdock said to MacKenzie, "Okay, Master Chief, you were wearing that happy face all during PT, and it wasn't just the extra atomic sit-ups you made Ed do for missing the count. What did you come up with?"

"We have to do a pseudo operation," said MacKenzie.

"Meaning?" asked Ed DeWitt.

"Meaning we dress up like the bad guys and drive right up to the front door. Like how the Israelis drove a duplicate of Idi Amin's Mercedes right up to the terminal at Entebbe. Like the Vietnam SEALs dressed their point men in black pajamas, coolie hats, and AK-47's to give them a little edge."

"By George," exclaimed Kos Kosciuszko. "I think he's got it."

"So we dress up like Syrian commandos?" asked DeWitt. "Or Hezbollah?"

"Neither," said Murdock, really warming to the idea. "You don't dress like someone they're going to want to stop and chitchat with. You dress like someone who makes them shit their pants and wave you right through."

"Syrian Presidential Guard," said Kos Kosciuszko.

"A big limo," DeWitt burst out. "And a couple of vehicles filled with Presidential Guards. Jeeps, land rovers, Russian Zils, whatever they use. Something we can fly in by helo."

"Tinted windows on the limo," said Kosciuszko. "Syrian flags on the bumpers. You don't know who's inside, but it's got to be someone you don't want to fuck with. That's the great thing about dictatorships."

Once the initial excitement passed, Razor Roselli, the wet blanket, weighed in. "That might get us into town without compromise," he conceded. "But we've still got to set charges and get out. And the problem with dressing up like Syrians and then having to deal with Syrians is like the Germans during the

Battle of the Bulge in World War II. They dressed up like Americans and caused a lot of confusion, but they nearly all got bagged because at close range they couldn't pass."

Razor Roselli had never yet failed to amaze Murdock.

"It's like North Korean Special Forces dressing up in South Korean uniforms and slipping over the DMZ," Roselli went on. "They get caught as soon as they open their mouths, because every Korean can tell the difference between a Northerner and a Southerner."

"Which means," Kos translated, "that the uniforms might get us all the way up to the warehouse if we showed up at night. But even if the CIA gave us someone who could speak fluent Syrian Arabic, we ain't getting invited inside without a lot of shooting."

That brought them back to earth. Then DeWitt suggested, "Maybe if we bring along something to shoot our way into the warehouse? Like a Russian BRDM scout car. The armor will stop small arms, and they pack a big-ass 14.5mm machine gun. We could ram our way right through the security."

"I'm sure the CIA could come up with one or two for us," said MacKenzie, giving DeWitt an approving nod.

Razor Roselli left the room and returned with the reference book *Jane's Armor and Artillery*. He flipped open to the Russian BRDM and said flatly, "It won't fit inside either an MH-53 Pave Low or an MH-47 Chinook. You'd have to sling-load it under the helo, and I don't know who we'd get to do a night low-level penetration with a slung load. Especially that kind of air defense threat."

They all groaned, mainly because they knew he was right. Murdock gave them a break, and everyone went out for coffee or a soft drink.

Except Ed DeWitt. He grabbed the book and thumbed through it, stopping at the Equipment in Service section at the back. Under Syria, and Reconnaissance Vehicles, there was BRDM-1, BRDM-2, and Shorlands (IS). What the hell was that last one? He tore through the index and then the page, and had it laid out when the others returned to the room.

"It's an armored car," DeWitt told them. "British, made by Short Brothers of Belfast. Basically an armored Land Rover with a machine-gun turret. The Brits use them in Northern Ireland, the Syrians use them for internal security." He shot a victorious look at Razor Roselli. "And it fits in an MH-47. I checked the dimensions."

"Shit hot, Ed," said Murdock. There were approving noises from the rest. Except one.

"Look, sir, that's great," said Razor Roselli. "So we can get to the warehouse and ram our way in with an armored car. But we still have to plant the charges and get the fuck out!" He was almost shouting now.

"Goddammit, we're a hell of a lot farther ahead than when we started this morning," Kos Kosciuszko bellowed. "And for all your bitching you haven't been any fucking help at all."

Roselli stood up. Kosciuszko took the challenge and came up out of his chair.

"All right!" Murdock said sharply. "That's it for today. Everyone get the fuck out and go home. I'll sanitize the room." Sometimes being a SEAL officer was like being a lion tamer. Except that being a SEAL officer was more dangerous than being a lion tamer. His SEALs all stood up and shuffled about nervously. "Get out," said Murdock. "Go home, cool down, and be back here tomorrow morning ready to work. Don't anyone say another fucking word."

Razor Roselli seemed to want to say something to Murdock, but he turned and followed everyone out.

They all left except George MacKenzie. He helped Murdock collect all the scrap paper, shred it, and put it in a burn bag. All the other materials went into a file box for storage in the classified material vault overnight.

"Boss, we are on *edge*," said MacKenzie.

"Razor's not pissing me off," said Murdock. "He's not Mr.

Tact, but you have to have a devil's advocate. If he wasn't doing it, you or I would have to."

"Razor is not why we're on edge."

"I know that, too. It's because this is shaping up like a suicide mission," said Murdock. He slammed the file box down onto the table. "But that's bullshit! Yeah, as a straightforward infiltration and raid mission, done the way we've always done it, it doesn't work. But we're the goddamned unconventional warfare specialists. It's time we started thinking unconventionally."

"I'll try, Boss," MacKenzie said pleadingly. "I swear I will."

They both started laughing.

"Buy you a beer?" said Murdock.

"No," said MacKenzie. "I think I better buy you one."

9

Tuesday, September 5

1815 hours
McP's Bar
Castle Park, California

Murdock and MacKenzie ended up at McP's, which was located on Orange Avenue just down from the Coronado Main gate. It was a popular SEAL watering hole, owned by a man who had been a corpsman in the teams during Vietnam. On the back of the bar menu was printed, "If you don't like crowds, don't come on Thursday night." Translated, that was when the place was packed with SEALs, and if you had a problem watching someone toss down a flaming drink without putting it out first, or eating glassware in front of you to win a bar bet, then maybe you ought to stay home.

Murdock and MacKenzie had no such qualms, having seen far, far worse while on liberty with the troops. And, of course, it was only a Tuesday.

The first beer went down fast. "Talked to Inge on the phone last night," said Murdock.

"Oh?" MacKenzie said warily.

Inge Schmidt was a special agent with the BKA, Germany's FBI. They'd met during an op in Europe, had nearly gotten killed together, and of course romance had flourished.

"We used to have phone sex once a week," said Murdock. "Now we talk once a month, if I'm not someplace like Sudan." He paused. "What the hell, I can't put my name in to be an exchange officer with the Kampfschwimmers until after this tour. I can't get out and move to Germany, and she can't quit her job and move here. So what the hell can we do?"

"As Razor Roselli would say, whenever you get some leave catch a MAC flight to Germany and screw each other's brains out."

Murdock clinked his mug against MacKenzie's. "Words to live by. Of course, I think Razor has more ex-wives than I have cousins."

"And you have a *lot* of cousins."

Murdock swung the subject around to something else. "You did a pump in Lebanon, didn't you?"

"Beirut, when I was a Second Class with Team Four. But that was before the truck bombing." He took a sip of his beer. "What a fucking zoo that was. And now we're back to Syrians, Iranians, and Hezbollah, the exact same bunch who did the truck bombing."

Even while he'd been talking, Murdock had seemed to be somewhere else. Now his focus was almost frightening. "Wait a minute, Mac, what was that?"

"Man, was I wrong when I thought people would listen to me after I made master chief."

"No," Murdock said urgently, as if he was about to climb across the table. "Truck bombs, Mac. You were talking about the truck bombs!"

"So you were listening after all."

Murdock sprang up and threw money onto the table. "Waitress, get this American hero another beer. I'd kiss you, Mac, but your wife thinks we spend too much time together as it is."

"What the *hell* are you talking about?" MacKenzie demanded. "And where the hell are you going?"

"Back to the office."

"I'll come with you."

"Nope, I'll see you in the morning."

Murdock walked off, and the waitress put another beer down in front of a very confused George MacKenzie. "What happened to your cute friend?"

MacKenzie looked up at her. "Somebody told him you were married. He was so disappointed he up and left."

She popped her gum. "Well, what mouthy son of a bitch went and told him that?"

10

Wednesday, September 6

0730 hours
Naval Amphibious Base
Coronado, California

Blake Murdock was waiting when everyone arrived at the planning room. He was freshly shaved and showered, but based on the amount of expended coffee grounds in the wastebaskets, he'd been there all night.

"Hey, sir," said Razor Roselli, "didn't you know SEALs are supposed to get ten hours of sleep every night?" A little joke from BUD/s, and Razor's way of apologizing for the previous day. During Hell Week SEAL trainees get a total of four hours of sleep in five days.

Murdock was in a dead serious mood. "Everybody take a seat. I've got something I want to run by you."

The SEALs began shooting little looks at each other.

A map of Lebanon was spread out on the table, along with a set of satellite photographs.

"We fly in to Lebanon on four MH-47E Chinooks," said Murdock. "Two Shorlands armored cars, two armored Mercedes limos; one vehicle in each helo. We terrain-fly all the way, and over the central mountain range. The helos drop us near the road south of Baalbek, so as we drive in it looks like we're coming from Damascus. We're in Syrian livery, and we roar past every checkpoint like we're king shit, all lit up."

Murdock pointed to a computer-enhanced close-up of the warehouse in Baalbek. "The entrance to the warehouse is fenced, sandbagged, and guarded. So is the loading area. But this road runs right up against the long side of the warehouse. We come up this road, and the two armored cars make a hard right, ram through the chain-link, and keep on going right through the flimsy-assed wood walls of the warehouse.

"The armored cars are filled with as much explosive as we can pack into them. From the specs I figure about seven hundred fifty pounds each, maybe more."

George MacKenzie was beginning to smile.

"As soon as they go through the wall," said Murdock, "the boys in the armored cars pop the vehicle smoke dischargers and pull fuses. They un-ass the cars and bolt through the holes in the walls and the fence. The limos provide covering fire and pop their own smoke.

"Everyone hops in the limos and we peel rubber. We blow out of town at high speed. If you look at the route I've marked, we have to go through two checkpoints, based on current intelligence. The limos still have Syrian flags, sirens blaring. Everyone's going to think really hard before taking a shot at us. On the way out of town we're throwing tire poppers and pursuit-deterrent munitions out the windows.

"We're out of town, and the helos are already on the way in. Two MH-60K Blackhawks, one primary and one backup, because we're not bringing the limos back with us. We'll rig them to blow when we leave.

"If we spend more than thirty seconds on the target, from the time the armored cars go through the fence to the time the limos pull out, you're all fired."

Murdock stood there expectantly, but there was silence in the room.

Then Ed DeWitt whistled through his teeth.

George MacKenzie's smile grew even larger.

Kos Kosciuszko was nodding happily.

All eyes turned to Razor Roselli.

Razor thought about it for a while. Then he said, "This could work. You know, Boss, this could most definitely work."

Murdock was unmoved. "We've just started working," he said grimly. "We're going to sit here and diagram every move we make every second we're in Lebanon. And then we're going to war-game absolutely everything that could go wrong, from a flat tire to Razor's hemorrhoids acting up on him. And we will figure out exactly what we are going to do in each situation. And only when we've got this plan airtight and polished like a diamond will we brief it back to the brass."

11

Monday, September 11

0925 hours
Naval Amphibious Base
Coronado, California

"I like it!" Admiral Raymond exclaimed. "It's about time a bunch of my young studs threw away the Ranger Handbook and did some *special* warfare." He cocked an eyebrow at Murdock. "You like planning for what might go wrong, don't you, Lieutenant?"

"Something always does, sir."

"You're right about that."

For this meeting it was just the admiral and the CIA. The Secret Service, the commodore, and Commander Masciarelli hadn't been invited. MacKenzie, DeWitt, Roselli, and Kosciuszko had come along to help Murdock with the briefing. It had taken just under an hour. Murdock had seen briefings go hours longer, but that was ridiculous. Briefers added a bunch of irrelevant crap just to show off for the brass. Anyway, the human brain couldn't absorb that much information.

Now the admiral turned to the CIA men. "This plan has my complete approval—*unchanged.* Can you get the lieutenant what he needs?"

"I don't see any problem," said Don Stroh.

"Well, I do," said Berlinger. "Do any of you realize how expensive the lieutenant's plan is compared with our original one?"

"Not too expensive compared to two billion in counterfeit currency a year," the Admiral observed. "Besides, this plan will work."

"With the expenditure of two armored cars and two limousines alone," said Berlinger. "Not to mention the increased helicopter assets."

"Excuse me, sir," said Murdock. "But if you'll recall, I said we needed *four* armored cars. Two reserved for the mission. And two to train with, of which one will be a mission backup and the other I plan on expending for demolition tests. And, of course, three limousines. One of which will be mission backup."

"And what's all this backup nonsense?" Berlinger demanded.

"In case one of the vehicles breaks down, sir. We wouldn't want to postpone the mission while we ordered a new one from the factory, would we?"

Berlinger still wouldn't quit. "Do you realize that you're using enough explosives to level a city block?"

"Yes, sir. It should do a really fine job on the warehouse."

"And you're not concerned with civilian casualties?"

Beside him, Murdock could hear Razor Roselli grumble, "Is this asshole with the CIA or the fucking Peace Corps?" Murdock quieted his chief with a sharp kick to the ankle.

"Let's move on, shall we?" Whitbread interrupted. "The rest of us are not about to pretend that we're concerned about any casualties to the Syrians, Hezbollah, or the good citizens of Baalbek. I, for one, remember that Baalbek was where those same people tortured to death William Buckley, our chief of station in Beirut and a good friend. Lieutenant Murdock, I'm prepared to recommend approval of your plan. Tonight I will present it to the Director and the . . . appropriate national authority."

Murdock hoped the President liked it.

"Don Stroh will be in touch with you when a decision is reached," said Whitbread. "Gentlemen, well done, and good day to you."

That did a very nice job of breaking up the meeting. Stroh came over to talk to Murdock, and the admiral moved to corner the SEALs before they could slip out of the room.

"Nice job on the briefing, Blake," said Stroh. "Love the plan. Berlinger's just bitchy because yours is light years ahead of the one his boys came up with. And you know," he said quietly, "the computer only gave his plan a fifty-five-percent chance of completion. Yours has got to be up over eighty percent."

"Great," Murdock said, without enthusiasm.

"Oh, I also wanted to tell you. That woman at the villa in Port Sudan? It turns out the French wanted to talk to her about the bombings in Paris earlier in the year. They think she might have planted a couple of bombs herself. Woman and a little kid, you know? You wouldn't figure they're packing a bomb that's going to blow up a few innocent people, would you?"

"I guess not."

"So if anyone was bummed about tagging a woman, you can let them know they didn't make a mistake."

"As far as I know, no one was bummed."

"Whatever. Our colleagues at the Direction Général de Sécurité Extérieure tell us, on behalf of the French Government, that they're very pleased not to have her running around anymore. They might even have sprung for a medal, except that it never happened, right?"

"Right."

"Okay, I'm going back to Langley and start putting your shopping list together. Don't worry about the big boys approving, it's in the bag. I'll see you at Niland, okay?"

"Okay."

Murdock started to walk over to the knot of SEALs that had the admiral surrounded, but George MacKenzie had already slipped away and was waiting to waylay him.

Mac looked around to see if anyone was listening, then said, "You still haven't told me if you're taking me along."

"You want to go?" Murdock asked innocently.

"Hell, yes," said MacKenzie. "How many ops do you think I have left before I retire?"

"You know I'd take you in a heartbeat, Mac. It's okay if you don't give a shit about Razor."

"What the hell are you talking about? What does Razor have to do with it?"

"The boys would all be looking to you. Really, it's okay if you don't give a shit about Razor's credibility."

MacKenzie was taken aback. Then he sighed. "Yeah, you're right. I wanted the op so bad I didn't think about the platoon."

"So you're not coming along?"

"You better be careful, *sir*. You go around making too much sense and they won't let you be an officer anymore."

"I'll just have to take that risk. You going to come to Niland and help us out with the training?"

"No," MacKenzie said reluctantly. "Razor and Kos can handle it. I've got to get back to work. But there is one thing I want you to add to the plan."

"What's that, Mac?"

"I want you to bring along a semiauto sniper rifle for every man that's going. I'd say M-21's, but you'll want to use sterile weapons that don't come from the U.S. German MSG-90's ought to do just fine. Have Magic Brown pack a .50-caliber. Put them in drag bags with one hundred fifty rounds each all loaded up in magazines, and stash them in the trunks of the limos."

"Okay, Mac. You think we might need them?"

"No, just something that kept me awake last night. On the off chance you get caught up in those hills with some free time on your hands."

"Consider it done, Mac. You know, we couldn't have put it together without you."

"You can get off the dick now, *sir*."

Murdock laughed and threw his arm around MacKenzie's shoulders. They walked over to the admiral.

"I asked your boys if they had any heartburn, and they said no," the admiral told Murdock. "Bunch of lying bastards."

The SEALs all laughed politely. Anything admirals said was automatically funny.

"What about you, George?" the Admiral asked.

"They're good to go, sir," MacKenzie replied.

"If George MacKenzie says you're good to go," the admiral pronounced, "then you're good to go."

"He's the man, sir," said Murdock.

"I want to wish all of you good hunting," said the admiral. "Now get on out of here and let me talk to your lieutenant."

The others left, and the admiral said, "Don't you worry about Berlinger, Blake. It's just politics. If the mission goes off without a hitch, no one will remember anything he said. But if it doesn't, he's positioned himself for the Congressional committees. He'll say that he had serious reservations about the mission, and was concerned about all the innocent bad guys who might get hurt. I'm sorry, son, but that's the way they play the game at this weight class."

The admiral obviously didn't know, so Murdock wasn't about to tell him, that he'd had a lifetime education in Politics 101 from the Honorable Charles Murdock, Congressman from Virginia. Blake had carried that albatross around his neck for years. The Congressman had planned on Harvard, Harvard Law, and politics for his son. He'd compromised on Annapolis, since a short stint of military service never did any harm when you ran for office, especially a nice safe job on a staff or in the Pentagon. But Blake Murdock had gone 180 degrees in the other direction and become a SEAL. And he intended to stay a SEAL. He and his father didn't talk much anymore.

"I understand, sir," he told the admiral.

"You remember what I said now. Any problems, and I want to hear your voice on the phone."

"Aye, aye, sir." As far as Blake Murdock was concerned, the admiral was his father, and his SEALs his brothers. He didn't need any other family.

12

Monday, September 18

0400 hours
Naval Amphibious Base
Coronado, California

Murdock wished that moving a SEAL platoon was as easy as throwing sixteen guys into the back of a truck, but it wasn't. Their equipment alone filled several aircraft pallets.

Their green light had come from CIA headquarters on the previous Thursday, and Murdock had immediately given the whole platoon the rest of the week and weekend off. Even though the majority had no idea about the upcoming mission, such a windfall only convinced them that something major was forthcoming. There just weren't that many good deals around, and they always had to be paid for.

Murdock had done it because they would be going into isolation until the mission was over, and the married men ought to have some time with their families. And the single SEALs, well . . .

The chiefs had wanted to move to Niland at night, for a lower profile. Then they couldn't get transportation on Sunday night, so they had to settle for the wee hours of the morning. The married men had come in with their game faces on.

Murdock didn't know how they did it, how you told your loved one: "Honey, I'm leaving. I don't know when I'll be back, and you probably won't be hearing from me. If something happens someone will show up at the door, but don't call the office because the duty might not be cleared for the operation, or might not even know I'm gone."

It took one hell of a woman to put up with that, which was why SEAL divorces were regular events.

Murdock was in his office finishing up platoon evaluations. The paperwork couldn't be ignored. Anyway, officers hopping around sticking their noses into things only screwed up an embarkation. Razor would come in when everything was ready, and then Murdock would go out and help the boys lug everything to the trucks.

Razor Roselli did crash into the office, but it wasn't to tell Murdock the platoon was ready. "Boss," he announced, "we've got a little problem."

"What is it?"

"Jaybird hasn't shown up yet."

"You sure?" Murdock asked. "General mayhem, yeah, but I can't picture Jaybird Sterling missing a movement."

"All I know is, he ain't here."

"What about Doc?"

"He's here, but he doesn't know where Jaybird is."

Now Murdock was concerned. For Jaybird to miss any action he'd have to be either in jail, in the hospital, or dead. Shit. "Okay, get some people on the phones. Check the brig and the base hospital, then the jails and hospitals out in town."

"Okay, Boss." As he went out the door, Razor was muttering, "He's dead. If he ain't dead now, he's gonna be."

About fifteen minutes went by before Razor blew back in. "If you can believe this, Jaybird just called the duty. He's at an apartment building in downtown Dago, and he needs a ride." Roselli's smile was terrifying. "I'll take care of this myself."

Murdock didn't think Razor was in the right frame of mind to go unsupervised. "We'll take my truck."

During the drive downtown, Razor seemed preoccupied, chanting, "He's dead, oh, he's dead," like some twisted mantra.

Murdock was getting sick of it. "Look," he said. "Would you rather have a pain in the ass who can really operate, or some Little Lord Fauntleroy who can't cut it in the field?"

There was just a smoldering silence from Razor Roselli.

"I love it when I'm right," Murdock chortled.

It was a very nice high-rise apartment building. As they entered the parking lot, Murdock aimed his pickup so they could stop in front of the lobby.

For some reason Razor Roselli happened to look up. Then he looked up again. "Wait a minute, Boss. Pull around the side of the building."

"How come?"

"Park right there," said Razor, pointing to an open space.

Murdock went along. He turned off the key, then followed Razor's finger, which was now pointing skyward.

"What am I supposed to be looking at?" asked Murdock. Then: "Oh, my God."

A man was climbing down the side of the building, balcony to balcony.

Murdock rolled down his window and pulled his body halfway out to get a better view. "You know," he said, "the son of a bitch is either wearing a pink jumpsuit, or he's bare-ass naked."

"It is Jaybird, isn't it?" Razor Roselli asked faintly.

Murdock slid back into the truck cab. "Yup, it sure is."

"That's good," said Razor, with evident relief. "The thought that there might be someone else just like Jaybird running around loose on the planet just bothered the fuck out of me for some reason."

Murdock went back out the window. "Good climbing technique," he said conversationally.

Razor stuck his head out his window and immediately regretted it. "I don't believe it," he moaned. "He is absolutely stark fucking naked."

"Actually," said Murdock, "that ought to help your climbing. You know, you're supposed to lean away from the rock. If you don't have any clothes on, you automatically lean away so your Johnson won't get scraped off." He paused. "I wouldn't want to be a tenant sitting out on my balcony right now, though."

"Am I even here?" Razor Roselli demanded of the heavens. "Why can't this just be a nightmare? What did I do to deserve this?"

"What didn't you do?" Murdock retorted.

Jaybird Sterling jumped down onto the second-floor balcony, swung out over the railing, and finished off his trip to the ground by shinnying down a drainpipe. When he hit the ground he spit something he'd been carrying in his mouth out into his hand.

Murdock honked the horn and flashed the headlights.

Jaybird made a loping run to the pickup. He tried the door, but Razor had it locked.

Sterling knocked on the window, grinning good-naturedly. "Hey, Chief, could you let me in?"

"Let him in, for crying out loud," said Murdock. "I'd like to get the hell out of here before the cops come."

"Only if you make it an order, sir," said Razor, while Jaybird waited patiently outside.

"Consider it so," Murdock sighed.

Razor unlocked the door and slid over. Jaybird hopped in and sat down. Murdock gunned the engine and pulled out.

"Morning, sir," Jaybird said pleasantly. "Morning, Chief. Sorry to drag you out here."

Razor began darkly, "You dirty—"

"Excuse me, sir," Jaybird interrupted. "You wouldn't happen to have a blanket or something?"

"No," said Murdock.

"Too bad," said Jaybird, crossing his legs delicately.

Razor Roselli was talking unintelligibly to himself.

"Your ass is going back out on the street," said Murdock. "Unless I hear a story right quick."

"Well, sir," said Jaybird. "I was in a bar last night, and I met this girl."

"Imagine that," muttered Razor.

"This was one in a million, sir," Jaybird reported. "I was just sitting there having a beer, and this beautiful girl walks right up to me. Brown hair, blue eyes, tits like . . ." He pantomimed with his hands to give them an idea of the general dimensions. "Before I could say anything, or even buy her a drink, she says, 'I've been watching you for a while. I think you'd better come home with me.' "

"Yeah, *right*," said Razor Roselli.

"Don't be too hasty, Chief," said Murdock. "Take a look at how our boy here is dressed, and judge for yourself how the story is shaping up."

"Well, when you put it that way," said Razor.

"I swear it's the truth, Chief," said Jaybird. "I was there with my buddy Hanson, from Team One. He was right there, and he couldn't believe it either."

"So what did you do?" asked Razor.

"I went home with her," Jaybird replied, as if he couldn't believe the question. "We went to the bar in Hanson's car, but she said she'd drive me back to base."

"Jaybird," Razor said wearily, "you must've come in on the noon balloon."

"SEAL groupie," said Murdock. "Nutcase."

"Anyway," said Jaybird, anxious to get back to his story, "we head for her apartment. And all the way there she's telling me everything she wants to do. She practically rips my clothes off in the elevator. Now, I'm figuring, this is that night, right? The one you'll remember when you're eighty and still get hard thinking about it. And if we ended up actually doing everything she was talking about, my picture was going up in some Hall of Fame somewhere, and I'd get a plaque to commemorate the event. And if I died, they'd retire my number."

"Get *on* with it," said Razor.

"Okay," said Jaybird, "we're in the apartment, then we're in the bedroom. You should have seen this painting she had over her bed; I don't even know where you could buy something like that. . . . Anyway, my clothes are off, and I'll tell you, Chief, I had a hard-on that could cut glass."

"And at that point," said Razor, "she tells you she needs a hundred dollars to pay her mother's medical bills."

"I ain't never paid for it, Chief," Jaybird protested.

Roselli shot him a disbelieving look.

"Well, not with money," said Jaybird, grinning, "just little pieces of my heart."

"That's why the chicks dig him," Roselli said to Murdock. "He's deep."

"Am I ever going to hear this fucking story?" Murdock demanded.

"Like I said," said Jaybird. "We're in the bedroom, naked. Then someone starts pounding on the door."

"Uh, oh," Razor said facetiously.

"I stay in the bedroom, she goes to answer it," said Jaybird. "It's her husband."

"Who she neglected to mention all this time," said Murdock.

"Must have forgot," said Razor. "It's the oldest one in the book. You're standing there at attention, he's got a gun, and it's going to take the contents of your wallet to make him go away."

"I wasn't hanging around for any of that," said Jaybird. "There was a phone right there, so I made a real quick call to the duty."

"Good presence of mind," Murdock conceded.

"Then I went out the window," said Jaybird. "And over the balcony. And you know, the whole way down I couldn't stop thinking about everything she said. Took a couple of floors to lose my hard-on."

"Thanks for sharing that with us," said Murdock. Then, just for the sake of clarity; "And you did all this without your clothes."

"They were in the living room."

"You're sitting here in the lieutenant's truck with your wallet and your pager," Razor said dubiously. "But your clothes are back in her living room?"

"I'm not that green, Chief. I might get separated from my threads, but not my wallet and keys. I stuck 'em in my mouth when I went over the balcony."

"I don't ever want to know how you got them into the bedroom," said Murdock.

Jaybird opened his mouth.

"I told you I didn't want to know," Murdock said.

"Yes, sir."

"Jaybird," Murdock said kindly, "do you remember how you got your nickname?"

"Ah, yes, sir."

"Tell me," Murdock ordered.

"Well, sir, this girl and I—"

"Sounds familiar, doesn't it?" said Razor.

"We were getting it on in the ocean, and these people came down to the beach and parked right where we left our clothes. So we had to swim down the beach and escape and evade back to my car—"

"Naked, right?" Murdock interrupted.

"Yes, sir."

"And you got caught?"

"Yes, sir."

"And you were Jaybird forevermore. Jaybird?"

"Yes, sir?"

"One time you can put down to carelessness. Twice is starting to look like a personal problem."

"I see your point, sir. Sir?"

"Yes, Jaybird?"

"I'm never gonna live this one down, am I, sir?"

"No, I wouldn't think so," said Murdock.

Especially when they arrived back on base, and Razor Roselli marched Jaybird Sterling right through SEAL Team Seven headquarters on the way to get some clothes. Jaybird handled it well. His general demeanor was the same as that of the Queen of England when greeting her subjects. The SEALs, however, demanded an explanation.

13

Monday, September 19—Tuesday, November 7

Chocolate Mountain Gunnery Range
Niland, California

The CIA had wanted all the mission preparations to take place at their training facility at Camp Peary, Virginia, known as The Farm. Murdock, suspecting that their real desire was to supervise him more closely than he wanted, used the excuse that the residents of nearby Williamsburg wouldn't take kindly to thousand-pound demolition shots going off at all hours. So Niland it was. The country was suitably arid and covered with scrub, and the mountain range was perfect to train for the helicopter part of the mission.

But one of the advantages to working for the CIA rather than Special Operations Command was that things got done in days rather than weeks. Murdock found plenty for the platoon to do. First, everyone had to be briefed on the mission, even though only half the platoon, eight men, would be going. Someone might get sick, or have a training accident, and one of the others had to be ready to step in. Of course, Murdock also had a more devious motivation behind the arrangement. The second eight, furious at being left behind, would bust their balls in training to prove to the lieutenant that he'd made a mistake in not picking them. They would push the first eight so hard that Murdock wouldn't have to as much as raise his voice.

And the first eight would be Murdock, DeWitt, Roselli, Kosciuszko, Jaybird Sterling, Doc Ellsworth, Magic Brown, and Professor Higgins.

Once the plan was briefed, they fell into a daily routine. In the mornings they did a hard PT while the desert was still fairly cool, and then fell to on the book work. Each man would have to memorize the entire route they'd be driving. From the insertion landing zone, to Baalbek, then out of town to the extraction landing zone. Satellite photos were put through a stereoscopic projector to give a 3-D view. Murdock insisted that everyone commit the entire street plan of Baalbek to memory. It would be night, there might be no street signs or time to consult them, and they might also have to deviate from the planned route. Getting lost was not an option. Neither was stopping at the nearest gas station to ask for directions.

In the afternoons they drove out to a secluded spot on the eastern side of the Chocolate Mountain range. A team from the CIA's office of Technical Service had flown in with some civilian contractors and heavy equipment. Near an old dirt auxiliary landing strip they constructed a wooden replica of the Baalbek warehouse. Any Russian noticing something new on a satellite photograph would have figured it for an airplane hangar target, since SEALs practiced air base attacks all the time. Inquisitive SEALs from other platoons were encouraged to think the same thing. The Technical Service people surrounded the warehouse with a chain-link fence, and graded in a rough dirt road in exactly the right spot.

Technical Service were the people in the CIA who did everything from supplying disguises to agents to planting listening devices in objects without leaving a mark or a seam. They also supplied the Russian AKM assault rifles and PKM machine guns, the same weapons used by the Syrians, that the SEALs would be taking on the mission. The pink-dappled

Syrian camouflage uniforms, Presidential Guard berets and insignia, boots, and web gear were fitted to each man and then packed away for the actual mission.

With Hummvees initially standing in for the armored cars and limousines, and man-shaped metal targets scattered about, the SEALs practiced the actual mechanics of shooting their way into and out of the area. It was all done with live ammunition—SEALs never used blanks.

The trick, as always, was not so much hitting the targets. It was not accidentally shooting one of your own in the smoke, noise, and confusion. If you wanted it to come off fast, you had to first walk your way through step-by-step in daylight. Then half speed, then full speed in daylight. Then with live ammo, and then at night. It took time, and was as complex as any grand ballet. If you didn't rehearse, the wrong people died.

A few days later they were joined by what the Army called a Special Operations Aviation Task Force.

The Army's premier helicopter unit was the 160th Special Operations Aviation Regiment (Airborne). It had formed in the aftermath of the botched Iranian hostage rescue mission, when everyone had realized that the skills to fly helicopters behind enemy lines had been lost after Vietnam. The 160th had three battalions. The 1st and 2nd were the "black" battalions, stationed at Fort Campbell, Kentucky. The 3rd Battalion was stationed at Hunter Army Airfield in Savannah, Georgia. It supported the Army Rangers, in particular the 1st Ranger Battalion, also located at Hunter.

The task force that showed up at Niland to support Murdock consisted of five MH-60K Blackhawks of 1st Platoon, Bravo Company, 1st Battalion of the 160th, all eight MH-47E Chinooks of Alpha Company of the 2nd Battalion, and a maintenance element from the maintenance companies of both battalions.

These were not plain-vanilla helicopters. Both the Blackhawks and Chinooks had the same avionics suites, optimized for low-altitude penetration of hostile airspace: a forward-looking infrared system for night flying, in addition to the pilots' night-vision goggles; a terrain-following/terrain-avoidance/digital ground-mapping radar; automatic target handoff and digital automatic flight controls; radar and laser warning systems, infrared jammers, and chaff and flare dispensers to handle any missiles that might be launched at them; six-barrel 7.62mm miniguns for the door gunners to shoot at anything else that might bother them; and several redundant precision navigation and communications systems. Both aircraft types had in-flight refueling probes, and the Blackhawks had pylons for extra fuel tanks or weapons.

The task force was led by a dapper little major who sported a full mustache that wouldn't do him much good with his next Army promotion board. He listened carefully while Murdock briefed the plan and then broke into a huge smile, visions of Distinguished Flying Crosses obviously dancing in his head.

Besides a captain and two first lieutenants, the rest of the major's pilots were warrant officers. While Army commissioned officer pilots had to follow career paths and only did three-year tours with their respective units, all the warrants did was fly. In a unit like the 160th, which was all volunteer and handpicked the best pilots in the Army, that told.

The warrants were the kind of people who enjoyed screaming over the treetops at more than a hundred knots in the dead of night, their only view through the green tunnels of their night-vision goggles. So of course they couldn't wait to fly into Lebanon and get their asses shot off.

In fact, like Murdock's SEALs, the pilots nearly got into a fistfight after the major decided who was going to fly the mission and who would be backup.

Unlike Air Force helicopter pilots, who sometimes acted as if the safety of their expensive aircraft was more important to them than accomplishing the mission, the pilots of the 160th were beloved by the SEALs, Delta, and Special Forces. All you had to do was point to a spot on a map and the 160th would take you there, and when you were done working, fly back through any kind of weather, ground fire, or the gates of Hell itself to get you out. They were shit hot, and bigger prima donnas than even the SEALs. They called themselves the Nightstalkers.

And while the SEALs trained to take down the target, the Nightstalkers got busy. The National Security Agency had electronically mapped the location of every radar and antiaircraft system in Lebanon and Syria, and the pilots carefully plotted their route through the gaps and dead spaces. Satellite radar mapping gave them the exact radar images they would see in their scopes as they flew the route. Their computer planning system digitized satellite photographs and gave the crews a virtual-technology view of the route as seen through any of the aircraft windows. It could stimulate daylight, night, and night-vision-goggle light.

The pilots slept during the day and flew at night, skimming over the desert and through the canyons of the Chocolate Mountain range. They didn't need Murdock and the SEALs. The helicopters were loaded with the equivalent weight of the vehicles and personnel they'd be carrying, and if one went into the ground only the crew would be lost. The 160th had lost more men in training than they had in Panama, the Gulf, Somalia, and other unmentioned places around the world combined.

Then the Office of Technical Service showed up with the mission vehicles. The Shorlands armored cars were painted in Syrian camouflage with all details correct, even the extra smoke dischargers Murdock had requested.

The Shorlands had the same general shape as the classic Land Rover, except the body was steel armor. The engine, suspension, and tires had been beefed up to take the extra weight. The Shorlands normally came with a machine-gun turret on the top, but it made the vehicle too high to fit in the back of a Chinook and had been removed. Even if they had kept the turret, there wouldn't be room for anyone to work the gun; the entire compartment would be filled with explosives. The front lights were covered by heavy wire grills, and the bumpers were reinforced to take a heavy impact. Top speed from the four-stroke V-8 engine was sixty-five miles per hour. Being a British vehicle, it was right-hand-drive. Being good Americans, the SEALS were driven absolutely crazy learning to shift with their left hands.

The Mercedes were big black sedans, with Syrian flags on the front bumpers and little lights to illuminate the flags at night. The sedans were equipped with the German GSG-9 protective detail package: armor, run-flat tires, fire-suppression systems, ram bumpers, sirens, and firing ports. In fact, they were almost identical to the cars purchased by the first commanding officer of SEAL Team Six, an act that he described in his book as getting him in Dutch with the chicken-shit SEAL brass. All true as far as it went, but the unmentioned part of the story was that the Mercedes were so spiffy, the SEALs of Team Six drove their official military vehicles out into town for nights of partying. That was a bit beyond the pale, and other C.O.'s had been fired for much, much less.

For the explosives that would fill the armored cars, the CIA provided the first production samples of Trinittroazetidine, or TNAZ. TNAZ was brand new, and projected to replace C-4 plastic as the special operations explosive of choice. It generated fifteen percent more energy, with twenty percent less volume and weight. With it, Murdock expected close to the equivalent of a two-thousand-pound bomb from each vehicle.

Almost six weeks from the day they arrived in Niland, after a final live-fire rehearsal, the vehicles were loaded into the helicopters and everyone flew north to Edwards Air Force Base. There they began a movement that had taken weeks of work and enough classified message traffic to fill a room to arrange.

The helicopters were loaded aboard four C-5B transports, and the entire force flew to Naval Air Station Sigonella on the island of Sicily. They landed at night, and the Chinooks were reassembled in enclosed hangars.

The next night the helicopters took off from Sigonella and flew onto the aircraft carrier *U.S.S. George Washington.* They were immediately whisked down into the hangar deck. To make room for them, a squadron of the *Washington*'s FA-18's had flown off to Aviano, Italy. The official statement was that they would support operations in Bosnia while the *Washington* made a scheduled port call in Haifa, Israel.

In reality, the *U.S.S. George Washington* was making thirty knots for the coast of Lebanon.

14

Friday, November 10

0000 hours, midnight
Aboard the *U.S.S. George Washington* (CVN-73)
Eastern Mediterranean Sea

Third Platoon was waiting, enjoying the comfortable padded chairs of the ready room of the squadron they'd kicked off the ship.

They were dressed in their Syrian camouflage uniforms and berets. The blouses were sized a little large to make room for Kevlar armored vests with ceramic plate inserts that would, hopefully, stop rifle fire. Two extra pockets were sewn inside the camouflage outer jackets to carry an MX-300 walkie-talkie and an AN/PRC-112(V) combination survival radio and homing beacon. They were leaving in half an hour, so everyone was wearing his Syrian load-bearing web gear filled with magazines and grenades. The Kalashnikov AKM assault rifles were lying across their legs. Everyone's gear had been inspected. They were ready to go.

None were wearing dog tags or carrying the military I.D. cards required by the Geneva Convention. There was no need. Considering how brutally the Syrian government treated its own people, they certainly weren't going to go easy on American SEALs caught trying to blow up their one-hundred-dollar-bill machines. According to Amnesty International, the Syrians' favorite interrogation technique was to sit you down on a box that rammed a red-hot rod up your ass. The only answer to that was to not let them take you.

Murdock looked over the room. Professor Higgins was deeply engrossed in *The Peloponnesian War,* by Thucydides. He occasionally paused to poke Doc Ellsworth on the arm and cackle gleefully, "Two thousand, four hundred years and nothing's changed! The shit is still the same!"

Each time he did that, the Doc's pencil skidded across the crossword puzzle he was working on. He looked as if he wanted to amputate Higgins's arm with his combat knife.

Magic Brown and Razor Roselli were playing a game of chess on Magic's travel board. Jaybird Sterling was doing a whispered color commentary on the match, as if it were a football game. Magic Brown, who had the intense powers of concentration of a master sniper, was delighted. Razor Roselli, more easily distracted, was getting angrier by the minute. Especially since his position was deteriorating alarmingly.

Ed DeWitt and Kos Kosciuszko were giving the route map a last bit of study.

The second eight were sitting around the periphery, left out, hoping someone would suddenly succumb to food poisoning. Failing that, if things fell apart on the ground, four of them would be going in with the extraction Blackhawks. They were all the reaction force there would be.

Don Stroh and Paul Kohler of the CIA were dressed in Navy officers' khakis and trying to look unconcerned.

Murdock decided to get Sterling out of Razor's hair. "Jaybird, come here."

"Yes, sir." Jaybird took the seat next to Murdock.

"The CIA gave me some word I want to pass along," said Murdock. "That woman in the villa in Port Sudan. She was wanted by the French. It seems that she went around Paris planting bombs. Used her kid for cover."

Jaybird's expression didn't change. "Thanks, sir," he said. "But you know, even if she was just an Avon lady out showing her samples, I would have had to pop her anyway. We couldn't take her along, and we couldn't let her go. The politicians can make up all the rules they want, but we have to deal with the real world." He shrugged his shoulders. "Just as well it's all secret, 'cause nobody else but us would understand."

Murdock was going to get out of the Navy if SEALs ever ceased to amaze him. He had no expectation of that ever happening.

There was a knock at the door, and a White Shirt Landing Signalman Enlisted appeared in his safety vest, hard hat, and earmuffs. The shirt color indicated that he was one of those responsible for safety on the flight deck. "Ready, gentlemen," he said.

The first eight threw on their gear, while the rest helped out and gave them a last word of encouragement.

Murdock grabbed Miguel Fernandez. "Stay close to the CIA guys. I'll call you if I need you."

"I'll be there, sir," Fernandez promised.

Murdock shook hands with Stroh and Kohler. They wished him good luck.

The SEALs followed the White Shirt down a passageway lit by red night-light. They went out the hatch and the flight deck was as dark as a cave, with only the silhouettes of the chained-down aircraft visible against the lighter horizon. The SEALs all put on their night-vision goggles, and the deck became a secret party that only the elect could see.

The flight deck was bathed in the glow of infrared lighting compatible with night-vision goggles. Four big two-rotor Chinook helicopters were waiting on the edge of the deck, turbine engines screaming. A fifth sat motionless on one of the elevators in case any of the four went down. Thermal strips on the end of each rotor blade made a solid circle of light as they turned. Other discreet strips on the fuselages were the only anticollision precautions. There wasn't a light showing in any of the aircraft. The flight deck crew were using infrared chemical light sticks instead of their usual illuminated wands to pass signals across the deck.

The weather report had indicated a low-pressure area over Lebanon; a light drizzle was falling and the cloud cover was very low. A bigger storm was on the way, maybe a thunderstorm. From a SEAL's perspective the weather was perfect, but Murdock had to defer to the helicopter pilots. They were willing. There would be few if any other aircraft flying, and the ground antiaircraft defenses would be accordingly relaxed. Unlike other aircraft, helicopters did not as a rule fly in non-visual flight conditions. The 160th's helicopters were among the few in the world capable of doing just that, and would be entirely on instruments. Forward-looking infrared could see through cloud and rain to a certain extent, but night-vision goggles couldn't.

The SEALs split up and followed individual white shirts to their designated aircraft. Murdock and Roselli headed for the first bird, with a Shorlands armored car inside.

Jaybird and Doc went to the second, which carried a Mercedes limo.

Magic and Higgins went to the third, with the second limo.

DeWitt and Kosciuszko went to the final Chinook, with the second armored car.

As they approached the helicopter, Murdock and Razor passed through a shroud of hot exhaust air that smelled like burned kerosene. They climbed in the side door just behind the cockpit. The helicopter crewman looked like a huge insect with the twin tubes of his ANVIS-6 night-vision goggles protruding from his helmet. He secured the hatch and went down to his gunner's window. He and his partner on the other side would be leaning out all during takeoff, giving the pilot helpful directions about any obstacles that might get in the way of the aircraft.

The Shorlands armored car was chained to the floor. It had been backed in so it was pointed right at the rear ramp hatch for a quick drive-off.

Murdock and Roselli strapped themselves into two jump seats on opposite sides of the fuselage near the front of the aircraft. They each had a headset plugged into the helicopter intercom system.

Murdock checked his watch. The second hand ticked over and, exactly on time, the cyclic pitch of the rotors increased, the fuselage shook, and they took off. The Chinook lifted straight up about twenty feet, then lurched to the left to clear the flight deck. Once they were out over water the bird picked up more height and speed.

Murdock sat back and accustomed himself to the peculiar feeling of going forward, up and down, and side to side all at the same time that made helicopter travel so interesting.

They made landfall, crossing a sparsely populated section of the Lebanese coast between Byblos and Jounié. Murdock looked out the window over his shoulder and saw only a blank wall of green through his goggles. He could almost hear the treetops scraping on the bottom of the helicopter. He and Razor took off their life preservers, since instead of crashing into the water and flipping over and sinking, now the only danger was the helicopter hitting the ground and exploding into an enormous fireball.

A short while later the helicopter pitched upward as the terrain-following radar led it up the slope of the Mount Lebanon range.

As they gained altitude, the turbulence rattled the Chinook around. They hit an air pocket, and the helicopter dropped like a rock. Murdock automatically put his head between his legs in the crash position. Then they were flying again, and Murdock straightened up to see Razor Roselli grinning maniacally at him. Through the goggles he could make out Razor carefully mouthing the words, "Kissing your ass good-bye?"

The cockpit chatter through Murdock's headset became busier. An E-2C Hawkeye radar aircraft from the carrier was providing regular reports on all the air traffic in the area, which aside from an occasional passenger jet and an F-15 combat air patrol over northern Israel, was nonexistent. The helicopters were just listening, and would not break radio silence even to talk to each other except in an emergency. They were also carefully monitoring their radar-warning receivers for any indications of hostile sets. The receivers gave off a tone when any radar energy hit the aircraft. There was just a regular chirp in their headsets as the AWACS radar swept over, but they were going so low and so slow it was doubtful that even the E-2 with digital signal processing could get a return off them.

They rattled between the peaks of the mountain range, and then lurched down the slope toward the Bekaa Valley.

The main highway of Lebanon led from Beirut on the coast over the mountains to Damascus, Syria. But a branch of that headed north along the entire Bekaa Valley, to Homs in northern Syria. That highway went right past Baalbek, and Murdock wanted to get on it south of the city.

Dirt roads led from the villages along the slope down onto the valley highway. The helicopters were going to land alongside one where there was enough room to set down and they would be out of earshot of the nearest village, a little place called Majdaloun, population 610.

"Five minutes," the pilot said over the intercom.

"Roger," said Murdock.

Razor Roselli unstrapped himself from his seat and carefully made his way to the armored car. He inched through the narrow gap between the vehicle and the fuselage, and squeezed into the right-hand driver's door.

Murdock went all the way down to the rear ramp of the helicopter. When they landed he'd walk around and check the ground, take a little look around, then guide Razor out. He braced himself next to the crew chief stationed at the ramp, and plugged his headset into the intercom jack.

He could hear the strain in the pilots' voices as they headed down. The copilot was watching the ground through the forward-looking infrared. The FLIR was mounted on a chin turret in the front of the helicopter. The copilot could swivel it around, and the image was projected on a cockpit panel display. He was giving directions to the pilot, who was flying the helicopter. The pilot couldn't see a thing outside, so he kept his eyes locked on the instruments.

"Trees on the right, we're drifting right."

"Roger."

"Fifty feet."

"Come back a bit, we've got a boulder right in front of us."

"Roger."

Murdock glanced at the crew chief. The man was trying to look nonchalant, and not succeeding. Murdock cocked his AKM and kept the barrel pointed at the floor. A helicopter's vitals were all above the fuselage, and it would be professionally embarrassing to accidentally shoot a hole in them.

"Okay, you're on."

"Twenty feet."

"Hold it steady."

The Chinook came to ground at a slight tilt, and then leveled off as all the wheels touched down.

The crew chief dropped the ramp. Murdock took off his headset and charged out into a cold rainy Lebanese night. The ground was firm enough for the armored car. He couldn't see anything, and doubted if anyone could see him. When he went back up the ramp the crew had the chains off the vehicle. Murdock signaled Razor to follow him out.

It had been a textbook insertion, brought off without a hitch. Razor Roselli turned the key, and the engine refused to start.

15

Saturday, November 11

0112 hours
Bekaa Valley
Lebanon

"Come *on*!" Murdock shouted.

Razor tried three more times, and all the engine did was flood itself.

Murdock was gripped by the most overwhelming rage of his life. He was not going to fail, and he was not going to let the helicopter fly back to the ship with that damned armored car inside. It didn't make much sense; there was plenty of room in the other Mercedes, but that was rage for you.

Razor had the armored flap window on his driver's door open so he could hear. "Throw it in neutral," Murdock shouted. "Push it out!" he screamed at the air crew.

Murdock and the crew chief got on each side of the front bumper, and the two gunners pushed from behind. The helicopter was slightly inclined, so it didn't take too much strength to get the car going.

The car was soon moving under its own momentum, and just before it reached the bottom of the ramp it gave a bouncing lurch forward and the engine roared.

Razor Roselli stuck his head out the door and gave Murdock a thumbs-up.

Murdock's only reaction was a warm but short-lived rush of relief. There was still too much to do. He gave the crew chief the "clear to take off" hand signal, then got in front of the armored car and guided Razor through the muddy field and out to the hard-packed dirt road. He could hear the other helicopters still on the ground. Two had landed in the fields on each side of the road.

One of the Mercedes, with Professor Higgins at the wheel and Magic Brown beside him, eased out of the brush on the opposite side of the road.

"Where are the others?" Murdock demanded.

"The birds landed back there but I haven't seen anyone yet," Magic reported.

"Join up with Razor and secure the road," Murdock ordered. As he ran up the road, the four Chinooks lifted off, one after the other. Murdock charged through the brush bordering the road and discovered the second Mercedes mired in the muddy field, spinning its wheels uselessly. Jaybird Sterling was out cutting some branches to throw under the wheels. "Sit tight," Murdock yelled.

The frustration was almost unbearable. He ran back through the brush to the road, just as DeWitt and Kosciuszko in their Shorlands emerged from the other side. Murdock gave them the "follow me" hand signal and guided them over to the Mercedes. He and Jaybird unwrapped the steel tow cable from the front bumper of the armored car and, diving into the mud, attached it to the axle of the Mercedes. The Shorlands skidded around, and they hooked the other end of the cable onto one of the armored car's rear tow loops.

The rain came down even harder. The armored car, in four-wheel drive, slowly dragged the Mercedes across the field and out to the road. Murdock walked in front to make sure they didn't hit any stumps or go into a ditch.

So Murdock was the first one out onto the road. His first sight was a pair of headlights coming on very fast.

Murdock held up a hand and brandished his weapon, but the Lebanese evidently felt the same way as American highway drivers about stopping at night for armed men.

The selector switch of the Kalashnikov AKM goes from safe directly to full auto. Which was convenient, as Murdock hit the lever with his left forefinger the same instant as he squeezed the trigger with his right. He emptied the entire thirty-round magazine into the car as it sped past him. The car skidded back and forth as the driver jerked the wheel under the impact of the rounds, but it kept going. Murdock watched helplessly as his mission was compromised before they'd even started.

Then Razor Roselli, at the wheel of the Shorlands, shot out of the darkness and broadsided the car in an explosion of glass and metal. It was no contest. The crumpled car spun off the road and slammed into a tree.

The automatic fire had left the barrel of Murdock's AKM glowing red. He changed magazines and rushed up. Through the rain he could see two white muzzle flashes flare up as Magic Brown and Higgins raked the car at point-blank range. When they ceased fire Murdock ran his red-lensed flashlight over the car's interior. It was a mess; he couldn't even tell how many people had originally been inside.

"Push it all the way off the road and throw some brush on it," Murdock shouted. "And hurry up, I want to get out of here before someone else shows up."

He ran back up the road and found the others sitting tight with their weapons ready, having heard the shooting but not knowing what had happened. "Let's go, let's go," Murdock yelled. He was starting to get hoarse.

They got the vehicles onto the road, and then had to unhook the tow cable and re-stow it on the Shorlands. Jaybird and Doc gave the Mercedes a quick once-over, and wiped off as much mud as they could.

To Murdock it seemed the faster they went the slower everything got. Finally the Lebanese car was concealed off the road and they were ready to get started.

Murdock checked out his Shorlands. The impact with the car had barely scratched the paint on the welded steel body. He jumped into the passenger seat, soaking wet, covered with mud, and shivering. His wool beret had sagged down over his ears, and the once-shiny emblem was dirtied by mud. There was hardly any room to move; the entire compartment of the vehicle from the two front seats back was packed solid with blocks of TNAZ explosive linked by detonating cord. "What a goatfuck," Murdock mumbled.

"The time isn't good," said Razor Roselli.

Murdock looked at his watch for the first time since they'd landed. Jesus, they'd used up almost fifty minutes of the precious darkness just getting unscrewed.

Cool down, now, Blake, he told himself. When you're pissed you don't think right, and you only make the boys nervous. Murdock took a deep breath. "Let's get going," he said evenly. He reached over and turned the vehicle's heater up to full blast.

With their armored car in the lead, then the two Mercedes, and finally DeWitt and Kos bringing up the rear in the second armored car, the SEALs started down the road into the cold Lebanese night.

16

Saturday, November 11

0204 hours
Bekaa Valley
Lebanon

"Don't forget Roselli's First Rule, Boss," Razor told Murdock as they sped up the highway. "The more fucked up an operation starts off, the more successful it's going to end."

"We've got nothing to worry about then," Murdock replied.

They'd gotten down off the mountain road, which was only slightly more improved than a goat path, without any more problems. The highway into Baalbek was two lanes, paved. There wasn't much traffic in the Bekaa Valley at one o'clock in the morning. Not many had the guts.

The occasional car they did encounter gave them a wide berth at the first sight of their markings. Syria kept its thumb firmly on Lebanon with the help of a forty-thousand-strong army of occupation. Ever since the civil war of the 1970's, their methods had been simple, effective, and ruthless. Whenever a faction became too powerful, the Syrians would ally with the faction's enemies and crush it. These alliances could shift with dizzying speed; friends would become enemies and then make friends again over the course of a week or two.

The Syrians currently had close links with Iran, whom they'd backed in the 1980's war with Iraq. And the Iranians were the founders, backers, and directors of the Lebanese Shiite Moslem Hezbollah, or Party of God, perpetrators of the Marine barracks bombing in Beirut, kidnappers of numerous Westerners in the 1980's.

Though Syria liked to protest to the world that the religious fanatics of Hezbollah were uncontrollable, their arms shipments and Revolutionary Guard advisors from Iran had to come into Lebanon through the Damascus airport. This gave Syria notification and veto rights over Hezbollah operations. And Syria used Hezbollah to keep up military pressure on the Israeli Army in southern Lebanon, through car bombs and ambushes. Conveniently, this meshed well with Hezbollah's stated goal of killing as many Jews as possible.

"Okay," said Murdock, hunched over his map. "Fork coming up. Right is the dirt road to Ain Bourdai, left is to the Roman ruins. We're going straight."

"We should be hitting a checkpoint pretty damn soon too," said Razor.

As they approached the outskirts of Baalbek, the checkerboard fields changed to tiny villages of low-slung stone buildings, thickets of roadside trees, and the large murals that were the Lebanese equivalent of billboards.

The first one they saw proclaimed, in English: *Hezbollah welcomes you by his pioneer values.*

It provoked some general snickering inside the car.

"Remember that intel report?" said Murdock. "The one about Hezbollah trying to persuade tour groups to come and visit the Roman ruins west of town?"

"The temples used to be a big tourist attraction," said Razor. Then: "Check this out."

The next mural was a crude representation of fists punching through American and British flags, and demanded: *Israel must be eliminated.*

"I think the tourism committee needs to sit down and take a meeting with the hate committee and the translation committee," said Razor.

"Come visit Baalbek," said Murdock. "We'll throw you in a cellar and chain you to the wall. You'll never want to leave."

"The whole family will love it!" Razor exclaimed. "It's really too bad their marketing campaign is going to be ruined in about an hour."

They both chuckled. It was good to release some of the tension.

"Checkpoint ahead," Razor said calmly.

Murdock shifted the Kalashnikov in his lap, and keyed his radio. "This is One, checkpoint three-hundred meters."

"Two, roger," Doc Ellsworth responded from the Mercedes behind them.

"Three, roger," said Magic Brown from the second limo.

"Four, roger," replied Ed DeWitt from the Shorlands bringing up the rear.

The transmissions were encrypted, so anyone who might be listening to a scanner was just picking up hums, clicks, hisses, and static.

The rain and the wipers beat against the windshield. The headlights fell upon a concrete shack, and a few figures, attracted by the light, began to emerge from it. Murdock could make out the familiar silhouette of the Kalashnikov in several hands. One of the figures balanced on his shoulder what looked like a piece of pipe with a cone on one end. An RPG-7 rocket-propelled grenade launcher, an antitank weapon with enough penetration to punch right through the Shorlands steel armor and probably continue right out the other side.

"No hesitation," said Murdock. "We're going right through, one way or the other."

"Drop the armored visors over the windshield?" Razor asked.

"No," said Murdock. "We're just driving along, we're not

concerned." He made sure all the external lights were on, and that the large Syrian flag flapping from the aerial hadn't fallen off. It was still there. A glance in the rearview mirror showed him that the limos had their flashing lights on.

They approached the checkpoint at a bold forty miles per hour, don't-screw-with-me speed. As they got closer Murdock could see the figures move more urgently and start to bring their weapons up.

0223 hours
Bekaa Valley

"The lieutenant's going too fucking fast," Jaybird said to Doc Ellsworth.

"So?" Doc replied calmly. "It's not like we can do anything about it, so why sweat it?"

Jaybird cocked the big Russian PKM machine gun lying across his lap and slid the barrel into the door gun port of the Mercedes. "I only see one RPG. When the lieutenant and Razor catch that rocket, try to go around them so they screen us from the checkpoint. I'll hose 'em down, and if we're lucky we'll all get through before they get the launcher reloaded."

"Hey," Doc said sharply, "enough of the bad karma, all right? Those motherfuckers pick up any negative energy from this car and I'll shoot you myself."

"Okay, okay," Jaybird relented. "I'll start thinking positively, I swear." Nothing else you could do, he thought, if the nuttiest one around was your medical corpsman. They should never have let Doc near California; he was way too cosmic to begin with.

Pleased, Doc smiled. "Good. Now put that weapon back on safe and shoot some warm and fuzzy thoughts at those ragheaded bastards."

0224 hours
Bekaa Valley

As they sped closer to the checkpoint, the silhouetted figures slowly changed into men. Murdock saw the rifles ready on their shoulders, the RPG gunner tracking them through his sight. They were about twenty yards away now. Murdock reached down and flicked the siren switch, just one quick arrogant blast.

They passed through the checkpoint, and Murdock waited for the rocket's impact. He looked again in the rearview mirror. Everyone was talking with their hands, gesturing wildly. He could almost hear them yelling at each other as the limos passed. Then the armored car. They were all through.

In retrospect, at least, it was clear that the psychology was perfect. Now matter how suspicious, paranoid, or dedicated the men at the checkpoint had been, they were much like the highway patrolmen watching the car of the governor's wife weaving down the road late at night. They knew they ought to do their job, but they also know just how sorry they could end up being.

"We're in," said Razor. "The Lebanese might fuck with each other, but no one fucks with the Syrians. And even the Syrians don't fuck with Syrian big shots."

"Let's get a move on anyway," said Murdock. "Before someone picks up the phone and calls down the line to see if any visitors are expected."

They sped through two more checkpoints, the men manning them exhibiting the same indecision. Then they were inside Baalbek. It was a town of a little more than sixteen thousand people. Green banners hung from houses. A huge mural of a woman in a full-body *chador* exhorted the ladies of the town to maintain Islamic modesty in their dress. If they knew what was good for them, Murdock thought. Iranian flags flew in the streets. Around Baalbek lay the remains of the fallen empires. The Phoenicians; the Romans, who had called Baalbek Heliopolis, the city of the sun; the Crusaders, whose forts littered the landscape; and in the 20th century the French. Now the Syrians, and Iranians far from home spreading a Revolution that hadn't managed to make it past a few poor towns in the Bekaa Valley.

There were occasional sandbagged gun emplacements in front of buildings, but they were unmanned. The streets were narrow and deserted. The rain and the Friday Moslem Sabbath had seen to that. Murdock doubted there was much nightlife in Baalbek anyway.

"Is this the turn?" Razor asked suddenly.

"Yeah, that's it," Murdock replied, counting the streets off in his head. He reached under his seat and took out a Kevlar helmet. He placed it on Razor Roselli's head. Razor tugged the chin strap into place. Murdock put on his own helmet. A hundredth look in the rearview mirror, and the others were still with him.

"There's the warehouse," Razor exclaimed.

They dropped the two steel shutters over the windshield, and now the forward visibility was restricted to two narrow armored glass slits.

Murdock keyed his radio. "This is One. Rattler, over." It was the code word to execute the primary attack plan. None of the contingencies they'd thought up would be necessary. The other three vehicles acknowledged.

The four separate fuses that led back to the explosives were taped to the dashboard in front of Murdock. He peeled off the tape and gathered them all up in a bunch in his left hand. He took a deep breath and let it out.

"Time to earn all that combat pay," said Razor Roselli.

Murdock noticed that the rain had stopped. He didn't believe in omens, but it gave him a little shiver.

17

Saturday, November 11

0249 hours
Baalbek
Lebanon

Razor Roselli stomped on the gas pedal and the heavy vehicle lurched forward. Blake Murdock's heart jumped as the wheels skidded on the wet road, but Razor straightened it out.

The chain-link fence, topped with barbed wire, bordered the right side of the road. The warehouse it protected was about twenty feet beyond.

When they were just past the midpoint of the warehouse, Razor twisted the steering wheel to the right and took the armored car off the road.

They hit the fence at a shallow angle; any more of a turn at that speed and they would have flipped over. The chain link snapped off the poles and then separated at its weakest point, but a big strip wrapped around the front of the armored car. It didn't slow them down very much.

Murdock hit a switch on the dash, and there was a hard thump as the four-barrel smoke dischargers on each side of the turret launched eight screening smoke grenades in a circular pattern around the vehicle.

The wall of the warehouse came up fast. Murdock braced himself against the impact, hoping there wasn't something large and solid, like a forklift, sitting up against the wall inside the warehouse.

The seven thousand-odd pounds of armored car going at forty-five miles an hour punched right through the wall in a cracking explosion of lumber and splinters. If Razor hadn't immediately stood on the brake, they would have gone out the other side.

As soon as they skidded to a stop, Murdock hit another switch and the second pair of smoke dischargers went off. Only four smoke grenades were launched this time. The other four barrels were loaded with 66mm Haley and Weller fragmentation grenades. These were designed to be launched the same way as screening smoke, but packed a bursting charge surrounded by several thousand steel ball bearings. Just the thing to take care of any unwanted enemy personnel who might be lurking around an armored vehicle.

Not intended for confined spaces, the grenades hit the ceiling and exploded. It didn't diminish their effect. Murdock and Razor were safe behind the armor, but anyone outside wasn't.

Murdock activated the fuses in his hand and tripped the last toggle on the dashboard. It armed a mercury switch that would fire the charges if anyone tried to drag the vehicle out or if it took a heavy impact—like the other armored car detonating.

"My door's jammed!" Razor yelled.

Murdock wrenched his open. "Follow me out!" He fell out the door with his AKM in his right hand and a box that looked like a full-size VHS camcorder in his left. It was a Marconi HHI-8 hand-held thermal imager. The warehouse was filled with the thick white smoke from the grenades, and the imager was the only way they'd be able to find their way out fast. It weighed about ten pounds, and saw objects on the basis of their heat, in varying shades of black and white. Because of this, it could look right through smoke.

Murdock swept the imager around and saw a line of printing presses, machinery, and wooden crates. At least they'd hit the right spot, a minor miracle in American intelligence terms. He could also see the other armored car: Ed and Kos had made it in.

The grenades hadn't got everyone; there were people still running around, but Murdock didn't shoot. If he did they would know where *he* was in the smoke. It didn't fit their public image, but operating in small groups with limited ammunition loads had taught SEALs to avoid firefights whenever possible.

Razor hopped out behind him and paused to lock the door. A small detail, but by the time someone dug up an acetylene torch to try to cut their way inside the vehicle, it would be too late.

The imager showed Murdock the huge hole they'd made in the wall, and he headed for it. There was just enough visibility for Razor to be able to follow him through the smoke, if he stayed close.

Then Murdock heard machine-gun fire start up outside.

0250 hours
Baalbek
Lebanon

The Mercedes was parked in the road right in front of the hole Murdock and Razor had left in the fence. Jaybird Sterling had his window down and his PKM machine gun set up on a homemade welded U-mount over the door frame. Another Marconi thermal imager was mounted atop his machine gun feed cover. Doc Ellsworth was still behind the wheel, occasionally tossing beer-can-sized white smoke grenades out his window.

Through his imager Jaybird picked up hot human figures running out from around the far corner of the warehouse. He had his radio set on voice-activated and called out, "Troops, warehouse, north corner," at the same time he opened fire.

Jaybird's first burst took two of the figures down. He'd removed the tracer ammunition from his ammo belts; tracer allowed you to see where your rounds were going, but also let everyone else know exactly where they were coming from. He didn't need it; the imager was so sensitive he could track the hot path of his bullets in the air. As the rounds impacted, the other figures slipped, stumbled, and ran back into cover around the side of the warehouse. The two crumpled forms lay motionless in harsh white contrast against the cooler ground.

Jaybird slowed his rate of fire, but kept shooting at the corner of the warehouse. Imagers couldn't see through solid objects, but it was easy enough to guess where they had taken cover, and the Russian 7.62-x-54mm rimmed rounds were heavy enough to punch right through the wooden wall.

It looked like the bad guys were pretty well pinned down. Doc Ellsworth was keeping an eye on the houses on the other side of the road, but no one was sticking their nose out.

Then someone started hollering over the radio.

0251 hours
Baalbek
Lebanon

Ed DeWitt, imager in hand, was leading Kos Kosciuszko out of the warehouse when an automatic weapon opened up off to their right.

DeWitt hit the deck at the first bullwhip crack of the rounds going by. Slugs kept snapping overhead, and a few ricochets skidded off the concrete floor. DeWitt made an instinctive decision not to return fire. Murdock and Roselli were somewhere in that direction, and might be in his line of fire. Besides, he could sense that the rounds were coming in blind.

DeWitt didn't have time to wait for the fire to taper off. Preparing to make a dash for the hole in the wall, he looked back to make sure Chief Kosciuszko was ready.

But Kosciuszko was lying face-down on the floor, unconscious. There was no time to check him over. DeWitt sprang to his feet and lifted Kos up bodily into a fireman's carry. Fortunately, both his AKM and imager were securely strapped to his body, SEAL-fashion, so he didn't lose them.

There was about a seventy-pound weight differential between them, in Kosciuszko's favor, but adrenaline and SEAL determination were wonderful things.

DeWitt shook one hand free and got the imager up to his eyes. Waddling as fast as he could under his burden, he headed out of the warehouse.

0251 hours
Baalbek
Lebanon

Magic Brown was firing his PKM at the southern corner of the warehouse. In the edge of his imager he saw DeWitt coming out with Kosciuszko on his shoulders. It looked like a huge body floating along under two tiny legs.

"Kos is down," he shouted. It went out over the radio net.

Without a word, Professor Higgins sprang out the driver's door of the Mercedes and charged through the hole in the fence into the smoke.

Higgins didn't have an imager. "Mister DeWitt!" he shouted.

"Over here," came the response.

Magic Brown went through a 250-round belt at the rapid rate to give them covering fire.

Higgins followed DeWitt's voice through the smoke until he found them. With two to carry Kosciuszko, the job went faster. They dragged him through the fence and threw him into the back seat of the Mercedes.

Higgins ran around the car to get back behind the wheel. The smoke had dissipated slightly in his absence and someone in a house on the other side of the road opened up on the now-visible car.

Rounds hit the Mercedes but didn't penetrate the armor.

Higgins ducked back around the car for cover and returned fire with his AKM.

The house was on the opposite side of the car from Magic and his PKM; there was nothing he could do but get off the gun and chuck smoke grenades out the window as fast as he could pull the pins.

The smoke billowed up. Higgins came in through Magic's door, crawled right over him in a thrashing, profane-rich tangle, and slid back behind the wheel.

Even though they could no longer see, someone still had the range. Rounds were hitting the vehicle but the armor was stopping them. It was time to get the hell out.

"Two, this is Three," Magic Brown spoke over the radio. "Lightning, Lightning, over." The code word for everyone present and ready to go.

0252 hours
Baalbek
Lebanon

Murdock and Razor had already made it to their Mercedes, and that was the word they had been waiting for.

"This is 1," said Murdock. "Roger Lightning."

"The bad guys are starting to stack up at the north corner," Jaybird Sterling informed them as he fired.

"Okay, then we won't go that way," said Murdock. "This is Two. Stand by for Route Echo. I say again, Route Echo."

"Roger on Echo," replied Magic Brown.

"Execute," said Murdock.

Doc Ellsworth swung the Mercedes into a screeching U-turn and sped back down the road the same way they'd come. Jaybird pulled the PKM back in the car and brought up the armored glass window.

Murdock was looking out the rear window. As they went past, Higgins yanked the second Mercedes into an identical turn and pulled in right behind.

They emerged from the smoke just in time to see and be seen by a startled group of Syrians huddled against the side of the warehouse. There was also a BMP-1 armored personnel carrier whose turret began to swing around as they passed.

"Floor it!" Murdock bellowed.

A rocket sailed over the top of the car. There was a huge flash from the BMP's 73mm gun, but the two Mercedes were moving faster than the turret could traverse and the shell fell behind them.

A line of slugs stitched the side windows of the Mercedes, but only made stars in the polycarbonate material. Razor Roselli had been looking out at the time and the impacts made him instinctively jump. He fell back against a very preoccupied Blake Murdock, who elbowed him out of his lap. Needing to vent some embarrassment, Razor stuck his AKM out the gun port and loosed off a burst. The hot cartridge casings ejected from Razor's weapon sailed right onto the back of Doc Ellsworth's neck.

The Doc yelped in pain and the car swerved. What effect that drive-by shooting had had on the Syrians was unknown, but the interior of the Mercedes was now filled with burned gunpowder smoke.

"Cease fire, for crissakes," shouted Murdock. "You'll gas us out."

Jaybird was trying to wave the smoke away so he could see out the window. "I think we're clear."

"Turn on the lights and siren," Murdock ordered, coughing. "And open the fucking vents."

18

Saturday, November 11

0253 hours
Baalbek
Lebanon

"How bad is he hit?" a worried Magic Brown asked Ed DeWitt.

"Give me a second," DeWitt replied.

The Mercedes was screaming through the streets of Baalbek, and Kos Kosciuszko was laid out across the back seat.

His flashlight held in his teeth, DeWitt began a search for wounds. It was best done by touch, and had to be thorough. Even a very small wound missed could mean a man bleeding to death.

DeWitt started at the feet, for no reason other than that was where he happened to be. He ran his hands up both legs—no blood, no wounds. He ripped open Kos's jacket and body armor. Nothing. Without moving Kos, he slipped his hands underneath and checked the back. No vertebrae out of place. What the hell?

Then his flashlight fell on Koscuiszko's helmet. There was a neat round hole in the front left side. DeWitt unsnapped the chin strap and gently eased the helmet off. There were no holes in Kos's head, but there was another one in the back of the helmet.

The round had hit the helmet, skipped off one of the kevlar layers, and gone back out at an angle. All it had done was knock Kos Kosciuszko cold.

DeWitt checked, but there was no blood in the ears or nose that would indicate a serious concussion. He opened Kos's eyes and flashed the light at them. Both pupils were responsive and symmetrical.

Kos gave off a low moan when the light hit his eyes.

"He took a round in the helmet and got knocked out," DeWitt announced. "The son of a bitch doesn't even have a bruise."

"You gotta be shitting us," said Magic Brown.

"No shit," DeWitt assured him. He hoisted Kos up and packed him against the corner of the rear seat. "Anyone got an ammonia capsule?"

There was no response.

"Fuck him, then," said DeWitt. He made himself comfortable, and they left Kos Kosciuszko to regain consciousness on his own. If you didn't require some major first aid, you couldn't expect much sympathy from a bunch of SEALs.

DeWitt keyed his radio. "Kos just got knocked out. He doesn't have a scratch."

"Roger," Murdock radioed back. He'd been pondering whether to stop somewhere and transfer the Doc to the other Mercedes. Now it was one less thing to worry about.

"Checkpoint ahead," Doc Ellsworth broke in. Then, cocking an eyebrow at Jaybird, he added, "And no, I ain't slowing down."

"*Out*standing," said Murdock.

Jaybird just shook his head.

They came up on the checkpoint with the Mercedes' police lights flashing and the sirens wailing. Even if there had been radio reports of raiders and a firefight, they looked like they were chasing something—not being chased. Enemy commandos certainly wouldn't be making all that noise. If not, they at least looked official enough to raise the same doubts as before.

The noise of the sirens had everyone out and ready at the checkpoint.

"Jiggle the siren switch," Murdock ordered. "Change the tone and let them know we see them."

Jaybird did it.

"Flash the lights and go on through," said Murdock.

The car filled with the metallic clicking of weapon safety catches coming off.

As they sped through the checkpoint Murdock saw one man raise his rifle and another yank it down. Even the visible bullet holes in the vehicles didn't tip the scales against them. Of course, you couldn't get that good a look at night and at that speed.

Where they had come up from the south, now they headed northeast. There was a hard-surface secondary road that snaked up into the mountains and all the way back down to Batröun and Tripoli on the coast. Murdock had identified a number of possible helicopter landing zones for the pickup, but he wanted to get as close to the mountains as he could. The valley was gently rolling and almost treeless, and the visibility extended for miles. As the land rose up toward the base of the mountains it became much more forested. Murdock wanted to get inside the screen of those trees, to minimize any exposure to the helicopters. It all depended on the time. The helicopters had to get in and out before daylight. That was definite.

In the second Mercedes, Kos Kosciuszko woke up. And like any good SEAL, he woke up fighting.

Ed DeWitt's first clue came when an arm the size of a country ham came swinging into his shoulder. DeWitt went sailing against the passenger door.

Magic Brown made a quick appreciation of the situation and dove over the front seat onto Kos. He was joined by DeWitt, and they tried to hold Kosciuszko down, shouting, "Chief, Chief, it's us, it's us."

Kos came to his senses fast, which was good, because Brown and DeWitt were on the verge of losing.

"Wha . . . what?" Kos stuttered.

"It's okay, Chief," said DeWitt, panting hard. "You took a rap on the head. You're okay."

Kosciuszko shook his head to clear it, and then grabbed his temples. "Man, my head hurts. Anybody got a couple of aspirin?"

Magic Brown crawled back over the front seat and rummaged around for the first aid kit, grumbling quietly to himself, "Fucking gorilla."

DeWitt fell back in his seat and took a little breather. He gingerly worked his arm. He thought that if he hadn't been wearing body armor, Kos's first shot would have broken his collarbone.

In the first Mercedes, Murdock was looking at his dive watch: 0258 hours. They had two minutes or so before the armored cars blew, and he wanted to be through the next checkpoint *before* that happened.

Then Ed DeWitt noticed headlights coming up behind them. So much for the breather. "We've got company in back," he reported.

Murdock heard it in his earpiece. "Get out some PDMs."

Ed DeWitt grabbed a bulging nylon bag from the rear seat storage area. Kos Kosciuszko was washing down three aspirins. "Get yourself together," DeWitt told him. "I'll take care of this."

The bag was filled with one-pound canisters about the same size as a nine-volt lantern battery, but with only three sides. The M-86 Pursuit Deterrent Munition had been designed to aid Special Forces teams being chased by larger enemy forces.

If you were running like a bastard, all you had to do was pull the pin and toss the mine back over your shoulder. When it hit the ground seven monofilament lines, each six meters long, were ejected from the casing. When anything touched one of the lines, a small charge kicked the M-86 one meter up into the air, where it exploded. It was guaranteed to make even the most hard-core pursuers lose their appetite for the chase. During the Vietnam War SEALs had improvised claymore mines with thirty-second time fuses for the same purpose.

The vehicles behind them were gaining. DeWitt could make out what looked like a Land Rover, and two more sets of headlights behind it. The winding narrow roads would have limited speed even if the Mercedes hadn't been carrying all that heavy armor.

DeWitt opened his door and, leaning out, lobbed three PDMs so they would land in the center of the road. For good measure he tossed out a couple of handfuls of caltrops, tiny three-pointed spikes that did the same damage to tires that they'd done to horses' hooves at the dawn of warfare.

The Land Rover hit one of the lines of an M-86, and the mine exploded in the air right behind it. The PDM also worked on vehicles. The fragmentation perforated the car and touched off the gas tank. The Land Rover exploded in a fireball. The second vehicle spun off the road trying to avoid it. The third hit another PDM.

Jaybird Sterling watched the whole scene in his side-view mirror. "Oh, shit," he exclaimed unhappily, because it couldn't have happened at a worse time. Everything was within sight of the upcoming checkpoint.

The Mercedes ran into a hail of fire. It sounded like rivets being driven into the car bodies, and so many rounds splattered into the polycarbonate that it was almost impossible to see out the windows. Murdock, Jaybird, and Razor opened up from the gun ports to try to suppress some of it, smoke be damned.

The two right-side tires blew out and the rear end started to swing around. Dancing the wheel lightly back and forth, staying off the brake, Doc managed to regain control. The hours they'd spent practicing at a California racetrack paid off.

The Mercedes kept going on the run-flat wheel inserts, just not as fast.

The Germans made good cars and good armor. Both cars passed through the checkpoint gauntlet, and perhaps there was even a faint expectation that they might make it.

Then, back at the checkpoint, a man stepped out into the road. He shut out the confusion around him and settled the crosshairs of his optical sight on the rear of the fleeing Mercedes, leading it just a shade high. He smoothly squeezed his trigger. There was no sensation of recoil, but a thunderclap of flame and smoke erupted from the rear of the RPG-7V launcher tube on his shoulder.

Everyone at the checkpoint watched the flare on the tail of the rocket as it seemed to float toward the Mercedes.

The road curved up ahead. The only question was whether the rocket or the Mercedes would get there first.

The rocket hit the car with a yellow flash. The checkpoint erupted with guns being fired into the air and shouts of "*Allahu Akbar!*" "God is Great!"

Then someone with their wits about them screamed, "Get them!"

The whole mob seemed to shake themselves awake and ran shrieking down the road.

19

Saturday, November 11

0301 hours
Vicinity of Baalbek
Lebanon

The Mercedes was just taking the curve when the rocket hit. An RPG shaped-charge warhead was capable of penetrating thirteen inches of solid steel. If it had hit the rear of the car straight on, no one inside would have survived. But as the Mercedes swung into the turn, the rocket hit at an angle near the right rear taillight. The plasma jet cut across the trunk and exited just behind the right rear passenger door. The door blew off, as did the trunk lid. The trunk armor contained most of the blast, but the plates still buckled and a great deal of energy was released.

Kos Kosciuszko was just starting to feel better. The explosion blew the rear seat off its mounting and threw him and Ed DeWitt toward the front of the car.

The Mercedes spun across the road like a top and smashed into a low stone wall. The Halon fire-suppression system activated. That was all well and good; the Halon kept the fuel tank from exploding and the ammunition and explosives from cooking off. But Halon gas, while wonderful on fires, is hard on human lungs.

The driver's air bag and the steering wheel to hold onto had left Professor Higgins in the best shape. The other side of the car was pinned against the stone wall, but his was clear. He held his breath as the high-pressure gas filled the car and dragged a stunned Magic Brown, and Ed DeWitt, who had ended up in the front seat, out his door. Kos Kosciuszko was already sitting out in the road, fully conscious but with a quizzical look on his face, as if wondering how he had gotten there.

Murdock was watching the whole scene, horrified. "Hit the brakes," he shouted. They were going back, if only to account for the dead. No SEAL had ever been abandoned on the field of battle, and Blake Murdock was not going to be the first to do so.

Doc Ellsworth threw the Mercedes into reverse and screeched back to the wreck. Murdock, Razor, and Jaybird piled out.

They found Kos still sitting in the road, bloody but blaspheming so fluently it couldn't be that serious. Magic Brown was puking his guts out onto the road. Ed DeWitt was just coming around. The Professor was dragging what weapons and ammo he could find out of the wreckage. Murdock was first amazed and then overjoyed to find them all alive.

Rounds were cracking overhead. Jaybird opened up with his machine gun to keep their pursuers at a distance. Razor picked up DeWitt while Murdock threw Kos Kosciuszko into the undamaged Mercedes.

Then there was a quick flash in the distance. Murdock counted off in his head: "Thousand-one, thousand-two." The shock wave and the loud rumble of the blast arrived at the same time.

0303 hours
Baalbek
Lebanon

The Syrian soldiers thought they had driven the raiders off by superior force of arms, causing them to abandon their vehicles.

Once they were sure the intruders were gone, they celebrated their victory in traditional fashion by firing their rifles into the air. Some were striking heroic poses atop the armored cars.

Since he had pulled his fuses a little sooner than DeWitt, Murdock's armored car went off first. But it didn't matter; the blast immediately set off the mercury switch in DeWitt's vehicle.

The power of an explosion is determined by both the mass of the charge and the velocity of the explosive. When black gunpowder is ignited, it changes from a solid to a gas relatively slowly, but few substances on earth do so faster than TNAZ.

The armored cars contained the blast only for microseconds, and then their steel broke into hundreds of thousands of high-speed fragments and added to the devastation.

The insides of the armored cars had been lined with sheets of zirconium, courtesy of the CIA. The same metal was used in cluster-bomb warheads to create an incendiary effect. When the zirconium ignited it added a fireball to the blast.

The warehouse and everything and everyone in it blew apart.

Unbeknownst to the CIA, the Syrians had housed the counterfeiting workers and technicians next to the warehouse, reasoning that it was easier to protect them there than transport them across Baalbek every day. The firefight at the warehouse had woken everyone up and caused all but the least prudent to hug their floors.

Those few who were looking out their windows died first when the shock wave caved in the front of the barracks. Then the building collapsed. Some of the others would eventually be dug out alive.

Pieces of wood, metal, and burning paper fell back to earth. The smoke settled, and the warehouse was just a mound of debris. An eighty-thousand-pound T-62 tank lay upside down. The turret of the BMP that had fired at the SEALs could be seen in the branches of some nearby trees; the body was nowhere to be found.

The houses surrounding the warehouse were flattened to one degree or another, depending on how shielded they were from the blast. The roads were blocked by trees and debris. The shock wave shattered windows in a mile radius around the warehouse.

Needless to say, everyone still living in Baalbek was wide awake. It was going to take quite some time to figure out what had happened, and even more time to get organized.

0304 hours
Vicinity of Baalbek
Lebanon

"Hoo-yah!" Razor Roselli screamed in exultation.

"Get in the car!" Murdock yelled.

"Eat that, motherfuckers!" Razor shouted down the road.

The explosion had temporarily silenced the incoming fire, and Murdock wanted to take advantage of it. "Get in the fucking car! Doc, get in the back and check 'em out. Jaybird, drive."

Murdock had tailored the assault force so they all could fit into one Mercedes in an emergency. They did, just barely, and it was madness: Jaybird behind the wheel, Murdock and Razor crammed in the front seat, the Doc stretched half over the front seat with a flashlight trying to sort out injuries from the packed mass in back. Magic Brown was fighting to get his head out a window so he could puke some more. The smell of sweat and fear and adrenaline was obscene.

And in the midst of it all, Razor Roselli was as happy as Murdock had ever seen him. "We did it!" he exclaimed. "We fucking did it."

"Excuse me, Chief," said Jaybird Sterling. "But if you take a second and look around you'll see that half our crew is at least half fucked up, and I'm not sure how long this car is going to hold together; most of the warning lights on the dash are lit up."

"Fuck you, Jaybird," Razor responded. "We fucking won. We finally rammed one up *their* ass, and it's gonna be a long time before they forget it. The mission's accomplished. Nothing that happens now is gonna change that."

"If it's all the same to you, Chief," said Jaybird, "I'd like to cap the mission off by living through the son of a bitch."

"Like I keep telling you, shitbird," said Roselli. "You picked the wrong line of work."

"Is everyone through now?" Murdock demanded. "We're going to live through it, but if we don't get our asses up into the hills with an hour window of darkness, we'll be walking out."

"Oh, I'd really hate that," Magic Brown groaned from the back seat, having just finished with the dry heaves. "Make haste, Jaybird, make haste."

"Doc, what's the score?" Murdock asked impatiently.

"Mister DeWitt's left arm is broken," Doc Ellsworth replied in a tone of clinical detachment. "Simple fracture, not compound, which is pretty amazing considering the way Razor threw his poor ass around."

"Hey, I got him out," Razor protested.

"Kos has half the skin on his back and ass ripped off," the Doc went on. "He's also got no pants; I don't know where the fuck they are. He'll be sleeping on his stomach for the next month or so. I wouldn't want to live with him while he heals, but outside of a general pissed-off mood, he'll be okay. The Professor's got a golden ass as usual; not a scratch. Magic's got some superficial lacerations, probably glass from the windshield, and he's sick to his little tummy." It was a fair example of SEAL corpsman bedside manner.

"Fuck you, Doc," Magic groaned.

"Can everybody move if they have to?" Murdock demanded.

"I'm fine," Ed DeWitt insisted through clenched teeth.

The Doc slid a clear plastic splint onto DeWitt's arm, inflated it with a tiny pump, and tied the whole thing across his body with an Ace bandage. "I don't think anyone has any major internal injuries, but it's not like I've got a lot of room to work in here. They've all got whiplash and torn muscles to one degree or another. If I don't get some muscle relaxers into them now, they'll be all twisted up and stiff as boards inside the hour. Mister DeWitt gets a shot, everyone else get a couple of pills. Other than that, we won't know until we try, and I'd just as soon we didn't have to."

"Thanks, Doc," said Murdock.

"Thanks, Doc?" Magic Brown said as he burped vomitus around the car. "You call that a diagnosis? I'd rather crawl my ass up and consult with the old guru on the mountaintop."

"Be my guest, asshole," the Doc replied calmly. "Piss me off any more and you won't get any drugs."

"Aw, you know I was just shittin' you, Doc," Magic said, instantly subdued.

What a mess, Murdock thought. He didn't share Razor's jubilation at the accomplishment of the mission. He had to get his men home. All of them. That was his responsibility. And the time, the goddamned time. It was now 0325. They were running out of time, and couldn't afford any more trouble.

There was an explosion behind them.

"What the hell was that?" asked Razor.

There was a general shrugging of shoulders, and then Higgins said quietly, "I rigged a charge to the car on my way out. They must've tripped it."

There were a few low, respectful whistles.

"That was very thoughtful of you, Prof," said Murdock. He was really quite impressed. *He* hadn't thought of it. "Consider yourself attaboyed."

"Thank you, sir."

From the darkness of the back seat there arose a chant. "Lieutenant's pet, Lieutenant's pet."

"We're back in fucking kindergarten again," Razor said, disgusted.

The siren and all the lights were shut off. They no longer

wanted to call any attention to themselves. Especially since now out in the open country any lights could be seen for miles. Jaybird was driving with night-vision goggles on.

The Mercedes crossed over the Bekaa highway and continued northeast. They drove around and past the small village of Iaat, and the former Lebanese Air Force base located north of Baalbek.

There was a drop in elevation; the road dipped lower into the Bekaa Valley proper, although the valley itself ranged in elevation from sixteen hundred to two thousand feet. Baalbek was around 3,800 feet above sea level.

The SEALs crossed the Litani River, which supplied the valley with its water. Fallow plowed fields broken up by stone walls stretched out for miles out in the moonlight, with hardly a tree to be seen. Only a quarter moon, but enough to see by. Small streams and wadis, dried-up streambeds, crisscrossed the road as it headed for the mountains in the distance. The road rose steadily up into the foothills.

The road forked, and they took the right. There was a left turn onto a dirt track coming up soon. They could have followed the paved road all the way over the mountains, but it ran right through at least one sizable village and the risk was too great. The dirt track went up into the forest at the base of the mountain range and simply stopped. That was where the helicopters would come in.

Murdock was intently studying his map. There was another stream that crossed the road, and then the turn.

"Here it is," Jaybird said abruptly. He'd already made the turn before Murdock could lift his head up.

"Wait a minute," said Murdock. It was too soon. But it did look like the dirt road. Maybe he'd missed the stream in the dark.

They drove about five minutes and the road stopped in the middle of a grove of low-slung olive trees.

Murdock felt like doing some yelling, but that wasn't how it was done. Besides, he was responsible—it was his screwup. "Turn around and head back," he said calmly. More time lost.

"Jaybird Sterling," Doc Ellsworth chortled from the back. "The human compass."

Jaybird burned with humiliation, but had the sense not to say anything.

They got back on the paved road and found the real turn about a quarter mile farther up. Just to be sure, Murdock checked the exact position on his GPS set.

The dirt road was slow going. It was narrow, and had been cut to the sides of hills and stretches of poor soil where crops would not grow.

They drove another quarter of a mile, and Jaybird came to an abrupt stop that caused everyone to lurch forward. "Rocks," he said in response to the inevitable razzing.

Several large rocks sat on the road, having fallen down from the hill that bordered the right side of the road. They weren't boulders, but there was no room to drive around them or get off the road.

"Back up fast!" Murdock ordered.

Jaybird rammed the Mercedes into reverse.

"Okay, stop," said Murdock, after they'd gone back about thirty yards.

"You think it's an ambush?" Razor asked.

"Don't know," Murdock replied. "But we can't go back and we don't have time to screw around. Jaybird and I will go out and move the rocks. Everybody but Ed get out and cover us."

Murdock and Razor took a minute to go through their moves. Nothing complicated, just on the order of: If this happens, I want you to do that; or if that happens instead, I want you to do this.

Then he and Jaybird trotted up the road, weapons ready. Not that that would do a lot of good if the two of them ended up in the killing zone of an ambush.

Murdock sniffed the air and let his senses pull in all the

available information. It didn't feel wrong, and he'd learned to trust that.

He and Jaybird rolled the rocks out of the way. Nothing happened. Murdock just hoped they wouldn't run into many more. They couldn't afford the time.

Everyone packed themselves back into the Mercedes. Jaybird kept it slow. There were more rocks, but small enough to either go over or around.

A half mile further and the road curved around the side of another hill. As they rolled around the curve Jaybird hit the brake again. The road was completely blocked by an enormous mound of mud and rock.

20

Saturday, November 11

0345 hours
North central Lebanon

Murdock got out of the car to take a look. After the door slammed, there was a moment of stunned silence.

"It's the karma," Doc Ellsworth said confidently. "Jaybird and all those negative vibrations."

"I told you I was thinking positively, goddammit!" Jaybird burst out.

"Someone's going to get shot in about a second," Razor Roselli warned.

Murdock got back in the car and unfolded his map.

"Why the fuck wasn't this in the satellite photos?" Magic Brown demanded. "We checked the whole route out."

"It was the rain," said Kos Kosciuszko. "The whole hillside is eroded. They must get mud slides all the time in the winter."

"Will everyone shut the fuck up for a second and let me think?" Murdock requested. He turned his flashlight on the map. They couldn't go around the slide. Going back would lose them time and distance, and even so, the nearest alternative road went right through a village. They couldn't afford another firefight.

It was time for one of what Razor liked to scornfully call the lieutenant's encounter groups. "All right," said Murdock. "Give me some ideas."

"We could drive around all night and not get any farther than we are right now," said Higgins.

"We can't bring a helo into this place," said Jaybird.

"They could drop a caving ladder," said Magic, but even he didn't sound too convinced.

"We couldn't even put Mister DeWitt on the hoist," said Doc. "Not with his arm."

"That's not it," Razor said impatiently. "The ground is as flat as a pancake and wide fucking open. There's a village within half a klick. As soon as the helos popped over the mountains everybody and his uncle would be shooting at us."

"We've got to assume that there are people chasing us," Higgins broke in.

"Either moving right now or in the process of getting their shit together," said Jaybird.

"We left so much fucking wreckage behind us, it's not going to be that hard to figure out our route," said Kos Kosciuszko.

"Oh, they'll show up soon," said Razor. "And pissed off to boot."

"We're too close to Baalbek as it is," said Doc.

"We've got to do some walking," said Ed DeWitt, giving voice to what was on everyone's mind.

"Can you walk?" Murdock asked him.

"I'd do anything to get off everyone's lap back here in this sardine car," said DeWitt.

"I guess we walk," said Magic.

Everyone seconded the motion. There was nothing else to do.

They opened up the trunk and removed their equipment. There were four nylon packs that had the same rough shape as guitar cases, only narrower. These were snipers' drag bags. A sniper occasionally had to move with his weapon over very rough terrain, sometimes crawling on his belly, and sniper rifles and optics had to be treated gently. Thus the drag bag. It was padded with foam, had shoulder straps like a pack, and could also be pulled along behind the sniper over rocky ground, hence the name.

Three of the bags contained Heckler & Koch MSG-90 semiautomatic sniper rifles in 7.62mm NATO. The other held a MacMillan M-87 bolt-action sniper rifle in .50 caliber, the same as a Browning heavy machine gun. All had been brought along at the insistence of Master Chief MacKenzie, who was looking more and more prescient as the night wore on.

The other four sniper rifles had been lost in the second Mercedes. Professor Higgins had only been able to salvage two AKMs, a bag of loaded Kalashnikov magazines, a few grenades, and his backpack radio. Razor carried an identical radio from the lead Mercedes. Each vehicle had been equipped redundantly.

They had a fast discussion about their body armor. With the ceramic inserts, each set weighed well over ten pounds. It was a question of protection or foot speed. The vests and helmets were tossed into the trunk of the car.

They passed around a camouflage stick and painted their faces and hands. Kos Kosciuszko borrowed a suture kit from Doc to try to quickly stitch his torn-up trousers together.

Jaybird gunned the Mercedes up the road and skidded it sideways into the mound of mud. Then they all quickly shoved as much of the mud as possible onto the car to conceal it from aerial observation.

Razor Roselli booby-trapped the vehicle.

"Hope no one comes along and decides to strip it," said Magic Brown.

"Then that's what they get for being thieving bastards," said Razor. "Fuck 'em if they can't take a joke."

They started off, in single file, with as much interval as possible between them over the open ground. As far away as you could still see the man in front of you and stay in contact was the SEAL rule. Jaybird was on point; he'd given his PKM to Kos Kosciuszko and received a lighter, faster-handling Kalashnikov AKM from Doc. Murdock walked right behind with an AKM and an MSG-90 in the drag bag on his back. As usual, Higgins dogged his heels with the radio and an AKM. Then Kos Kosciuszko, with the machine gun and close to seven hundred rounds linked, all that had been left in the Mercedes. Doc followed with Ed DeWitt. With the shortage of weapons due to the destroyed Mercedes, DeWitt just had his backup Russian Makarov pistol; it was all he could handle anyway. Doc had removed an MSG-90 from a drag bag and was carrying it at the ready. Magic Brown and then Razor Roselli finished off the file as rear security, both with AKMs. Magic had the MacMillan .50 in the drag bag on his back, Razor an MSG-90.

The temperature was about thirty degrees, and the night air was still wet-cold from the rain. They cut around the side of the hill and then between two fields, keeping close to the dividing stone wall for cover.

Murdock was watching his men carefully as they patrolled along. DeWitt seemed to be moving all right. And there was a confidence to the others, as if they were all more comfortable being out of the car and back on the ground. It made him feel better too.

As he looked across the fields, Murdock could see trees in the distance and the mountain range farther away, covered with snow.

A dog barked, too far away to worry about. There were no other sounds but the occasional boot crunching lightly into the frost-covered earth of the field.

21

Saturday, November 11

0400 hours
Near Btedaï
Lebanon

The SEALs soon left the fields and cut back across one of the forks of the dirt road. Murdock had been very uncomfortable with the tracks they were leaving.

There was a ritual to crossing what was known as a danger area. Jaybird and Murdock went across the dirt road first, while Kos and Higgins, on either flank, trained their weapons up and down the road. Murdock secured the far side while Jaybird scouted out even farther ahead. On Murdock's signal the rest crossed, one at a time, with Kos and Higgins still covering.

Murdock was waiting when the last man, Razor Roselli, made it across the road.

"We're heading onto more solid ground," Murdock whispered to him. "Let's put some CS across our trail."

Razor nodded, and took a small plastic bottle out of his trouser pocket. It was filled with powdered persistent CS tear-gas crystals. Razor sprinkled the powder sparingly in a zigzag pattern across their trail. Just in case any dogs were tracking them. One tiny whiff of the CS crystals and a dog would no longer have a sense of smell. Rain would not wash the CS away.

Murdock went back to his place at the front of the column.

They edged around the village of Btedaï, population 554. There were a few slivers of light visible from the village, even at that hour. Farmers got up early. The SEALs stayed far enough away to keep from alerting the ubiquitous village dogs.

The SEALs crossed another dirt road. It was expected. This one cut past Btedaï to the south and simply ended.

Just past the road they entered a grove of trees. This patch was the beginning, the edge, of the larger woods. There were pines and oaks; the legendary cedars of Lebanon were not present. It was not a forest in the American sense; the trees were too sparse and widely dispersed. It was cover, though, and a welcome change from the wide-open fields.

As Razor Roselli at the end of the file slipped into the trees, loud voices speaking Arabic were suddenly heard further ahead. The SEALs dropped flat to the ground.

It was the type of situation that required the most careful exercise of judgment. If you started shooting when you could have let someone pass unknowingly by, you alerted the entire neighborhood to your presence. But if you allowed a large force to walk right up to your position, you risked being pinned down, overrun, and wiped out.

Unless one of the SEALs was stepped on or otherwise compromised, it was Murdock's call. He lay with one ear to the ground, breathing quietly and shallowly through his mouth to keep from sending up a cloud of condensation. He smelled pine needles. His weapon was pointing toward the voices.

And the voices came closer. It only sounded like one or two. Then again, maybe it was more and only one or two were talking. Not for the first time, Murdock wished he spoke Arabic. He added it to his list of early New Year's resolutions.

None of the SEALs shifted even slightly on the ice-cold ground, or so much as twitched a muscle. Discipline was perfect. The only real discipline was self-discipline, as they said in BUD/S.

The voices seemed to be coming right at them. Murdock's finger edged toward his trigger. The SEAL platoon's standard signal for triggering a hasty ambush was the platoon commander opening fire. No whistles or shouted commands. Nothing that would give the enemy time to make any move. Just rounds on target.

The voices abruptly angled off to Murdock's right, as if they were now moving across the SEALs' front. It would be the perfect moment to spring an ambush.

Murdock resisted the temptation. He could now hear as well as feel feet moving on the ground. Not like troops moving tactically, just clumping along. It sounded like just a couple of pairs of feet, not more than three. They were so close he could actually smell sour body odor and garlic.

Murdock set his finger back across the trigger guard and let them pass on by. The voices faded off in the distance, but the SEALs waited for a solid minute of dead silence before lifting themselves cautiously from the ground. Murdock noiselessly crawled down the line to Magic Brown, who had the best Arabic. "What was all that?" he whispered in Magic's ear.

"Couple of farmers heading back home," Magic whispered back. "They spent the night at another village, helping someone out. The sheep are lambing right now."

Murdock squeezed his arm in acknowledgment.

When they got moving again, Murdock noticed a narrow but well-worn footpath that curved right around where they had lain. It headed back to Btedaï. They avoided it as they would all paths and trails, and resumed patrolling into the woods.

Murdock was becoming more and more anxious. There seemed to be a running conspiracy against them making any time.

The woods opened up into a clear grassy area. It was like a firebreak, though not man-made. A stream ran through the middle of it. Even though time was crucial, some instinct told Murdock to have his men fill their canteens. The Russian-style Syrian web gear only carried a single canteen, and everyone had to be dry or close to it. They formed a circular security perimeter. Then, one by one, they drained their canteens, filled them in the stream, and dropped in an iodine purification tablet.

It only took a few moments. Then they crossed the stream, slipped through the tall grass, and disappeared back into the woods.

22

Saturday, November 11

0425 hours
West of Btedaï
Lebanon

The SEALS had entered a thin strip of woods only a few hundred yards across with open areas on either side. But it led deeper into the forest.

Murdock peeled the nylon cover off his watch and checked it yet again. About another kilometer further and it would be time to get on the radio and call in the helicopters. They had just enough time, with a nice little cushion.

Professor Higgins was the first to hear it. A low scratching sound off to his right that could have been whispering. Then a drawn-out metallic click that, despite someone's best efforts, sounded like a safety catch coming off.

Higgins wheeled about, brought up his weapon, and squeezed off a long burst. Known as an immediate-action drill, it gave everyone time to get down. "Ambush right!" he screamed as he fell forward, but it was lost in all the noise.

A line of muzzle flashes lit up about twenty yards away. Green tracers streaked across the intervening space.

In a short-range ambush, with the element of surprise lost,

neither side is usually able to assault forward or withdraw. Survival is awarded to those who first establish fire superiority. That is, those who put out such a heavy volume of *accurate* weapons fire that their opponents' ability to return fire is either suppressed or eliminated. Easy to discuss in the classroom, hard to do in real life.

Ed DeWitt lay flat on his stomach. A tree in his path provided convenient protection. He had his pistol in hand, but was saving his rounds in case someone came assaulting through their position.

Beside him Doc Ellsworth was squeezing off rounds from his sniper rifle at the rapid rate. Fortunately the MSG-90 carried a twenty-round magazine.

Magic Brown was firing his AKM single-shot, but so fast it sounded like automatic, putting fire everywhere he saw tracers coming from. His concentration was so intense that he didn't even notice the incoming rounds kicking up dirt all around him.

Razor Roselli was looking for an opportunity to flank the ambush from the right, but he was solidly pinned down. He couldn't maneuver, so he fired.

Unless very well trained, everyone shoots high at night. The SEALS were superbly trained and shooting straight. It began to tell with a slackening of fire from the other side. Then at least four more rifles joined in, firing on automatic, as if reinforcements had just come up. That shifted the odds dramatically.

Sensing it, Kos Kosciuszko raised up on his knees and held down the trigger on his PKM machine gun. He worked a continuous stream of fire down the line of muzzle flashes in front of him. Dirt flew, brush and saplings were literally mowed down. The PKM barrel glowed red, then white. It would soon melt, but if they didn't survive the next few seconds it wouldn't matter.

It was devastating, and the opposition immediately concentrated all the fire on him.

For Kos the world slowed down until almost nothing was moving. He saw the tracer coming at him, so slow that it seemed he could dodge it, but he couldn't. Then it felt like he'd been hit by the world's hardest punch, but red hot. He was a huge man, and strong, and he kept the trigger of that machine gun down, weaving back and forth, up and down the line. Then he wasn't firing the machine gun anymore. His first thought was that the belt had run out. Then he felt the ground, and somehow he had fallen back down onto it. Then he felt cold, so cold. Then he couldn't feel anything at all.

Murdock and Jaybird, at the front of the column, had been completely out of the ambush killing zone when Higgins initiated the immediate-action drill. When the shooting started they did not open fire. Instead they began crawling to their left in a wide hook, trying to come around on the enemy's flank.

They scuttled on their bellies as fast as they could. Brambles tried to hold them up, but they yanked their way free.

Only seconds had passed since the beginning of the firefight, but their crawl seemed to have taken hours. They knew they were getting close because the bullets snapping over their heads were coming from their own side. They came up through the trees, and suddenly they were looking straight down the length of a line of shooters maybe ten yards away. It was the perfect spot for a flank attack. In such a position two men could take on many times their number, because while Murdock and Jaybird could shoot straight down the line of firers, only the man closest to them could twist around and get an unrestricted shot at them.

But if Murdock and Jaybird were to go assaulting down the enemy line just then, they would be cut down by the incoming fire of their fellow SEALs. But not if a signal was given for the SEALs to cease fire first. No human voice could rise above the din; a radio call might not be received by everyone. But there was a signal that every SEAL would recognize immediately, because it came right out of their standard operating procedures.

Murdock and Jaybird fumbled in their pouches and came up

with two Russian M75 hand grenades each. Small, barrel-shaped, with ribbed plastic bodies, the grenades were Cold War copies of an Austrian model.

They pulled the pins, rose up from the ground, and distributed the grenades evenly down the line. At the fourth explosion Murdock and Jaybird got to their feet and charged forward, assaulting down the line.

Murdock passed by grenade-torn bodies that he fired into just the same. Then, out of the smoke, a man was on his knees with arms outstretched, begging with what sounded like, "Hai, hai, hai."

Blake Murdock was not dispensing mercy. His burst blew the man down. Murdock dropped to one knee to change magazines, and then continued on. He reached the end of the line. He heard the thrashing of someone running through the brush, but didn't fire. From some long-ago training class he heard: Don't fire unless you can identify your target; it might be a SEAL.

"Jaybird," he yelled.

"With you, sir," came the call to his left, right where Jaybird was supposed to be.

Murdock marveled for a brief moment at Jaybird using the word "sir" when he wasn't in trouble, then keyed his radio. "Jaybird and I have the ambush site secure. Come up on line, and don't shoot us when you do."

A series of acknowledgments came over the net, and then the rest of the platoon surged forward in a classic skirmish line. They reached Murdock and Jaybird, and then swept onward into the trees to make sure they hadn't missed anyone. Murdock and Jaybird now faced around to cover their rear.

Murdock heard a short spasm of firing, then everything quieted down.

"Two more tangos and a bunch of donkeys," came the unusual message over the radio.

With only one good arm and a pistol, Ed DeWitt prudently hadn't gone on with the others. He walked up and put his hand on Murdock's shoulder. "Kos is dead," he said.

23

Saturday, November 11

0440 hours
West of Btedaï
Lebanon

"Are you sure," Murdock demanded, grabbing DeWitt's jacket. It immediately occurred to him that he had never asked a more stupid question in his entire life. He let go of DeWitt. "I'm sorry, Ed."

"He was gone by the time we got to him. He saved our asses."

The rest of the SEALs reappeared out of the darkness.

DeWitt took things in hand. "Let's get their ammo," he said crisply. "From what I heard, they were all using AKs."

Jaybird and DeWitt stood security while the rest of the SEALs went down the line of corpses and stripped them of weapons and magazines. Razor Roselli stayed with Murdock.

"Smugglers," Razor reported. "They had a string of donkeys loaded with hash. I think they stopped to take a break, and we just ran into each other in the dark."

"It was my fault," said Murdock. "We were patrolling too fast. I was pushing Jaybird too hard. If I'd been scanning with the imager, we would have picked them up with enough time and space to go around."

"We don't have *time* for this," Razor said firmly. "That's all over and done with. We have to get out of here, and fast."

Murdock knew Razor was right. They had to clear the area. Some of the smugglers had undoubtedly gotten away. There were always survivors in every engagement. It never happened that way in training, but it always did in real life.

The SEALs formed a hasty perimeter and redistributed Kalashnikov magazines. The grenades the smugglers had been carrying were so old and beat up no one wanted to mess with them. Doc Ellsworth and Ed DeWitt took two AKMs that seemed in the best shape.

"Use the grenades to booby-trap the bodies?" Magic Brown suggested.

"No," Murdock replied. "We don't want to make it look too professional. If we're lucky, anyone who finds them won't make the connection. They may write it off as a business disagreement."

Kos Kosciuszko's body was wrapped in Doc Ellsworth's German nylon poncho. It had six stout carrying straps on each side and doubled as a stretcher.

Murdock took point. DeWitt followed him. Jaybird, Razor, Higgins, and Doc carried Kos. It took that many to bear his weight and still cover the ground at a decent pace. Magic Brown took over the tail-gunner position.

Despite what had happened, they pushed harder. The firefight had to have attracted attention, and the nearby road networks would allow a fast response. And the fast-approaching dawn was on everyone's mind. The ground was rising fast as they headed up higher into the mountain highlands. It was hard going.

The time only permitted a mile and a half advance before Murdock called a halt. They formed another perimeter with Kos's body in the center. Professor Higgins broke out his backpack radio.

It was a piece of gear that had only recently come into SEAL service, the AN/PRC-117D. Extremely compact at fifteen inches high, eight inches wide, three inches deep, and fifteen pounds total, it was one of the most sophisticated tactical radios in the world. Capable of operating in a number of modes and multiple frequency bands, the PRC-117D combined the functions of the three different radio sets it had replaced in SEAL service.

It could send and receive UHF satellite communications, or SATCOM, capable of reaching literally anywhere in the world. It also used UHF line-of-sight, to talk to aircraft and direct airstrikes, and VHF, or FM, the band used for tactical communications by most of the world's armies, the same band the Motorola MX-300 walkie-talkies operated on.

Changing bands was as easy as flipping a switch and deploying the right antenna. The radio's power could be adjusted anywhere from ten watts maximum down to .1 watt to reduce the probability of enemy interception. It could also be switched to automatic frequency hopping in the VHF band. The encryption system was embedded in the radio, and the crypto keys could be changed daily by simply punching in a new set of numbers.

The radio could transmit in a number of modes: voice, data, video. A special interface could even link it into the worldwide cellular telephone system.

The capability was incredible, but it also allowed everyone in the chain of command to contact and supervise you to an extent that Murdock did not care for at all. The Vietnam ploy of turning off the radio or pleading poor reception was no longer a viable option if you could talk in real-time with the admiral in Coronado or the President at the White House from the middle of the Lebanese hills.

If it had been a straight SEAL mission, Murdock would have been transmitting code words to mark his progress at each step in the operation, from landing onward. But as he'd told the CIA, if they weren't going to provide him with any external fire support, then he didn't need to be talking to them every five minutes—no matter how much they might want him to.

Higgins unfolded the satellite antenna, which was just a collapsible wire facsimile of the familiar dish. The radio set told him when the antenna was in line with the communications satellite overhead.

A signal sent straight up to a satellite was hard for an enemy to direction-find, but not impossible. Especially if you were dealing with a paranoid dictatorship like Syria, which had the best signals-interception and direction-finding equipment money could buy. So the SEALs would send their message by data-burst. Instead of talking over a handset, Murdock wrote out his message and Higgins typed it into a small keypad. Previously agreed-upon code words were used to reduce the length of the message. It went something like this, but in a continuous line of traffic with STOP where any periods would have been:

E70: *Phonetically, Echo Seven Oscar, 3rd Platoon's call sign for that day.*

SWITCHBLADE: *Target destroyed.*

ZEBRA-1: *One friendly killed in action.*

SEATBELT-1: *Request immediate helicopter extraction. No change from mission brief.*

PENGUIN: *Landing zone is secure.*

857682: *Their current location, in map grid coordinates.*

END.

Murdock reviewed the message in the keypad's liquid crystal display and nodded to Higgins. Higgins pressed a button and entered the message into the keypad. Another button automatically encrypted it. Then he pressed the SEND button and the message went out over the air in a compressed burst of less than a millisecond in duration. Now there was nothing to do but wait for confirmation and any return message to come back from the aircraft carrier.

24

Saturday, November 11

0503 hours
Aboard the *U.S.S. George Washington*
Eastern Mediterranean Sea

The huddle of men packed together in the dull gray intelligence center of the *George Washington* was becoming both more hyper and more despondent, if such a thing was possible. The coffee they'd consumed by the gallon had done its own small part to jack up the general mood.

Don Stroh of the CIA couldn't sit down in his institutional Navy chair for more than a minute before springing up to pace. He wouldn't call it pacing, though, just a continuing process of checking in with the line of Navy communicators at their consoles, or talking to the ship's bridge or Combat Operations Center on the phone.

Paul Kohler, his CIA counterpart, had gone through what seemed to be about five cartons of cigarettes, based on the contents of the ashtrays. The fastidious young sailors in the room, high-IQ types one and all, appeared to be on the verge of donning breathing apparatuses.

The Army major from the 160th was sitting with his legs crossed and reading a paperback novel, to all intents and purposes the very picture of professional calm. But that crossed leg was bouncing up and down so fast it might have been hooked to an electrical current.

Miguel Fernandez, the lone SEAL, was catching up on some sleep. His feet were up on the worktable, his head thrown back, and every minute or so he let loose with a few seconds of loud honking snores. Whenever it happened the others threw him looks that were part disgust, part envy.

One of the communicators suddenly shot forward in his chair. "Message just came in," he announced excitedly.

They all practically climbed over each other to reach the terminal and read Murdock's message off the display.

"They did it!" Paul Kohler whooped, sounding very much like Razor Roselli.

Miguel Fernandez, whom the platoon called Rattler in honor of his favorite cuisine during desert operations, stared at the screen and wondered which one of his friends was dead.

Don Stroh had a handset up to his mouth, and was passing the news over a satellite link to the operations center at CIA headquarters in Langley, Virginia.

The major was on an internal ship's phone giving the word to his pilots waiting in the ready room.

Stroh put down the handset and picked up another one that connected to the ship's Combat Operations Center. "Is it still there?" he asked. "Okay, thanks." He hung the phone up. "We've got a real problem." He turned to the communicator. "I want you to send, 'WAIT ONE STOP STAND BY FOR MESSAGE END,'" he ordered.

"Aye, aye, sir," the sailor replied.

A Russian Sovremenny-class destroyer had shown up in the area about a half hour before, attracted to the *Washington* and trying to discover what she was doing. Intelligence photographers shooting through night-vision equipment had been lined up on her rails the whole time. The Russians had been going through one of their we're-a-great-power hypernationalistic phases lately, and had been causing more mischief than they had in years.

The presence of the destroyer meant the *Washington* couldn't launch the helicopters without permission.

"If only we'd gotten that message an hour ago," the major lamented.

"The COC says we can lose her," said Stroh. "But the Navy can't do that, get back into helicopter range, and go to flight quarters all before daylight."

"Then we have to launch anyway," said the major. "Screw the Russians."

Fernandez was glad the major had said that because otherwise he would have had to. And one of the facts of life was that majors got more favorable hearing than first-class petty officers.

"We can't do that without permission from Langley," said Kohler.

"Well, fucking get it then," Fernandez blurted out. Heads turned and all eyes fell on him, and he added rather lamely, "Sir."

Well used to SEALs, Don Stroh only chuckled. "I'm going to do just that, Miguel."

The communicator handed him the handset to Langley, and he explained the situation in detail. After Stroh finished he listened for quite a while. His face darkness. "I'd like to point out, sir," he said, "that if any SEALs are captured, the mission will be even more compromised that it would be by the sighting of a few helicopters. Any number of cover stories could explain that away."

Fernandez's stomach turned to ice.

Stroh listened some more. "Yes, sir, their equipment is sterile, but that won't matter if the Syrians get a chance to go to work on them." More listening. "Yes, sir, we *will* stand by, but allow me to remind you that our launch window is closing rapidly. Yes, sir." He gave the handset back to the communicator. "They're going to get back to us."

"The fuck!" Fernandez said fiercely. "The dirty work is done, so now no one gives a shit anymore."

One of the Navy intelligence officers seemed on the verge of having words with Fernandez, then perhaps thought better of it.

"I can launch at any time," the major said. "I'm *willing* to launch right now," he added pointedly.

Don Stroh just shrugged helplessly and shook his head.

The minutes ticked off. Five. Ten. Fifteen. Twenty. The tension in the room was unbearable.

"Sir," the communicator said, giving the handset over to Stroh.

"Yes, sir," Stroh said into the handset. There was conversation on the other end, and Stroh finally broke in to protest, "Yes, sir, but we have no idea what the situation on the ground is right now . . . sir, I don't care where the order came from, this is murder. Yes, sir. Yes, sir, I understand perfectly." Stroh gave the handset back to the communicator. "We don't launch while the Russian ship is here," he told them. "So that means the earliest we can launch is after dusk. Tonight."

"They got to sit out there all day?" Fernandez shouted.

"Well, screw that," said the major. "I'm launching right now. I'll take the responsibility."

Fernandez could have French-kissed him—and an officer at that.

Another phone rang, and it was handed over to Don Stroh. "Yes? Yes, Captain? You did? Very well, thank you." He hung up. "The Captain just got a flash message from Washington. No Army helicopters will be launched until End of Evening Nautical Twilight. Tonight."

"Those bastards don't miss a trick, do they?" Fernandez asked bitterly. If they had turned the major down he'd been considering pulling his pistol and making some demands. Now even that wouldn't work. "I'll tell you something. You all better make out your wills, 'cause you do this to Razor Roselli and I wouldn't put odds on your life expectancy once he gets back."

"I'd be glad to have Razor take a shot at me, as long as we get him back," said Stroh. He sounded completely worn out. "Be that as it may, now we have to sit down and put together a message to the SEALs."

25

Saturday, November 11

0535 hours
North central Lebanon

The light on the keypad blinked. Murdock and Razor were both huddled over the tiny display.

"What the fuck took them so long?" Razor whispered in Murdock's ear. "They bring in Shakespeare to compose the fucking message?"

Murdock reached over and hit the button to review the message.

They watched eagerly as it ran across the narrow strip window of the display:

UNABLE TO LAUNCH AIRCRAFT STOP CANNOT LAUNCH IN DAYLIGHT STOP REMAIN HIDDEN OR ESCAPE AND EVADE AT YOUR DISCRETION STOP WILL LAUNCH ON ORDER ANY TIME AFTER EENT 11 NOV STOP SORRY STOP ORDERS STOP GOOD LUCK END

Razor couldn't believe it, and reviewed the message again. Murdock felt like he'd been kicked in the balls.

Razor took a moment to regain his composure, then whispered, "Well, this has to be the best fucking I've ever taken, bar none."

"I think I'm finally starting to get a handle on the drawbacks to working for the CIA," Murdock whispered back to him.

"Fuck 'em," Razor whispered. "We'll get our own selves out."

"Acknowledge the transmission," Murdock told Higgins. "And don't tell them to go fuck themselves."

"Roger that, sir," the Professor replied. "I'll keep it professional."

With that, as might be expected sitting in the Lebanese woods with dawn approaching, it was back to business.

Murdock crawled to each man and gave him a whispered briefing. They were SEALS, so no one went hysterical. At first some of them thought Murdock was playing a really bad joke. Then there were a few whispered oaths, followed by a general shrugging of shoulders, as if all that could be expected from the powers that be was a good hard shot up the ass anyway. The SEALs knew what kind of situation they were in but, since they were SEALs, it was the kind of situation they *expected* to find themselves in.

Murdock briefed them because they needed, deserved to know. And because, as usual, they picked his morale right back up. Jaybird Sterling wanted to know if it meant an extra day of combat pay. Murdock said only if it went past midnight the next day. Jaybird then asked if the lieutenant would take that into consideration in his planning, since he was thinking of buying a motorcycle.

Then Murdock, Razor, and DeWitt pulled a poncho over their heads, turned on a flashlight, and broke out their maps for an impromptu conference.

"Let's get the hard stuff out of the way first," said Razor. "We have to leave Kos here."

Murdock started. He knew it would eventually come down to that, but it would have taken him a while to bring the subject up.

"He's too big," said Razor, "and we've got too many people

hurt and sick to carry him, move fast, and still keep good security. If he was alive we'd take him, no matter what. But you don't die for the dead. Kos would understand." He paused again. "I'll handle the boys."

"All right," said Murdock. The fact that you got paid to make the tough decisions didn't make them any easier.

DeWitt closed his eyes and nodded.

"Okay," said Razor. "Now, which way do we go? Right now we got our backs up against the mountain range to our west. Not a damn piece of cover on the whole mountain range. We're coming from the east, the bad guys are following us from that direction. So east is out. I guess we can go either north or south."

"South is Israel," said DeWitt.

"It's not the U.S.-Canada border," Razor said dubiously. "There's minefields, fences, and a shitload of people with guns. Just to get to their security zone in south Lebanon we'd have to go through a lot of Hezbollah country. Plus it's a long goddamned walk."

"Let's not get off the track here," said Murdock. "We just have to hide out for twelve hours or so."

"So they say," Razor retorted.

"Looking on the bright side," said DeWitt, "they Syrians are going to think that anyone slick enough to pull off what we did would be long gone by now."

"If we were Israelis, we would be," said Razor. "Good thing they don't know what a stupid bunch of dicks we really are."

"A few klicks south the forest disappears and we're back in open country," said Murdock. "I vote we head north, stay in the woods. And we get moving right now, make as much distance as we can before daylight."

"This is a vote?" Razor inquired.

"It's a vote," Murdock confirmed.

"Then I vote we go north."

"Don't look at me to disagree," said DeWitt, grinning in the red glow of the flashlight. "I'm just the j.g."

"We love you all the same, sir," said Razor, trying to lighten the mood like a good chief.

26

Saturday, November 11

0520 hours
North central Lebanon

The SEALs found a small depression in the ground and scraped out a shallow hole with their knives, piling the dirt onto a poncho. They laid Chief Boatswain's Mate Benjamin "Kos" Kosciuszko into the hole, covering him with earth, then pine needles and branches. They sprinkled CS crystals around to keep the animals off. The rest of the dirt was carried away and scattered.

Murdock took several GPS readings at the grave site, and everyone recorded the coordinates on their maps in case there was ever an opportunity to recover the body.

In the meantime, another SEAL family would be told that there had been a diving accident and the body lost at sea. An empty casket would be buried with full military honors.

They left him and patrolled away. That was the way it was. No beating of breasts, no inability to function. The SEALs just got a little tighter, a little colder. Kos Kosciuszko would be mourned when it was all over. Violent death was not an unanticipated event among SEALs. A great many earmarked money in their wills for a final party that they would not attend.

They headed northeast. Although still within the cover of the woods, this meant they had to cross numerous ridgelines that steadily increased in elevation. These all ran east-west, and the constant up-and-down climbing was both exhausting and time-consuming. It was known as going cross-compartment. Murdock wanted to spend as little time in the ridge valleys as possible. The low areas were where people walked, and eventually trampled paths. And the SEALs wouldn't walk anywhere they expected to meet anyone else. The same was true for the tops of hills or ridgelines. Whenever you passed over them you were completely exposed. It was better to walk halfway up and then traverse around, no matter how long that took.

Running parallel to the ridgelines were a whole series of dirt roads that connected the mountain and highland villages to the Bekaa Valley highway. One of them was the cross-mountain paved road they had originally taken such pains to avoid.

Crossing that road was a particular problem. It forked into two separate directions, and crossing the nearest and most heavily wooded portion would require crossing both forks, which was tactically unwise. The SEALs had to patrol far out of their way to find a section where there wasn't too much open area on both sides of the road. Another consideration was that the crossing site couldn't be within view of anyone driving further up or down the road. This usually meant crossing at a curve or bend.

Jaybird found the right spot just as the first halo of dawn began to light up the horizon. The SEALs followed their danger-area SOP. Great care was necessary because it was exactly the sort of place *they* would pick to set up an ambush. As they approached, Murdock designated near- and far-side rally points where the unit would re-gather if split up in either the crossing or a firefight.

Higgins and Doc secured the right and left flanks of the

crossing point. Jaybird sprinted across first, followed by Murdock to secure the far side.

DeWitt had just bolted from the tree line when a glow came through the trees and headlights began to emerge from around the bend. DeWitt dropped flat. Murdock cursed. If anything happened now he was separated from the bulk of his men by the open road.

The lights flashed past and headed down the road. DeWitt got up and scrambled across. Murdock gave silent thanks for Lebanese drivers. They went so fast they'd miss an elephant grazing by the side of the road.

DeWitt slid into the trees and found Murdock.

"How's your arm?" Murdock whispered, worried that DeWitt had damaged it even more when he'd hit the deck.

"Hurts," DeWitt replied bluntly.

Ask a stupid question, thought Murdock. When Doc came across, he sent him over to DeWitt.

Doc checked him out and came back over to report. "He landed right on the arm, but the fracture still didn't go compound. I gave him another shot. Don't know how he kept from yelling when he hit the ground. Tough little bastard." Having dispensed his highest praise, Doc slipped back into formation.

No more cars showed up, and the rest of the SEALs crossed without any difficulty. They pushed on. It was getting alarmingly bright. Murdock called a halt for another conference.

"If we stop here," he said, "we're right in the middle of a box of roads, with another road cutting across the box. I don't like it, but to get out of the box we've got to patrol in daylight and cross another dirt road."

"The roads all form boxes," Razor replied. "One after the other." He pointed to the map. "But the box after the next, a little over ten klicks away, is a hell of a lot bigger. The ground is higher, and at least there aren't any villages nearby if we keep going."

"So what you're trying to say is that you want to go?" Murdock asked.

Razor nodded.

"Staying here doesn't feel right," said DeWitt.

"Okay," said Murdock. "Then we go nice and easy. I want to take two hours to move the ten klicks. If we take three, I won't be pissed. Right?" he asked Jaybird, who had been brought into the circle.

"You got it, sir."

Murdock pointed his pencil at a spot on the map. "I want to establish a patrol base near this high ground, and an observation post on the high ground. Any problems with that?"

There were none. In a perfect world Murdock would have preferred to establish the patrol base while it was still dark. It was a shame the world wasn't perfect.

Jaybird set a careful pace. Take a step, carefully scan your assigned sector of observation, then take another step. The SEALs were spread so far apart that it would take an ambush the size of two full platoons, around sixty men, to catch them all in a single killing zone.

They refilled their canteens in a stream and crossed another dirt road. As Razor had said, at least it was a bigger box, about six miles east-west by three miles north-south. Five ridges ran east to west across it.

It took a little time to find the right spot for a patrol base, a secure area where they could hide out. The rules were that a patrol base had to have good cover and concealment and be away from human habitation. It ought not to be ground that a military unit could easily move through, or would even choose to move through. All roads, trails, or natural lines of movement had to be avoided.

They found it in a large thicket of brush and brambles in low ground that probably held water during the spring rains. The SEALs didn't head right in, instead patrolling past the thicket.

Then they circled back onto their own trail and set up ambush to snare anyone who might be following them.

They sat motionless for an hour and a half. No one showed up.

Doc Ellsworth went into the thicket first, on his hands and knees. He didn't trample and break down the bushes, instead parting the branches and working his way through carefully. The rest of the SEALs followed, in his exact path. Razor Roselli went in last, smoothing out the marks in the earth and bending the branches back into place. When he finished there was no trail, and no open spots in the thicket. Anyone following would have to pass along the original trail that led past the thicket, thereby alerting them.

Murdock and Jaybird had remained outside. By necessity, the patrol base had to be located in an area where visibility was restricted. Murdock intended to find an observation point where he could get a good look at what was happening in the surrounding countryside.

There was a dominating hill nearby, within MX-300 walkie-talkie range. And if by some chance they couldn't return to the others, Jaybird was carrying the second, backup PRC-117.

When the two of them reached the hill, Murdock carefully circled around the entire base, looking for trails or any sign of human presence. They found none, so they worked their way up.

They avoided the top. While observation might be best there, it would be equally easy for someone else to observe them. It had to be a place they could move out from under cover if they detected the enemy observing them.

They found an out-thrust corner of the hill that afforded a good view in three directions. Murdock removed his MSG-90 sniper rifle from the drag bag and set the rifle up on its bipod legs. The Hensoldt 10-power telescopic sight would be his observation device. Jaybird cut some brush to camouflage their position.

The sun had risen far enough to use the telescopic sight without fear of a reflection off the glass. SEALs used the sniper's trick of fitting lens hoods to the ends of their scopes; just a piece of plastic tubing that extended out from the objective end of the sight. With the hood in place, there would be no lens reflection unless the sun was directly in the scope's field of view. It took a lot of effort to be that careless.

Perfectly concealed, Murdock scanned the area through the scope. It took some time, because the telescope had a very narrow field of view.

They were around six thousand feet up, and the surrounding hills and ridges were in the four-to-five-thousand-foot range. Murdock could even see Baalbek. He couldn't make out the warehouse, but a pall of smoke still hung over the town from the fire, or fires.

Vehicles were racing around the town, and up and down the Bekaa highway.

Then Murdock was alarmed to see a long line of military trucks, armored personnel carriers, and even a few tanks speeding up the same route they'd taken in the Mercedes. They were heading straight for the village of Btedaï.

27

Saturday, November 11

0945 hours
North central Lebanon

The Syrians were responding a hell of a lot faster than Murdock had expected them to. He'd been counting on it taking at least a day to get their shit together. Perhaps the firefight with the smugglers had attracted even more attention than he'd thought.

Murdock couldn't see what the trucks did when they reached Btedaï; a ridgeline was in his way. Several light observation helicopters that looked like the French Gazelles flown by the Syrians were buzzing up and down the valley. Confident of the SEALs' camouflage, Murdock wasn't worried about the helicopters.

Finally, the strain on his eyes from the scope was too much. Sitting still made him aware of the twenty-four hours worth of stress and fatigue he'd been fighting. He turned the rifle over to Jaybird and dug in his pockets for the mocha energy bar he knew was there somewhere.

The sun was warming up the ground wonderfully. Murdock was even enjoying the smell of the brush Jaybird had cut to cover them. It was like rosemary.

Then he was in the midst of a dream about being chased; he ran and ran and couldn't make any progress no matter how hard he tried. Then he shot awake. Jaybird was shaking him.

"Sorry to wake you up, sir."

"Why did you let me sleep?" Murdock grumbled, furious with himself for giving in to it. Doubly furious for sleeping while one of his men had to stay awake.

"Thought you ought to see this," said Jaybird, scooting out from behind the rifle.

Murdock locked the stock against his shoulder and followed where Jaybird's finger was pointing. It was the secondary road Ed DeWitt had had so much trouble crossing. A long line of troops was crossing the road, along what seemed like its entire length.

"Looked to me like at least a battalion, maybe two," said Jaybird. "And check this out."

All the villages within view and most of the road intersections were occupied by at least a couple of military vehicles and milling troops. They were on every road that came off the Bekaa highway, every road that led into the mountains, from Btedaï all the way up to a secondary road that passed far north of their hill. The box of roads, Murdock thought. How fitting he'd called it that. Because they were in the damn box.

Jaybird gestured around. "There's the cordon, to hold us in," he said. Then he pointed back to the troops, who had by now crossed the road and disappeared into the trees. "And there's the sweep."

"Sweeping toward us," said Murdock. "To flush us into the cordon."

"Yup," Jaybird agreed. "From Baalbek to the checkpoint we busted, the Mercedes, and then on to the smugglers. Pretty soon to Kos's body. The sons of bitches are just connecting the dots."

28

Saturday, November 11

1215 hours
North central Lebanon

From his vantage point, Murdock considered the situation. He thought the Syrian sweep was a serious development but not a catastrophic one. The advance on line was the most difficult military formation to control. Anyone who had tried it with only a few troops over a short distance knew how hard it was. To do it with more than a thousand troops over miles of woods and broken ground was well-nigh impossible without breaks in the line, units getting ahead of or behind each other, and frequent stops to sort things out. Seven men ought to be able to either evade or slip through that force. It was something SEALs specialized in.

The main problem, as Murdock saw it, was bringing helicopters into the midst of such a concentration of enemy, even at night. It was going to be tricky. And, like all ground commanders in the age of the helicopter, he wasn't quite sure how much information to give out. If you told the truth about how bad it was, they might not come and get you. If you didn't, they might come in using the wrong routes or tactics and get shot down, also putting you in the lurch. He wasn't worried about the 160th. It was the CIA's timidity that had gotten them into the present situation, and Murdock didn't intend to test their resolve any more than he had to.

He would have loved to consult with Razor Roselli just then, but he had to assume that the Syrian electronic warfare units had also come out to the field that Saturday. With modern equipment, even a short transmission from an MX-300 was way too easy to get a fix on.

The essence of war was the right place and the right time, and Murdock intended to choose well. He estimated that the Syrian sweep line would reach the patrol base in an hour and a half, two hours at the outside.

"As nice as it is up here," he said to Jaybird, "I think we'd better get back to the platoon."

"Yes, sir."

"Hey, Jaybird?"

"Yes, sir?"

"Stop calling me sir, will you? After all this time it just makes me think you're fucking with me."

Jaybird's grin was enormous. "Yes, sir."

Murdock sighed.

They eased their way down the hill and back to the patrol base. And after an exchange of birdcalls, the backup signal to a radio message, they got into the patrol base without being shot by their fellow SEALs. It had happened.

"I love it how the breaks just keep getting better and better," said Razor Roselli after Murdock gave him the news.

All the SEALs were in a tight circle. Shoulder-to-shoulder, face-to-face.

"Comments?" Murdock requested.

"Make some hides, let them walk right past us?" Higgins suggested.

"We don't have time to dig good ones," said Doc. "These woods are so open, if a Syrian took a wrong step and fell into just one hide, we'd all be screwed."

"What the Syrians are counting on," Magic Brown weighed in, "is that we've got the wide-open valley and fields to our east, and another thousand feet of mountains that are just bare rocks to our west. These woods aren't more than three miles across at the widest point. Look how long we had to patrol to find enough cover to cross the damn roads. We're going to have a hell of a time maneuvering around to find a gap in their lines."

"I was watching how they're doing the sweep," said Jaybird. "Every time they came to a road everyone would automatically stop. That way whoever fell behind got a chance to catch up. Then, when they were all on the road, all covered and aligned, they'd start up again. It worked pretty good, 'cause there's dirt roads cutting across these woods every couple of miles. So if we're going to make a move, it has to be just before they reach a road and get themselves unfucked. That's when they're the most disorganized and vulnerable." He looked around the circle to see what everyone was thinking.

"Keep going," Murdock urged. "You're on a roll."

"Okay," Jaybird said, feeding off the enthusiasm. "What we've got to do is think a couple of moves ahead of them, like Magic does in chess."

Imagining he was hearing his game slandered, Razor's eyes narrowed.

"Now," said Jaybird, "What I was thinking is this. . . ."

Listening, Murdock felt once again that any officer who thought he had all the answers was an asshole.

When Jaybird finished, Razor Roselli was the first to speak. "You know something, Turdbird? I think you're starting to work your way off my shit list."

29

Saturday, November 11

1305 hours
North central Lebanon

The SEALs were spread out among the trees, and not coincidentally had located themselves on the far western portion of the woods. Except for the quarter-mile-long portion they were in, a ridgeline stretched across that entire length of woods and continued down into the valley.

Out ahead of them they could hear the shouting of frustrated Syrian sergeants and platoon commanders trying to keep their troops together. Murdock took some comfort from the fact that the Syrians were having a long day too, and had probably reached the point where their heads were concentrated on maintaining the formation, not preparing to engage the enemy. And the SEALs were all dressed in Syrian uniforms, which was about the only bit of gratitude he could work up for the CIA just then.

But the sounds kept coming on, and Murdock began to get worried. Something should have happened by now.

A few minutes passed and Murdock could now hear the Syrians crashing through the brush. If they got any closer he was going to have to make a tough call. If he pulled back,

Jaybird's plan was blown. But if he stayed there and nothing happened they were committed to a firefight.

Like one of those "find all the animals in the barnyard" puzzles, Murdock could make out the green camouflaged faces of his SEALs among the trees. They were all looking over to him for a signal. He could have all the discussions he wanted, but in the end he would always be the one in charge. And the SEALs would do exactly what he decided, whether it got them killed or not. In training that ultimate responsibility was a lot of fun. Now it felt like being slowly crushed by a large rock.

He decided to throw the dice and stay put. But when he was able to pick out the uniforms of the Syrian troops moving toward him through the trees, he knew he'd chosen wrong, and his stomach flipped over. Then he heard the explosions in the distance, and was reprieved.

1314 hours
North central Lebanon

A mile to the east of the SEALs, the line of Syrian commandos looked up at the ridge they would soon have to climb and shook their heads. Although called commandos, these were not special forces like the SEALs or Green Berets. In the October 1973 War with Israel, the performance of Syria's conscript infantry had been disappointing. So the Syrian Army decided to form independent commando battalions to which they assigned their best and most reliable soldiers. The commando name was for morale and esprit; the units performed conventional infantry missions. The decision paid off. In the 1982 War in Lebanon, the Syrian commandos performed extremely well. Although present on the battlefield only in small numbers, they fought effective delaying actions, retreating only when ordered—a minor miracle for Arab armies up until that time. The commandos also sprang effective ambushes on the Israeli armor as it tried to negotiate the narrow Lebanese roads and rocky hills.

Now their sergeant shouted at them, and the commandos

started up the ridge. They didn't notice the monofilament fishing line snaking across their path. One of the Syrians snagged the line and tripped two hand grenades rigged with instantaneous fuses—the sort of toys SEALs carried in their pockets. The grenades blew and threw up a cloud of black smoke. Three commandos went down screaming.

Almost instantaneously, right in front of them there was a series of fast popping explosions, like the concentrated fire of a number of automatic weapons.

The Syrian soldiers hit the dirt and opened fire on the ridge. Nearby units, thinking that the enemy had been found atop the ridge, opened up also. Whenever a Syrian stopped to change magazines he still heard firing going on, so he continued shooting. It was a very common phenomenon and linked to the necessity of gaining fire superiority. No one wanted to slacken their fire and let the enemy gain an advantage. It happened more often than not in the confusion of battle. In the past even SEALs hadn't been immune to it.

What the Syrians had actually heard after the initial grenade explosions were 7.62mm M43 Kalasknikov bullets looped around a long piece of explosive detonating cord that had been taped to the grenades.

Certain that they had finally discovered the enemy, all the Syrian units along the line followed their orders. They began to maneuver to surround the enemy force and pin it down. It was the first step toward its destruction. Two more grenade booby traps were hit, convincing the Syrians that they were on the right track.

1316 hours
North central Lebanon

Once the firing started up, the Syrian soldiers in front of Murdock stopped dead in their tracks. Murdock visualized the radio conversation that had to be taking place.

Then orders were screamed. The Syrians faced about. Where

they had been sweeping northeast now they headed southeast, in the direction of the firing.

Murdock looked around and saw SEALs grinning at him. He waited, giving the Syrians time to get out of the way. A few hand signals, and Jaybird was back on point with the others formed up behind him.

The SEALs patrolled southwest, right through where the Syrian sweep line had originally been. A few hundred meters more and they were behind the sweep line, in the area the Syrians had already cleared.

Murdock had the completion of a perfect fantasy in mind. The Syrians would take their time, pound the living crap out of the ridge with mortars or artillery, and then assault. When they found nothing, they would eventually get sorted out and decide that the booby traps had only been intended to delay them. Angered by their losses, they would get back on line and renew their sweep with greater vigor, totally convinced that the enemy was up ahead. Which would be perfect, now that the SEALs were safely behind them.

Murdock made a mental note to name his first child Jaybird.

30

Saturday, November 11

1330 hours
North central Lebanon

The SEALs had made it out of the noose, but the main roads were still covered by the Syrians, and the section of woods they were now forced into was alarmingly small.

Now Murdock had to decide whether to sit tight or keep moving. There seemed to be no contest. There wasn't any assurance that the Syrians had finished moving around the area. If the SEALs kept moving there was always the risk of bumping into some random unit. Better to lay low and keep their heads down until dark.

But first they had to find the right place. The SEALs patrolled excruciatingly slowly, making no noise. They didn't follow a straight route, zigzagging back and forth instead to make it more difficult for anyone trying to trail them.

Jaybird found a spot that looked good, and Murdock was unwilling to keep patrolling in order to find something better. Unlike the previous patrol base, this one was on higher, more defensible ground: the side of a high but gently sloping ridge, covered with boulders, brush, tall grass, and scattered scrawny saplings clinging desperately to the rocky soil.

The SEALs arranged themselves across the nose of the ridge, settling in among the boulders with good 360-degree security.

After twenty minutes of peace and quiet, a small group of men passed by at a distance of several hundred yards. They were armed but scruffy, wearing combinations of military uniforms and civilian clothing. Murdock thought they had to be Hezbollah.

Another half hour passed. Murdock had no intention of allowing himself to fall asleep again. He chose the most uncomfortable position he could find.

A single shot was heard, not far away. Murdock was so keyed up that it made him jump slightly. It wasn't a rifle shot, though. It sounded like a shotgun. Then there was another shot, closer. It was definitely a shotgun. Murdock couldn't figure it out, and he didn't like it when that happened.

Fifteen minutes later he had his answer. Two Lebanese civilians appeared, carrying shotguns and accompanied by a dog. Murdock couldn't believe it. Half the Syrian Army in Lebanon was pounding the hills on a major manhunt, and these dumb bastards were out hunting. He'd heard amazing stories about recklessly stupid and fatalistic Lebanese behavior during the civil war, but this was ridiculous. Then again, if you lived in a country where armed soldiers regularly roamed the hills, maybe that wasn't reason enough to make you postpone your Saturday outing.

Go away, Murdock ordered them in his head, go the fuck away. The dog flushed a bird at the base of the ridge. Both hunters fired, and missed, but their shotgun pellets rained in among the SEALs' position. Murdock was glad that shotgun pellets didn't travel far before losing velocity. Considering that it was Lebanon, he supposed he ought to be thankful that the two yokels weren't out hunting with machine guns.

The dog picked up a scent and bounded up the ridge. Murdock didn't know whether it was scenting an animal, the mass of Syrians who had already passed through, or the SEALs.

The dog kept coming, and Murdock knew the animal was on their trail. They had made the usual question mark maneuver before heading into the rocks, so the dog went almost all the way around the ridge before heading down and then coming back toward them.

Then the dog ran into the line of CS crystals Razor Roselli had thoughtfully sprinkled down.

The dog didn't take a few tentative sniffs, then call it a day and head for home. No, it took a deep drag of CS and went absolutely berserk.

The dog nearly did a complete back flip. It yelped and howled and rolled in the grass. Then it chased its tail in tight frantic circles, howled some more, and began rubbing its eyes and muzzle in the dirt.

The two hunters were running up the slope to see what was the matter with their dog. And the dog, in the course of spazzing out, had come within twenty yards of the SEALs' position.

By the time the hunters reached it, the dog's muzzle was caked with dirt. They got ahold of the dog. One of them, clearly the owner, began wiping the dirt off the dog with a rag while the animal whimpered. And the other hunter just had to take a look around and see what had caused all the fuss.

The hunter literally stepped over Professor Higgins. If the man hadn't seen him, Higgins never would have moved. But the hunter's eyes went wide, and before the man could move his shotgun an inch Higgins shot him in the head.

Higgins, like the rest of the SEALs, was carrying as a backup weapon a sound-suppressed Russian Makarov pistol, which they called the P-6. The weapons were part of a stockpile inherited by the Germans from the former East German Spetsnaz special forces.

Although the shot was quiet, Higgins couldn't do anything

about the dead body rolling back down the hillside. As soon as that happened all the SEALs were up and blazing away with their pistols at the other hunter.

Even if it had been the hunter's first scrape, which it probably wasn't, his reflexes were perfect. As soon as he saw the green and brown apparitions bouncing up out of the very earth, he instantly abandoned his dog and his shotgun and launched himself down the ridge at a dead run.

Twenty yards or more is a long pistol shot, especially with a suppressed weapon designed to be used at point-blank range. It was professionally embarrassing, but all the SEALs who were able to get a clear shot missed.

Twigs and leaves clipped by the bullets fell all around the man, but he remained untouched. He hit the base of the ridge without breaking stride and smashed into the brush.

Murdock passed hand signals down the perimeter. They said in essence: "Let's mount up, we're out of here." It wasn't going to take that hunter very long to find someone to tell his story to.

The situation was that the Syrians were off to the northeast, and the hunter had run southwest. Murdock looked at his map to try to figure out which village the man would head for. There was one to the east, and another almost equally distant to the west. Great.

Murdock's choices were even more limited than that, being determined by the available terrain.

The SEALs headed northwest, Jaybird setting the pace as fast as he felt secure. They had to put some ground between themselves and that ridge.

Jaybird zigzagged wildly across their base course, to throw off pursuit. Razor spread the last of the CS crystals behind them.

In a fairly open forest glade Murdock gave a signal. Everyone turned ninety degrees to their right and kept walking. Where there had been one trail now there were seven. A hundred meters or so and they all turned back onto the original course, the seven separate trails returning to one. It was enough to buy them a little time while any tracker stopped to try and figure it all out.

To make better time and keep from leaving tracks, Jaybird angled the formation around a stretch of boggy ground. They came across a tiny stream, filled their canteens, and walked in it until it disappeared into the earth.

As Jaybird was elbowing his way through some streamside brush, he suddenly came face-to-face with an equally surprised Lebanese carrying a Kalashnikov.

31

Saturday, November 11

1408 hours
North central Lebanon

In a gunfight, the one who shoots first usually wins. Jaybird Sterling, who like all SEALs patrolled with his rifle at his shoulder and ready to fire, got off a burst before his opponent even had a chance to start work on the cumbersome Kalashnikov safety catch. The force of the rounds threw the man back into the brush.

Jaybird didn't know if the man was alone or had fifty buddies following along behind, and he didn't intend to stick around to find out. He began a maneuver called the Australian Peel. He emptied his magazine into the bushes in front of him to force everyone who might be in there down on their faces, then turned tail and ran, changing magazines as he went.

This left Murdock on point. He knew the drill. When Jaybird opened up he had automatically dropped to one knee. As soon as Jaybird moved he fired several shot bursts to his front, then followed right behind Sterling.

Higgins, now in front, did the same. Then Doc. Then DeWitt, who threw a grenade in lieu of firing one-handed. The explosion threw up a nice bit of smoke, so Magic Brown and Razor didn't waste time on a lot of shooting.

Soon the whole file of SEALs was sprinting in the opposite direction. It had all been neatly done, and without a word of command being spoken.

But there was fire coming from behind them, and they were obviously being chased.

They kept running, and the firing continued. Whoever it was was right on their ass. The SEALs had to break contact or the pursuers would dog their heels until, inevitably, they ran right into a larger force.

As he ran, Jaybird kept looking back over his shoulder to make sure everyone was still with him. When he went over a small rise in the ground Jaybird saw that Murdock had stopped, so he stopped also.

As each SEAL ran up and saw Murdock on his stomach, they instantly spread out on both sides of him. It only took a few seconds, not even long enough to catch their breath, before the screaming pursuers broke through the trees.

Murdock fired, and all the SEALs joined in. The pursuers dropped to the ground or behind the trees and began firing back a few moments later.

As soon as that happened, Murdock slid back down below the cover of the rise and had Jaybird and the SEALs up and running again.

The hasty ambush had put the first of their pursuers down, but the ones behind must have started running again as soon as the firing stopped. The SEALs had bought themselves some time and distance, but not enough. It wasn't that their pursuers were good; it was that they were Hezbollah and didn't mind running into a few rounds. Paradise was automatic for those who died in battle with the infidel, which covered just about everyone besides themselves.

Murdock yelled over his shoulder to Higgins, "Throw a PDM!"

The order worked its way back to the end of the line of

runners. Razor Roselli tossed one of their two remaining Pursuit Deterrent Munitions over his shoulder.

A key element of human psychology, of which the SEALs were well aware, was that when you chased someone you assumed they were running in a straight line and would continue to do so. And when you were being chased, you *did* tend to run in a straight line and at a constant pace.

So after Razor threw the PDM, Murdock yelled to Jaybird and Jaybird veered hard to his left. He quickly slowed down to a fast walk to minimize the enormous racket they were making.

Now the SEALs crept along quietly. They heard the PDM explode. There was a pause, and then they could hear the shouting of the Hezbollah continue along their original route.

Another hundred meters and Jaybird made another hard change of direction. They continued on for a while, and then Murdock flashed him some more hand signals. Jaybird circled around in another question-mark maneuver and they came back on their trail.

The SEALs set up an ambush and waited, slowly getting their wind back. A fifteen-mile run through beach sand was a lot less tiring than a relatively short run for your life.

No one came down the trail. They were safe. Again. For the moment.

32

Saturday, November 11

1435 hours
North central Lebanon

Murdock crawled from man to man. He needed to get an idea of their ammunition situation. He also needed to take everyone's temperature, in a manner of speaking.

"Four magazines," Jaybird whispered. "A hundred and twenty rounds. If it wasn't for those smugglers, I'd be out. One frag grenade, one smoke."

"Five mags," Higgins reported. "Three frags, about six feet of time fuse, a few igniters, five caps. Used up all the det cord on the diversion."

"Four magazines," said Doc. "Four frags. I also used up forty rounds of 7.62 match on the smugglers."

"Three magazines," said Magic. "Three frags. I'd like to use up some of this .50-cal. ammo; it's weighing my ass down."

"You ever try running with your arm strapped to your chest?" DeWitt wanted to know. "Really slows you up. Magic almost ran me down from behind."

Even under unbelievable pressure, that almost cheerful, cocky-ass attitude was what Murdock had been expecting to hear. It was why there was a BUD/S, and a Hell Week. The instructors made sure the quitters quit back at Coronado, not in Lebanon. And that the officers who wanted to wear the pretty badge but would sooner or later say, "I'm tired, I don't want to be in charge any more . . . you guys do what you want," never made it out of the program.

"I got four magazines," said Razor Roselli. "The last PDM and two frags. Don't these fucking people know we don't want to be disturbed until it's time to leave?"

"I guess someone didn't tell them," Murdock whispered in reply.

"You know what's going to happen now?" said Razor. "They're going to get on the radio and all the Syrians are going to turn right around and come sweeping back down here. And they ain't going to fall for the same trick twice."

"You've got something on your mind," said Murdock. "Don't keep it to yourself."

"We've got to head for the mountains."

"It's wide open," Murdock protested. "The biggest piece of cover is a knee-high bush."

"They'll close in on us eventually. We'll keep getting chased around these fucking woods until we run out of room, and all it'll take is one good firefight to pin us down. Then they'll close in and keep throwing troops at us until we're either overrun or out of ammo. And that's all she wrote."

"I don't like it."

"I don't like it, either," said Razor, "but we gotta do it. These woods are nothing but a trap."

Murdock didn't take his chief's counsel lightly. He thought hard on the problem. It *would* be easier to bring the helicopters in without getting them either shot down or shot out of the landing zone. The SEALs only had enough ammunition for one more firefight. And not a long one at that.

He decided, and they began patrolling west toward the mountains. At least in that direction they weren't having to cross one ridgeline after the other. But the woods quickly opened up, and Murdock felt even more exposed.

A helicopter flew overhead and all the SEALs froze. Movement was more easy to see from the air than shapes, especially well-camouflaged shapes. Even the very act of throwing yourself to the ground could mean compromise. The helicopter disappeared and they resumed patrolling.

Then Jaybird signaled enemy ahead. Murdock signaled the file to halt, then get down. Jaybird was very close to the edge of the trees. Murdock slipped in beside him, and Jaybird pointed to their front.

There was a road just beyond the trees. A low-slung BMP-1 armored personnel carrier was parked diagonally across the road. The paint job was Syrian brown and sand. The top hatches and the two rear doors were hanging open. The crew, seven men, were slumped casually against the outside of the vehicle. Some were sleeping, the rest were brewing tea. Their weapons were casually propped up against the tracks. Murdock decided that there had to be at least one man inside the BMP monitoring the radio. Maybe two.

Using hand signals, Jaybird asked Murdock which way he wanted to go to patrol around them.

Murdock signaled back to wait. He had an idea, an idea that didn't seem too outlandish once he considered all the angles. Murdock slid back into the brush, and then signaled Razor to come up.

It took him some time; he didn't make a sound. Then Murdock pointed to the BMP. Razor checked it out and shrugged, as if to say, "So what?"

Using his finger, Murdock drew a diagram in the dirt. One of Razor's eyebrows shot up, and then he nodded approvingly. He slid back and brought up the rest of the SEALs.

They were all briefed on what Murdock wanted without a word being spoken. It took a bit of diagramming, but soon they all signaled their understanding.

The Syrian mechanized infantrymen had no inkling of what was going on when what seemed to be a group of their fellow soldiers burst from the tree line. The uniforms made them freeze for a crucial few seconds, but they realized something was wrong. The weapons were pointed at them. They had no chance, which was exactly how Murdock had planned it.

The SEALs opened fire as they charged. The prone Syrians weren't even able to lift themselves up, let along get to their weapons.

The SEALs could have shot them from inside the cover of the tree line, but Murdock needed to get to that vehicle fast.

While the rest of the SEALs made sure the Syrians on the outside were dead, Razor Roselli leaped up onto the top of the BMP, stuck his AKM into the driver's hatch, and fired. Only then did he risk a peek inside. No one was there. He quickly shifted his weapon over to the nearby vehicle commander's hatch and repeated the process.

As did Magic Brown atop the weapons turret. But when he inserted his barrel into the hatch a pistol shot was fired out at him. Magic didn't expose himself in the hatch; he just worked the barrel back and forth, firing continuously.

At the same time Murdock was charging around the rear of the vehicle. He fired at an angle into one of the rear doors. When he stopped he could hear the *ching-ching-ching* of his rounds continuing to ricochet around the interior. After that sound stopped he leaned in the door to finish the job, but the troop compartment was empty.

Grenades would have done the work much easier, but a catastrophic explosion of all the BMP's stored ammunition was the last thing Murdock wanted. He had other plans for the vehicle. As soon as Jaybird had pointed it out to him, a question had presented itself. Why walk up the bare hills where everyone could shoot you at their leisure, when you could drive right up them in the armored comfort of one of the enemy's official vehicles?

When Murdock emerged from the troop compartment, he saw Razor and Magic pulling the deadweight of a blood-soaked Syrian out of the turret hatch. He had been the only one inside the vehicle.

The rest of the SEALs were stripping the other Syrians of their equipment. The bodies were then dragged off into the trees. The weapons and equipment were tossed into the troop compartment.

"Okay," Murdock said, anxious to be on the road. "Who knows how to drive a BMP?"

It was not outside the conceivable range of skills possessed by a SEAL platoon.

"I drove a T-62 at Aberdeen Proving Ground one time," said Higgins.

Jaybird came out of the trees, wiping the blood off his hand onto his trousers and grinning triumphantly. "I drove a BMP at National Training Center," he announced.

"Well, what the fuck are you waiting for, an invitation?" Razor Roselli growled impatiently. "Get in and drive the motherfucker already."

Jaybird did just that. It had been a while since enemy vehicle familiarization training at Fort Irwin, and it took a minute to get reacquainted with all the controls and instruments. Then he worked the engine's pneumatic starter, and the six-cylinder, three-hundred-horsepower water-cooled diesel roared to life.

Murdock went over to the turret first, but the entire compartment was drenched with blood and splattered bits of flesh. He had no idea how to operate the 73mm gun and Sagger antitank missile system anyway. At least that was how he rationalized his decision.

Instead he jumped into the vehicle commander's hatch located directly behind Jaybird. Lying across the seat was a padded wool Russian armored vehicle crew helmet. It smelled like it had been worn continuously and not washed since World War II. Not inconceivable, since the Russians had worn the same model helmet fifty years back. Murdock put it on anyway; otherwise he wouldn't be able to hear over the vehicle intercom system.

Hanging on a hook was a microphone that also looked like it dated back to World War II. In good Russian fashion there were diagrams denoting the function of the switches and dials, for those who couldn't read. The communications switch was set on radio. Murdock turned it to what looked like intercom. He keyed the microphone and, a little apprehensive at the prospect of mistakenly transmitting to the entire Syrian Army, tentatively asked, "Jaybird?"

"Yes, sir?" came the reply.

Murdock was able to look back over his shoulder and see into the troop compartment. The rest of the SEALs had climbed in. They had closed the clamshell rear doors and were in the process of opening the four troop-compartment roof hatches to let in some air. Razor Roselli gave him the thumbs-up to let him know they had everyone and were ready to move.

"Let's go, Jaybird," Murdock said over the intercom. He'd jacked his seat up until his head was sticking out the hatch. If you stayed down inside the vehicle you couldn't see squat out the thick glass vision blocks.

"Where to, sir?"

"Swing this thing around and head south. Take the first real road you see on your right. That's the one that heads up into the mountains."

"Aye, aye, sir."

Because it was a tracked vehicle, the BMP was steered by a clutch-and-brake system. Each track had an independent brake. So to make a left turn, the driver locked the brake on the left track while allowing the right track to continue to roll. The longer the brake was held down, the tighter the turn. It took a little getting used to.

Jaybird shifted the transmission into first gear, locked the brake on the left track, and released the clutch on the right.

The BMP lurched around 180 degrees, on a dime. A large dime, but still a dime. It lurched around so quickly that Murdock's head went clanging off the side of the hatch opening. Smelly or not, he was grateful for the padded helmet. He could hear the SEALs and equipment spilling around the inside of the troop compartment, and decided not to look back.

As the BMP finished its turn, Jaybird popped the clutch on the left track and headed them straight down the road. A heavy tank rides very smooth, but a light armored vehicle takes bumps surprisingly hard.

Fourth gear on the BMP topped out at around thirty-five miles an hour. In a rare flash of prudence, Jaybird decided not to shift into fifth gear or get anywhere near the top speed of fifty miles an hour until he got the hang of the vehicle.

"This is the turn," Murdock said into the microphone.

Jaybird waited just a bit too long before downshifting and braking the right track. The BMP went right past the turn. Jaybird turned anyway, and the BMP went up and over a grassy embankment and made a teeth-shattering drop back onto the road.

The BMP bounced nicely, and this time Murdock's head hit the front of the hatch ring.

"Take it easy, goddammit!" he shouted into the intercom.

"Sorry, sir," came the reply. Jaybird straightened the BMP out and headed up the road.

Murdock looked up ahead, and could see the road snake up into the mountains. He felt better than he had all afternoon, and was almost enjoying himself. If you considered staying alive the ultimate expression of luck, then theirs had been pretty good. But with all the trouble they'd had staying alive, it could have been a lot better. Murdock thought he could feel everything turning around.

The BMP climbed steadily upward. Hot shit, Murdock thought.

33

Saturday, November 11

1550 hours
North central Lebanese mountains

"Careful, Jaybird," Murdock cautioned over the BMP intercom. "We slip off this road and we'll all be playing harps." He chuckled to himself and keyed the microphone again. "And Razor'll be ramming his up your ass for the rest of eternity."

"I get the picture, sir," Jaybird replied over the system. "Thanks."

The road zigzagged along the sides of the switchback ridges. Fortunately, the steep slope meant that Jaybird couldn't get the BMP much over twenty-five miles an hour. Murdock was glad that at least nature was able to exert some influence over Jaybird.

Murdock turned around in his hatch and looked out over the valley. Razor had been right. He could almost picture the Syrians down below beating the brush for them. At least the sun was starting to drop into the west. It felt like the longest day of the whole fucking year.

All the SEALs were hanging out of the troop compartment roof hatches. The BMP was not a large vehicle. It was designed to tightly accommodate eight small Russian infantrymen sitting four back-to-back in the troop compartment. To give an idea of the fit, the Russians were in the habit of donning their gas masks and sliding the hoses out the roof hatches in order to get some air. Staring at the steel wall while the BMP bounced up and down was almost guaranteed to induce vomiting.

Now the road was on a long, straight uphill run along the side of the mountain range. The right side of the road sat snug against the sheer side of the mountain. The left side was a long drop into the canyon below. Of course there were no guard-rails. Just short of the top, the road made a hard right turn in the opposite direction, still heading up. That put the mountainside on the left, the drop on the right. It would continue that way right over the top and down the other side of the mountain.

Jaybird made the turn very slowly, jiggling the right-track brake and left-track clutch on and off so the BMP turned a few degrees, stopped, turned a bit more, stopped, and then moved slowly forward. When the turn was accomplished, Murdock reached out and gave Jaybird a complimentary tap atop the helmet.

Then Murdock looked out and saw one of the Gazelle helicopters sweeping up the valley. It seemed the size of a golf ball in the distance. Then Murdock was looking down at fluttering rotor blades as the Gazelle rose toward the mountains, following the road.

The SEALs disappeared into the troop compartment, which was good because the group included a few fair-haired and fair-skinned types who weren't about to pass for Syrians.

Murdock picked up the microphone. "Jaybird, there's a helicopter coming up to take a look at us. Just be cool and keep driving at a steady pace, like we're going someplace we're supposed to."

"Roger that, sir."

The helicopter approached cautiously. Murdock could make out the sand, brown, and blue camouflage, and the red, white, and black Syrian bull's-eye roundels. He saw the clear bubble front, the skids, the protruding tailpipe, and the finned fan-rotor tail. Murdock took no comfort from the fact that the copter was an antitank variant, armed with six French HOT heavy wire-guided missiles with a four-thousand-meter range; three tubes mounted in-line on each side of the cabin.

Murdock gave a friendly wave. The Gazelle moved up even with the BMP, but far enough off to the side to keep the rotor blades away from the side of the mountain. Murdock could see both the pilot and copilot/gunner looking over at him.

Murdock stood up higher in the hatch and pointed to the BMP's whip radio aerial mounted on the roof of the vehicle at the left rear. Then he pointed to the earpiece on his crewman's helmet, shaking his head and stretching his arms out in a gesture of helplessness. As if the reason why he wasn't talking to them was that his radio was broken.

He could see the helicopter crew talking in their microphones.

It was a cold November day in the mountains, yet Murdock could feel the perspiration trickling down his back. Something tapped his right leg. He looked down, and Razor Roselli's face was looking up at him.

"Everyone's got their gear on," Razor shouted. "You want us to shoot the motherfucker down, just let me know."

Murdock was still smiling and waving at the helicopter. "No shooting," he said through his teeth. "Just stay ready and keep out of sight."

Razor gave him a reassuring tap on the leg and disappeared back into the compartment.

Murdock pretended to speak into his microphone, as if giving it another try, then pointed to it and shook his head sadly. He decided it was time to ignore the Gazelle, so he gave a final wave and shrug of the shoulders and turned back to his front.

After a very long minute the Gazelle began a slow, sweeping turn away from the mountain and back toward the valley. It grew smaller in the distance, but wasn't losing any altitude. Murdock noticed that the BMP had almost reached the top of the mountain range.

Then, off in the distance, the helicopter made another turn. It was in a stationary hover, and its nose was pointing directly at the BMP.

A small puff of gray smoke appeared in the sky beside the helicopter.

Murdock screamed into the microphone and the troop compartment at the same time. "Stop! Everybody out! Bail out, bail out, bail out!"

34

Saturday, November 11

1620 hours
North central Lebanese mountains

With his drag bag in one hand and the AKM in the other, Murdock leaped from his seat right over the side of the BMP. He'd been counting in his head the whole time, and was up to thousand-six, thousand-seven.

He hit the ground and rolled to his feet. Thousand-nine, thousand-ten. Jaybird Sterling was in front of him, trying to get up off the ground. Murdock shifted his gear in his hands, grabbed Jaybird by the belt, and lifted him up bodily.

The SEALs in the back of the BMP didn't bother with the rear doors. They poured out the top hatches while the BMP was still rolling.

Razor Roselli actually saw the missile coming in at them. He grabbed Professor Higgins and threw him off the road. Higgins slid down the gravel slope face-first, with Razor and DeWitt close behind him.

Doc and Magic went out the other side of the BMP, which faced the side of the mountain. There was nothing they could do but run down the road.

Now Murdock and Jaybird were running up it. Thousand-thirteen, thousand-fourteen. The explosion picked them up and threw them face down onto the road.

The Gazelle's pilot had been careful to pull back out of cannon and machine-gun range before he allowed the gunner to launch the HOT missile. HOT time of flight to three thousand meters was thirteen seconds. To four thousand meters max range, it was 17.3 seconds.

When armor-piercing shape-charge warheads are tested, they leave holes in steel over a yard deep but less than an inch in diameter. Very much like a stream of water coming out of a hose and boring a hole in mud. But when a fast-moving missile with a shape-charge warhead hits steel, the dynamic impact effect is quite different.

The HOT hit with a blinding flash and blew a hole in the top of the BMP large enough for a man to climb through. The shape charge jet went all the way through the vehicle and out the floor. The forty rounds of 73mm cannon ammunition, two thousands rounds of machine-gun ammunition, and four Sagger missile reloads chain-detonated in rapid succession. White-hot flame blasted out all the hatch openings. The diesel fuel ignited in a fireball.

Murdock rolled in the dirt in case he was on fire. This time Jaybird dragged him to his feet, and they were running again. After a thirty-yard sprint up the road, they were able to get off it and into a wall of boulders that spread up into the mountaintop. After a short climb, they threw their weapons over the top of a boulder and scrambled over themselves. They landed in a sizable crevice in the rocks.

Explosions blow up and out, so Razor, DeWitt, and Higgins had been spared the force of the blast. But now flaming metal and debris was raining down all around them.

"Across the slope," Razor shouted. "We gotta get up the road. Cut across the slope."

Magic and Doc weren't far from the BMP when the missile hit. Magic could feel the heat right through the soles of his boots. His head hurt. The back of the heavy drag bag had cracked him across the skull when he hit the ground.

They crawled down the road away from the flaming vehicle. Magic looked over and saw Doc's trousers smoldering. He leaped up, pinned Doc down, and threw dirt on him to put it out. It was only then Magic realized that his clothing was smoking too. He rolled off Doc and threw handfuls of dirt over himself.

Doc was already up, and he saw what was on the way. He grabbed Magic by the webbing harness and pulled him over to the side of the road. After the first tug Magic rolled back onto his feet. They got off the road just as a second HOT missile exploded with an earsplitting roar. Right where they had been.

Doc shook his head to clear it. Talk about trying to kill mice with a howitzer.

Magic saw Higgins, Razor, and DeWitt sprint across the road higher up and start climbing up the rocks. Well, at least they knew where to go. He got Doc's attention and pointed; both of them were still pretty deaf from the blast. Doc gave him a thumbs-up. They headed up across the slope, staying well below the surface of the road. They had to get past the destroyed BMP, which was still spitting flame and small explosions.

Murdock had heard the second HOT explode. It sounded as if it had been guided onto the road to try to take out some SEALs with the blast. He had no idea where the others were. He sprang up from the rocks to try to see what was happening, and immediately had his wind knocked out when Professor Higgins came sailing over and landed right on top of him. Murdock curled up into a ball and fought that terrible feeling of really needing to breathe air and not being able to.

Jaybird, meanwhile, was leaning over the rocks bellowing, "Up here, up here, on me, on me."

While Murdock wheezed around in the dirt, people began climbing over the rocks.

He was grabbed and turned over. Ed DeWitt's imperturbable face appeared before him. "You okay, Blake?"

Murdock only nodded. He'd just regained the ability to draw breath, and was fully occupied doing that.

"What the fuck happened to him?" he heard DeWitt demanding.

"I did it," Higgins admitted. "I landed on him."

"*You* fucked up the lieutenant, Higgo?" DeWitt asked, bewildered.

"Sure," Jaybird broke in. "Did you think it was the Syrians?"

"Fuck you, Jaybird," said Higgins.

"No, fuck *you,*" Jaybird replied.

"Shut up and spread out!" Razor Roselli screamed. "Get those long rifles broken out."

Magic and Doc made it across the slope and past the BMP. Doc gave Magic a hand signal: "You first, and I'll follow." You had to stay spread out, so if you had a misfortune the other guy wouldn't get sucked in too.

Magic signaled OK, and sprinted across the road. He reached the rock and started climbing. Hands reached over the top to grab him. Doc showed up a few moments later.

"About time," said Jaybird.

Doc, panting hard, fought off the urge to shoot him.

Razor got everyone positioned and then came over to check on Murdock.

"Have we got everyone?" Murdock demanded between gasps.

"Yeah, Boss." Razor was talking fast, as he always did when he was excited. "We were watching through the periscope in back. We saw that helo turning around, and while you were still yelling me and the boys were blowing out of every hole in that BMP like shit through a goose. We just had to wait a bit; couldn't head up the road until the ammo finished cooking off."

"Anyone hurt?" Murdock demanded.

"A little shrapnel, a few burns. Just made us run faster. I think we broke the Iraqi Army's world record for un-assing an armored vehicle under fire. Chicken-shit son of a bitch launched from max range. If he had the balls to get in close we'd all be ashes right now."

"Shouldn't have said that so loud, Chief," Jaybird called out. "He's coming in."

35

Saturday, November 11

1625 hours
North central Lebanese mountains

While his fellow SEALs were scrambling among the rocks, Magic Brown was removing his massive rifle from the drag bag.

The McMillan M88 was a highly tuned bolt-action sniper rifle, scaled up in size to handle the huge .50-caliber machine-gun cartridge. It was fifty-three inches long, with a bulbous muzzle brake on the end of the barrel, an adjustable bipod, and a fixed five-round magazine. To make that great length more manageable, the black fiberglass stock broke down at a joint just behind the trigger group. The rifle weighed twenty-five pounds, including the Leupold Ultra Mk 4 16-power telescopic sight. Magic had screwed a 2-power converter onto the end of the scope to bring the total magnification up to 32-power. That much magnification threw up a lot of haze and mirage in the field of view, but was necessary for a rifle designed to shoot accurately beyond two thousand yards.

Although McMillan rifles were close to being a SEAL trademark, the M88 had been brought along on the mission because a great many had been sold around the world.

Particularly to the French, who used them for countersniping in Bosnia. Magic had been careful to bring along the M88 instead of the similar but lighter and improved McMillan M93, which was almost exclusively in the SEAL inventory.

There was no flat place to set the rifle on its bipod, so Magic threw the empty padded drag bag over a rock and used it as a rifle rest.

Now that the BMP and its cannon and machine guns had been destroyed, the pilot of the Gazelle felt more comfortable about moving in close. He intended to use the high-magnification HOT sight to pick out the enemy in the rocks. His remaining missiles would blow them to bits. A range of one thousand meters ought to do just fine.

Razor Roselli was beside Magic acting as spotter. But the compact laser range finder the size of a small pair of binoculars wouldn't be much use. The Gazelle's range was changing every second. It was all going to be up to Magic.

Quartermaster First Class Martin "Magic" Brown was a black man who had grown up in the Chicago projects. His fiercely protective mother had made sure he maintained the clean police record that allowed him to escape into the Navy.

At boot camp in Great Lakes he'd watched the SEAL recruiting film and decided that was for him, even though at the time he could barely dog-paddle across the pool. Swimming pools and swimming lessons were hard to come by in the projects, one reason why there were proportionately few minority SEALs. But you didn't need to be an Olympic swimmer to be a SEAL. You just needed to be determined. Martin Brown was determined.

Because nothing came easy, Magic got in the habit of listening carefully and doing things exactly the way he was taught. Not only was this the right formula for making it as a SEAL, it also happened to be the characteristic of a great rifle shot. After he pinned on the Budweiser, a smart platoon chief sent Seaman Brown through the SEAL sniper course. He later went on to Marine Corps Scout Sniper Instructor School, and the Army Special Operations Target Interdiction Course. A kid who had barely made it through basic-level high school math now did ballistic trajectories, windage compensations, and moving target computations for a range of ammunition loadings—in his head, and in minutes of angle. Magic liked to say he just needed a practical application for those numbers.

The McMillan was capable of Minute of Angle accuracy, which meant a group of rounds would fall in a one-inch circle at one-hundred yards, a ten-inch circle at one thousand yards, and a twenty-inch circle at two thousand yards. With the right ammunition it could do better than that. No matter how good the rifle was, most men couldn't shoot Minute of Angle. Custom-built sniping weapons in the conventional rifle calibers could produce ½ Minute of Angle. Magic Brown could shoot ½ Minute of Angle.

Magic worked the heavy bolt and racked a round into the chamber. The Gazelle was approaching leisurely; it was bright and clear in the fine black crosshairs of his scope. Magic watched the clouds to see which way the wind was blowing and how fast. His brain was working on the math, and the compensation for the difference in altitude from the Chocolate Mountains, where he'd last zeroed the scope. Long-range marksmanship was both art and science. Magic Brown was both artist and scientist, and, as the platoon liked to say in frequent awe at the results, part magician.

Magic didn't aim at the helicopter. He practiced the sniper's trick of aiming at a particular spot on the target, in this case a square of windscreen. He clicked the elevation drum of the telescopic sight to fifteen hundred meters.

The Gazelle gunner was scanning the rocks through his own crosshairs, looking for signs of life. His finger was on the firing button.

In order to shoot Magic had to be exposed. The gunner picked him up.

Magic fired. The time of flight for a .50-caliber slug at fifteen hundred meters was 2.4 seconds. Plenty of time for a helicopter to move.

"Miss, low," said Razor.

Magic had already worked the bolt and made a new set of calculations. The SEALs in the rocks were silent, like any appreciative audience. But that made no difference. No matter what the noise or distractions, there was only Magic, the rifle locked against his body, and the helicopter.

At that range the Gazelle crew had no idea they were being fired at. Now the gunner had *his* crosshairs on Magic, and unlike a sniper's bullet, a HOT missile could be continuously guided to its target. The pilot was hovering now. The gunner pressed his firing button.

Magic fired again. What he fired was an armor-piercing explosive round. Explosive rounds in .50 caliber had previously been unavailable because no one could make a fuse small enough to fit in the round with enough room for the charge. This one was made by Raufoss of Norway, so of course the SEALs called it a Rufus round.

It hit the plexiglass windscreen of the Gazelle and passed between the pilot and copilot. Even if the pilot hadn't lost control when the windshield shattered—it was the last thing in the world he was expecting—the round slammed into the engine compartment behind them and exploded.

"That looked like a hit," said Razor.

The helicopter wobbled in midair, then rolled upside down and headed for the earth.

The copilot grabbed the controls and kicked the foot pedals, trying to coax the rotors into auto-rotation. But the helicopter was already aerodynamically unstable. It crashed into the base of the mountains and exploded.

The SEALs acknowledged Magic Brown with a round of subdued golf claps, as if they were the gallery and he had just two-putted the ninth hole at Augusta. Magic turned around and grinned at his audience.

But he quickly got back behind the rifle when Razor informed them, "Two more Gazelles coming up from the valley."

Magic peered through the scope. "No missiles on these, just 20-millimeter gun-packs."

"Terrific," came Jaybird's voice from the rocks. "*Just* 20-millimeter cannons."

"Are you starting up with those negative thoughts again?" Doc Ellsworth shouted angrily.

The rest of the SEALs actually began chuckling. Jaybird found the wisdom to remain silent.

"Everyone get some cover," Magic said helpfully. "We may end up taking a little incoming." He pressed two fresh rounds, both as long as his entire hand, into the magazine.

Murdock and Razor set up their MSG-90 rifles. Doc had left the third MSG-90 behind in the BMP, choosing to save his medical pack instead. Doc had made the right choice, but Murdock wouldn't have blamed him even if he'd left everything behind. If it came down to your ass or some gear, you had to go with your ass. No sense in losing both.

Murdock knew his MSG-90 wouldn't do much good in the present situation. He was a good shot, but unlike Magic, not a one-thousand-yard shot. Eight hundred yards was the limit of his skills. It was all in Magic's hands.

The pair of Gazelles didn't know what had happened to the first one, but their tactics were a little better. One made a run straight at the rocks where the SEALs were hiding, but zigzagging this time. The other split off and came at them up the long axis of the mountain range.

Magic decided on the Gazelle coming right at them. It was zigzagging, but in the most regular back-and-forth pattern imaginable. The French 20mm cannon had an effective range of about two thousand yards, but in the absence of the high-powered optics of the HOT system, it would have to get in closer to identify targets.

The Gazelle wasn't sure where the SEALs were. It opened fire at max range and worked bursts up the road, trying to flush them out.

Magic Brown fired.

"Miss, right," said Razor.

The cannon rounds splattered up the road.

Magic Brown fired again.

"Miss," said Razor. "Wait for it, he's going to have to stop juking once he gets on target."

The only problem with that, Murdock was thinking, was that *they* were the target.

Magic fired again.

The round hit the Gazelle low, and took the copilot's left leg off at the knee. It exploded behind his seat.

Despite the screams of the copilot and the arterial blood spraying around the cabin, the pilot kept control of the Gazelle and yanked it into a hard right turn, quitting the fight.

The SEALs heard the *boom-boom-boom* of the other cannon, and knowing what was coming, Magic grabbed his rifle and dropped beneath the cover of the rocks. The rest followed suit.

The high-explosive cannon shells exploded among the rocks like small grenades.

Just as they'd taught him in the demo pit during Hell Week, Murdock clapped his hands over his ears and kept his mouth open.

The shells would come in breaking the sound barrier, followed by the explosions, then tiny pieces of fragmentation and rock splinters singing by.

Then the Gazelle pilot did a very foolish thing. Perhaps he was overconfident, perhaps he was used to targets that didn't shoot back. Instead of standing off and pouring cannon fire into the rocks, he continued his gun run and made a high-speed pass overhead. Murdock had seen Marine Corps Cobra pilots do the same thing. Maybe the pilot planned on making a quick turn and then shooting straight down on them.

As the Gazelle passed overhead the SEALs all rose up shooting. They used the old Viet Cong technique of picking a spot in the sky ahead and letting the helicopter run into the fire.

The Gazelle shuddered and then sped off to the east, trailing smoke.

"I guess we've done our part in writing down the Syrian Air Force inventory," said Razor Roselli as he peeked up to watch the helicopter go. He patted Magic on the back.

Then, from the rocks off to the side an urgent cry rang out. "Doc, over here!"

Murdock felt sick to his stomach.

36

Saturday, November 11

1639 hours
North central Lebanese mountains

Doc Ellsworth leaped over the rocks, his medical pack in hand and Blake Murdock on his heels.

Razor Roselli shouted, "Everybody stay put and keep your eyes open. The Doc don't need no help. Now sound off!"

"Jaybird."

"Magic."

"DeWitt." And then the same voice. "I'm here with the Professor."

Murdock found DeWitt applying direct pressure, with his only good hand, to a wound in Higgins's side.

"I didn't see any other wounds," DeWitt said to Doc. And then: "I . . . I tried to get a battle dressing open, but I couldn't."

"You did just fine, sir," the Doc said soothingly. "Don't worry, Higgo, we're under control here."

Murdock stripped off Higgins's radio pack, then elevated his legs to force blood back into the upper extremities and prevent shock.

Doc cut away part of Higgins's jacket so he had room to work. "Okay, sir," he said to DeWitt. "Take your hand off."

Doc took a close look at the wound, then inserted a woman's tampon into the hole. It was a little battlefield medical trick. The tampon absorbed blood and swelled outward, sealing off the wound and effectively stopping the bleeding. The size and shape were perfect for fitting inside wounds.

Higgins was staring into the sky, blinking hard, groaning through gritted teeth, but not saying a word.

Then Doc placed a four-by-seven-inch battle dressing compress over the wound, winding the two long green gauze strips around Higgins's torso and then tying the ends together over the compress. He checked Higgins for other wounds. Finding none, the Doc listened to Higgins's chest with his stethoscope and slid on a blood pressure cuff. He gave Higgins a shot of morphine, clipping the empty syrette to his collar to keep track of the dosage. Finally, Doc started an intravenous line and hooked up a clear plastic bag of Lactated Ringer's solution. DeWitt held the IV bag up.

"No sweat, Higgo," the Doc said confidently. "You're going to be fine."

Higgins nodded. The morphine was starting to kick in.

Doc slid his nylon stretcher underneath Higgins in case they had to move fast. He covered the Professor with a green foil space blanket to keep him warm, and then wrapped the stretcher straps around the whole setup. Then he slipped away to give the Murdock the score.

"It doesn't sound like the fragment's in the thoracic cavity," Doc repeated. "Lungs are clear, and thanks to Mister DeWitt he didn't lose too much blood. He's stabilized. Other than that, I'm not psychic."

"I know you'd like to get him out now," Murdock said. "Can he wait until dark?"

"He's got to," Doc replied, putting it as simply and bluntly as a SEAL corpsman could. "If he stays stable, he should be all right. But not too long after dark, okay, sir?"

"Do my best," said Murdock.

37

Saturday, November 11

1650 hours
North central Lebanese mountains

"They know where we are now," Murdock said to Razor Roselli. "And I don't like that one bit, no matter how defensible the position is. Not with only five of us in fighting shape."

Razor nodded in agreement. "If we move two or three klicks south down this mountain range, we'll still be in a good position to dominate the road up."

"You're reading my mind again," Murdock replied.

SEAL officers did not delegate the grunt work. Murdock sent Jaybird out ahead to scout a good route. He, Razor, Magic, and Doc would carry Higgins on the stretcher. It would take all four of them to negotiate the rocks. Ed DeWitt would have to cover the rear single-handed. In more ways than one, as Razor humorously told him.

Moving two kilometers, or little over a mile, was no easy matter when you were doing it across the top of a rocky mountain range in thin high-altitude air while carrying a wounded man on a stretcher. And despite their superb physical condition, the SEALs were already exhausted. Since the early hours of the morning they had been walking and running a marathon over the Lebanese hills under almost constant enemy pressure.

The enemy pressure was the key. When SEALs did a for-real combat swim during the invasion of Panama, they found that the increased stress caused them to use up the air supply in their Draeger rebreathers at twice the rate of regular training swims.

They had been out of drinking water for some time, and were all dehydrated. There was snow on the peaks, but it had to be melted. And that took time and heat, both of which were in short supply. You could operate a long time without food, but not without water.

The air was cold and dry, which made their thirst worse. There were only the rocks for shelter from the whipping wind on the peaks. The solution was movement, fast enough to keep their body temperatures elevated and prevent hypothermia. As long as they kept moving, their relatively light dress would be no problem. As a matter of fact, light dress was a necessity since sweat-soaked clothing caused dangerous overheating and then rapid cooling. The result was a potentially fatal drop in body temperature—hypothermia.

Having been pushed to the limits of physical endurance in their selection and training, the SEALs were used to constantly monitoring their bodies and staying alert for danger signals. But what made them so formidable was the extreme outer threshold of their physical limits.

The snow was patchy, mostly accumulating among the rocks that were out of direct sunlight. Jaybird moved along gingerly. The snow might be concealing holes or crevasses; he knew that a broken leg and one more man down would mean disaster for the whole unit. The four carrying the stretcher were careful to follow in Jaybird's footprints.

There was nothing approaching a path available to them as they trudged down the mountain range. Jaybird chose the easiest going, but all that meant was having to climb over the smallest rocks.

After the first few halting attempts, a system was developed. Murdock and Razor would take the stretcher themselves while Magic and Doc climbed up the larger rocks. Then they passed the stretcher up and climbed on their own. Occasionally they had to stop and give DeWitt a hand up.

After lifting Higgins up and over a particularly narrow boulder, Razor said smugly, "Now you know why they made you carry those rubber boats and logs around on your head during BUD/S."

Magic winked at Doc. "And all this time I thought they did that just to fuck with us."

"You hang around with Razor Roselli," Doc pronounced, "and you learn something new every day."

"Disrespectful bastards," Razor grumbled good-naturedly to Murdock. "You know, sir, that gets me to thinking. Master Chief Mac was looking for a couple of guys to give one of the gear lockers at Chocolate Mountain a fresh coat of paint. Money's tight these days. Uncle Sam can probably swing the paint, but the two guys who volunteer just might have to use their toothbrushes."

"You know the Master Chief," said Murdock, joining the act. "He wouldn't care how you did the job as long as it got done."

"This is the thanks we get for sustained superior performance in an operational environment," Magic complained.

Razor grunted as they handed Higgins up again. "Hey, Magic, you know what they say. One fuckup cancels out all those pats on the back. As a matter of fact, I'm starting to forget about those three helicopters already."

"That really hurts my feelings, Chief," Magic replied with a grin. "I'd hate to have it affect my aim the next time."

Razor accepted Murdock's hand up the rock. "That's the problem with all of us sitting down at the same table, Magic. If we eat it, you eat it."

Razor Roselli was not in the habit of relinquishing the last word. Magic and Doc grinned at each other and accepted that.

Higgins was out of it. Knowing the move wouldn't do him any good, Doc Ellsworth made sure he was well medicated. Though his fellow SEALs were doing their damnedest, Higgins was still taking jolts.

The ground rose up toward a small peak. The stretcher-bearers found Jaybird waiting for them.

"This peak blocks the way down the range," he said. "We can't go over, we've got to go around. I checked both sides, there's no ledge. The slope isn't bad but the footing's slick; only a few cracks for handholds. It's got to be single file."

"Okay," said Murdock. He thought for a few seconds. Ed DeWitt had just come up behind them.

"Okay," Murdock repeated. "Jaybird, you go first. Doc, you and Magic grab ahold of Mister DeWitt's belt and help him across. Razor and I'll watch how you go and then bring Higgins over."

DeWitt, who had been privately steaming about his helplessness, seemed on the verge of protesting. But without a better idea to offer, he didn't.

The SEALs approached the peak, which was in the shape of a dome. They were able to easily walk up to it. But then both sides of the dome extended out and down about a hundred feet. One side was sheer and the other sloped gently. Walking across the sloping side was the only way around. That in itself wouldn't be a problem, even with the chance of ice. The problem was negotiating it with the stretcher.

Like all SEAL officers, Blake Murdock was a graduate of U.S. Army Ranger School. And there, during Mountain Phase in the Chattahoochee National Forest near Dahlonega, Georgia, they taught all the tricks of moving up, over, and down rock. Especially with casualties. Unfortunately, virtually all those tricks required climbing rope, which the SEALs did not have. Oh, well, Murdock thought.

Jaybird went first. He faced the rock with both hands and boot soles pressed flat against the slope. He moved without crossing his legs. He crabbed across by stretching his right leg out, making sure of his hold, and only then bringing the left leg over beside it.

Melting water had frozen into seams of ice in the channels and cracks in the rock. Jaybird occasionally paused to break up the patches of ice with his boot.

Magic, DeWitt, and Doc followed him, except they made the move together. Magic first, his left hand grasping DeWitt's belt. Then DeWitt, his good hand on the rock for support. Then Doc, his right hand hanging onto the other side of DeWitt's belt.

Doc slipped. As he felt his leg slip off the icy rock he instantly released DeWitt's belt. As he dropped all he could do was splay his feet outward and hope the friction arrested him. He slid about twenty-five stomach-churning feet, and then stopped in a shower of ice and rock chips.

"You okay?" DeWitt called down.

"Yeah," was all Doc managed to get out.

Now that he knew Doc was all right, DeWitt said, "You're supposed to be helping *me*."

Doc wasn't receptive to SEAL humor just then. His face was ash gray. He slowly made his way across to one of the ice channels running down the rock. Doc took out his knife and chipped out the ice, exposing a crack in the rock about an inch and a half wide. He wedged his fingers into the crack and used it as a handhold.

Doc slowly climbed upward. Chipping with the knife, climbing, stopping, chipping some more. It wasn't fun. His hands were already abraded and bleeding from the drop. He lost two fingernails on the way up, and had to keep tucking his hands in his armpits when they became numb from the cold.

When Doc reached the level he'd dropped from, he continued on across the dome. Jaybird and Magic were waiting on the other side to pull him over.

Doc collapsed onto the ground. "If you guys don't mind, I'm going to take a little break here."

"No problem, Doc," said Jaybird. "We had a nice rest ourselves waiting for you." Then he reached around for the medical pack and got to work wrapping up Doc's hands.

On the other side of the dome Murdock and Razor were looking at each other.

"I don't know about you," said Razor. "But I didn't pick up a lot of pointers watching that."

"Well," Murdock said laconically. "We can pause here for a short moment of prayer, and then we can head across the rocks before I get any more hypothermic."

"Skip the prayer," said Razor. "God's already made up his mind what he's going to do with my ass. Besides, he's a SEAL God, he doesn't like to listen to any sniveling."

Razor Roselli *was* the Old Testament type, Murdock thought. "Let's go then. But if I fall you let us go. There's no way you can hold Higgins by yourself and no sense in going down with us, you understand? That's an order."

"You've been doing just fine, Boss," Razor said calmly. "Let's not ruin everything by giving orders at this stage of the game."

Murdock just shook his head and gave up. He grabbed the handles on both sides of the head of the stretcher in his left hand. He stepped off first, facing the rock with the entire weight of the front of the stretcher in that one hand.

Razor followed, holding the rear of the stretcher with his right hand.

They eased across an inch at a time. With half of Higgins's deadweight hanging on it, Murdock's arm felt like it was coming out of its socket. A bitter cold wind was whipping across the face of the rock. Murdock felt himself tensing up; his knees began to wobble. He couldn't stop to sort himself out;

he and Razor had to keep moving in unison. Be cool, he kept telling himself. Take it easy.

Razor Roselli's right foot slipped. He threw his entire body flat against the rock. That and his left leg held him up; he didn't go down. To Murdock's enormous relief.

Razor regained purchase with his right foot. He pushed himself back off the rock and nodded to Murdock. They resumed their inch-at-a-time rhythm.

As Murdock came around the dome, Magic and Jaybird reached out to grab the stretcher. When Razor got closer, they worked their way down the line of carrying straps on the stretcher, trying to take as much of the weight onto themselves as possible.

Razor got off the rock and joined Murdock slumped on the ground. Doc checked Higgins out.

Jaybird clapped his hands together with exaggerated enthusiasm. "Okay, Chief, we're ready to go."

Razor treated him to a single arched eyebrow. "Then get out there and do some scouting. And work a little goddamned harder on the route selection this time."

Jaybird nodded happily, as if he would have been disappointed with any other response. "You got it, Chief."

Murdock and Razor rested until they felt themselves cooling down, the body's signal to get moving again.

The going was easier now. They went a few hundred meters further, and Jaybird came bounding back.

"I found a position with a good view of the road," he announced.

When they reached the spot Jaybird had picked, Murdock used his GPS set to find out exactly where they were. They'd traveled a whisker over two kilometers.

Jaybird had been right. They had a perfect view of the road, just short of the dogleg where Jaybird had made that very careful turn in the BMP.

When Murdock announced the halt, Doc Ellsworth issued

orders. "Everyone drink your IV bag and put your space blankets on."

All the SEALs carried a bag of intravenous fluids as part of their belt survival kit. It was just as effective swallowed as injected into the veins. They also carried a vacuum-packed foil space blanket. It folded down to the size of a pack of cigarettes and weighed only ounces.

The SEALs broke out the blankets and wrapped themselves up.

Murdock already had the vise-grip headache that was one of the warning signs of dehydration. He cut the top off his IV bag and sipped steadily until it was gone. The survival credo said to ration your sweat, not your water. You drank whatever you had; your body would handle the storage and use it as needed.

Murdock immediately had to urinate, which was a good sign. The urine was dark and therefore concentrated, which wasn't a good sign.

Jaybird, who knew he'd had it the easiest, came around and collected everyone's canteens. He'd discovered a frozen pool of collected water. He chopped up the ice with his knife and filled the canteens with the ice and slush. The SEALs would keep the canteens under their space blankets. When the ice eventually melted they'd have at least a little water.

Murdock joined Razor in the rocks overlooking the road.

A column of BMPs was stacked up at the base of the mountain, but none had started up the road.

"I can't wait to see what happens next," said Razor.

He said it with a definite lack of enthusiasm, which Murdock shared.

38

Saturday, November 11

1745 hours
North central Lebanese mountains

"The bastards are waiting on something," Murdock said of the BMPs down below.

"What's your call?" Razor asked.

"Infantry in helicopters," said Murdock. "Land 'em further up and down the range and have 'em sweep together. Couple of rifle companies ought to do it."

"Nope," Razor said confidently. "That would be the smart thing, which is why they won't do it. They don't want to lose any more expensive helicopters. They're going to come up that road. They're just waiting for the tanks to lead the way."

"That's your call?" Murdock asked.

"Yup."

"For ten bucks?"

"You got it, Boss."

"Wait a minute," said Murdock. "I might have gotten carried away there. I think betting with subordinates is one of those things they told us not to do at Annapolis."

"Does that mean you're pussying out on the bet, sir?"

"No, fuck it." He paused. "It would be sweet if they came up that road."

"What about the tanks?"

"Tanks would just clank around on the road. They could shoot their guns all they wanted; they don't know where we are. They'd run out of ammo before they found our position. I'm worried about infantry, though. Either in helicopters or BMPs."

The answer didn't take long in coming. The falling sun illuminated two small dots in the eastern sky. Razor Roselli spotted them right away.

The dots grew larger, and noisier, and turned into two swept-wing Russian MiG-23BN Flogger ground-attack aircraft.

Razor looked at his watch. "It takes two hours to scare up some air support?" he said with professional disgust. He and Murdock stuffed their space blankets under the rocks. They were invisible among the brown boulders in their brown camouflage, completely motionless. The other SEALs were out of sight.

The two MiGs went across the range at very high altitude. It seemed like they were trying to get their bearings while staying out of range of ground fire.

Then they came back across the valley, wings swept fully forward and popping flares to confuse shoulder-launched infrared guided missiles.

Murdock thought they were still pretty high up for effective bombing. As it turned out he was right.

Two small dark objects dropped from the belly of the lead MiG. The bombs landed just above the hulk of the burned-out BMP on the road. One hit the side of the mountain. One blew a crater in the road. The ground shook beneath the SEALs.

Razor Roselli shook with silent laughter. "That's good," he chortled. "That's really good. Nothing like creating a fucking antitank obstacle for *us*. We ought to put these dumb bastards on the payroll."

"No balls at all," said Murdock. "Son of a bitch was flying so high it was a wonder he could see the ground."

The MiG's wingman screamed in and dropped two bombs of his own. One landed where the road cut across the top of the mountain range. The other just barely missed and sailed over the other side.

"With any luck some Syrians were coming up the other side of that road and it landed in their laps," said Razor. He wiped his eyes with his sleeve. "Oh, this is too much. We could have saved ourselves all that trouble and stayed right where we were. These fuckheads would never hit anything they were aiming at. Shit, we're probably in more danger here out of the line of fire."

"I think you're missing the point," Murdock said dryly. "We don't *want* them to be any good."

Razor's sharp eyes spotted two more planes in the distance. "Here comes the second team. Let's see if they can do any better."

"We don't *want* them to do any better," Murdock insisted.

There were two more MiG-23BN's. These two didn't make an orientation pass over the target to advertise their presence. They came in very low across the valley, their camouflage blending well with the ground.

The MiGs made hard banking turns and streaked up the long axis of the mountain range. When the lead MiG was almost over the SEALs' heads, strings of black smoke belched from its wing roots and underside, and sixty-four 57mm rockets rippled into the rocks where the SEALs had last been.

The second MiG waited just long enough to let the smoke clear away, and then fired its four pods of rockets right onto the target also. The two MiGs made high-G turns and streaked back toward Syria just over the treetops.

Murdock allowed enough time for a good dramatic pause. "You were saying, Chief?"

"All right," Razor conceded. "So someone threatened to

shoot them if they didn't do better. And maybe it wasn't too safe staying where we were."

"They did pretty damn good," said Murdock. "We would've been in a world of hurt."

"I guess the Syrians are going to decide that we're either dead or pretty well suppressed," said Razor. He took a look over the rocks. "Better get your wallet out, Boss. Guess what's coming up the road."

39

Saturday, November 11

1785 hours
North central Lebanese mountains

"I don't see any tanks," said Murdock.

"So they're even stupider than I thought," Razor replied.

A Syrian mechanized infantry company was heading up the road. A platoon of three BMPs, in column, was in the lead. Then a gap, and the second platoon of three BMPs. Then the company commander's BMP, and the third platoon bringing up the rear. Ten BMPs in all.

"Oh, Magic?" Razor called sweetly.

"I see them," came Magic's voice from the rocks.

"Let me tell you what I want to do," said Murdock.

The Syrians weren't in any hurry to drive up the hill. They must have thought they were just going to clean up what the rockets had left. Another mistake, Murdock thought. He would have rushed the vehicles up while the MiGs were still firing, arriving at the position while the enemy was sucking dirt and bleeding from the ears. But that was him.

Murdock pulled his MiG-90 from the drag bag. It was a substantial weapon, except when compared to Magic's McMillan M88. Unlike most sniper rifles, which were bolt-action weapons, the MSG-90 was a gas-operated semiautomatic. It was less accurate than a bolt-action, but faster at engaging multiple targets. The caliber was 7.62-X-51mm NATO. By way of comparison, the .50-caliber round was close to five and a half inches long. The 7.62mm NATO was two and three-quarter inches long.

The MSG-90 weighed fourteen pounds unloaded, and was forty-six inches long with an adjustable bipod, stock, and cheek rest.

Murdock stacked the eight twenty-round magazines filled with Lake City match ammo beside him. There was an opening in the rocks just large enough to accommodate the rifle barrel. Murdock dropped the bipod legs and adjusted them to the correct height. He took a square of camouflage cloth from the drag bag and placed it beneath the muzzle, so when he fired the gas wouldn't kick up the dirt and dust and give his position away. At any range beyond six hundred yards it was almost impossible for anyone to tell where the bullet had come from. He grabbed cocking handle mounted on the left hand side of the stock, pulled it all the way back, and released it, chambering a round. Then he stuck a set of foam earplugs in his ears. No sense in going deaf.

The lead BMP was approaching the still-smoldering hulk of the SEALs' hijacked vehicle. It had to ease around very slowly and carefully; there wasn't much room left on the road.

When the BMP came even with the hulk Murdock heard a boom from Magic's McMillan.

Designers of armored vehicles have to make trade-offs in where they allocate the protection. Any vehicle equally armored all around, on top, and on the bottom would end up either underprotected, or so heavy it would be immovable under the highest-power engine able to fit inside.

The BMP was designed to be able to defeat up to .50-caliber rounds over its frontal arc. The rear was proof only against small arms. As in any armored vehicle, the armor was thinnest on the roof and belly.

In the mountains of Afghanistan the Russians quickly discovered how vulnerable the BMP was to fire from above. But these Syrian BMPs did not carry any of the add-on armor panels the Russians had developed.

Magic put his first round right through the roof of the BMP's engine compartment. It was easily identified by the ventilation and exhaust grills at the right front of the vehicle.

The BMP came to a dead stop and black smoke began pouring out of the grills.

The rest of the BMPs halted and began firing their cannon and machine guns at the rocks near the top of the road.

Magic smoothly worked his bolt, sliding a new cartridge into the chamber. He made a small adjustment to his scope, and his next round punched into the engine of the very last BMP in the column. That BMP lurched forward a few feet and then stopped, also shedding smoke.

Murdock watched in amazement as the BMPs stayed frozen on the road. No one emerged, even from the smoking vehicles; the troops inside weren't as stupid as their leaders. But none of the other BMPs tried to push their way either up or down the road.

And so they wouldn't get the idea, Magic put his next round through the vehicle commander's hatch of the company commander's BMP.

The other vehicles continued to fire rapidly, but at the wrong place.

Magic's fourth shot went into the engine of the second vehicle in the column.

His fifth round took out the third vehicle. Scratch one platoon. Not to mention creating a nice set of obstacles for anyone trying to come up the road in the future. Magic paused to reload.

His sixth shot, into the engine of the first BMP of the second platoon, triggered the stampede.

BMPs had the capability of making their own smoke screens by injecting diesel fuel into the exhaust manifold. Billowing white smoke gusted from the BMPs spinning around on the road.

Murdock heard Razor say scornfully, "Of course they're running away."

The mountain wind was dissipating the smoke as fast as the BMPs could generate it.

Magic kept working his bolt, firing, reloading, picking his spots through gaps in the smoke.

The rear BMP that Magic had killed was blocking the way of the others. Murdock watched in amazement as two BMPs *of the same platoon* rammed the disabled vehicle off the road so they could escape. Panic was contagious.

The disabled BMP slid sideways down the slope, and then hung up on something and stopped. Murdock was almost glad.

Their way now clear, the BMPs roared down the road a lot faster than they'd come up. Magic didn't want to waste any of his scarce .50-caliber ammunition.

The smoke cleared and seven BMPs sat immobilized in the road. Three had managed to escape.

Murdock could imagine what was going on inside those immobilized vehicles. But he didn't want any of the Syrian troops suddenly growing themselves a set of balls and deciding that charging up the road was better than sitting around and waiting to get killed.

"Let's get it done," he said.

Magic called out range and windage numbers, then asked, "You all ready?"

Murdock was peering through his scope, the crosshairs settled on the rear of the first BMP. He thumbed off the MSG-90's safety. "Flush 'em out."

Magic fired a single round into the troop compartment of the first BMP. Murdock could imagine it punching through the roof armor and exploding inside.

The rear doors swung open and the troops rushed out. At that range, even with a 10-power scope, the intersection of the crosshairs was as wide as the human figures.

Murdock knew that when shooting downhill it was important to aim low. The pad of his forefinger flattened against the wide trigger shoe. He took a deep breath, let it out halfway, and held the rest.

The rifle bounced against his shoulder, surprising him. That was good; the trigger break should always be a surprise. When the scope settled back down he saw his man on the ground. Magic's firing dope was right on the money, as usual.

Murdock shifted to another target, a Syrian trying to hide behind the BMP, and fired. He could hear Razor's MSG-90 hammering away.

Their fire drove the Syrians down the road. Magic put a round into the back of the second BMP, then the third.

The Syrians in the other BMPs didn't wait for the Raufoss rounds to come smashing in. Those who weren't dead or wounded were charging down toward the valley in a terrified screaming mob. They could have saved themselves by jumping off the road and taking cover behind the slope. But the Syrians were beyond reason, and therefore playing follow the leader. Murdock and Razor helped that happen by concentrating their fire on anyone who looked like they might shoot back or try and rally the others. Wounded fell. The lucky ones were abandoned by their comrades. The unlucky ones were trampled underfoot by their fellow Syrians running from behind.

One of the BMPs was still defiantly firing its cannon, though nowhere near the SEALs. Murdock admired the gunner. Magic fired a round through the turret roof and the cannon fell silent.

For the life of him, Murdock couldn't understand why the Syrian commander down in the valley didn't crank up his mortars and fire some smoke shells onto the road to screen his retreating troops.

In any case, Murdock kept on firing. Every man he killed was another less that would be shooting at him later.

Soon the mob was out of range. The BMPs sat quietly smoking. The road down the mountain was littered with tiny brown figures. Some were still moving, crawling slowly down the hill. The SEALs let them go, but not out of any misplaced chivalry. The wounded men were already out of action, and any more firing would be a waste of ammunition. SEALs had no illusions about fighting fair, as if there was such a thing. They were coldly professional warriors, and if they had a chance to kill an enemy by shooting him in the back they accepted it eagerly, because then there was less chance of being shot themselves.

40

Saturday, November 11

1820 hours
North central Lebanese mountains

The bottom edge of the sun was just touching the western horizon. And not a moment too soon, as far as Murdock was concerned. It had been quite a day, and was not over by any stretch of the imagination.

"Hey, Boss," said Razor. "Remind me to kiss the Master Chief's ass for making us bring these long rifles along."

"You'd better thing of another way to express your appreciation," said Murdock. "Otherwise you'll never kiss anything again." They did owe their survival to Mac. It wasn't every day that three SEALs took on a ninety-man company and rendered it completely ineffective.

Razor leaned back against his rock. "If I just had a six-pack and a lawn chair, I wouldn't mind hanging around to see what else these hammerheads have up their sleeves."

Murdock could recognize false bravado when he heard it. "Okay, you can stay here. Be sure and drop us a postcard."

"It's like I said, Boss. I don't have the lawn chair and the six-pack."

"Well, these boys aren't done," said Murdock. "They're determined, I'll give them that."

"Oh, we pissed them off good," said Razor. "And we just keep pissing them off. They ain't going to be happy until they have our heads up on the wall. I'll really be upset if we don't get out of here tonight."

"We don't get out of here tonight," Murdock said coldly, "there's some CIA sons of bitches who better hope I *never* make it back."

"The kind of mood I'm in?" Razor growled in agreement. "If they did it again I'd walk all the way to the coast and swim to Cyprus with Higgins on my back just for the pleasure of getting even."

"Speaking of getting out of here . . ." said Murdock.

"Yeah, I know. I don't like the idea of tackling those rocks in the dark, but each time we've pulled off a score, the Syrians made me glad we left right afterward."

A creaking, clanking sound rose up from the valley below. The dusk had deepened, and it was hard to see the road. Murdock removed his night-vision goggle from his jacket pocket. Three tanks were coming up the road. From their shape they looked like T-72's. Through the NVG Murdock could see the beams of the tanks' active infrared driving lights and main gun searchlights sweeping the road ahead.

"Man," said Razor. "They're going to drive right over their wounded in the dark."

Murdock slid his MSG-90 back into the drag bag. "All Magic's .50 could do is scratch the paint on those things. Let's get saddled up." He slung the drag bag across his back and carefully made his way across the rocks to where Doc was attending Higgins.

"How's he doing?" Murdock whispered into Doc Ellsworth's ear.

"Not good. His vitals are all dropping."

"Can we move him?" Murdock asked, that familiar sinking feeling returning.

"Only to a helicopter." Doc paused. "Or only if it's the difference between everyone else making it."

Murdock got the Doc's meaning. If they bounced Higgins around any more he was going to die. Murdock wasn't prepared to give that order—yet. Only if, as the Doc said, it meant saving the lives of the rest of his men. He hoped it didn't come down to that. Sacrificing his own wounded was something he never dreamed he'd have to do.

"Everyone else is shivering," said Doc. "Dehydration's making it worse. I don't think we could stay tactical and still live through the night up here. I don't want to step on any toes, sir, but . . ."

"You're doing what I want, Doc," Murdock assured him. "Your job."

He made his way back to Razor. "Change of plans. We're staying."

"Higgins?" Razor asked.

"Not good. He can't take another move."

"Then we stay," Razor said flatly.

"I was going to move and then get on the radio," said Murdock. "Now I think I'll just get on the radio."

"I'll rub my nuts for luck," said Razor.

"You rub your nuts for *fun*," Murdock retorted. He'd been carrying Higgins's radio pack. He took it off and began unfolding the satellite antenna.

Just then there were a series of quick flashes along the valley floor.

"Uh, oh," said Razor.

Murdock began to count off in his head once again. Just under a minute later there were a string of explosions farther up the mountain range, near the top of the road.

"Mortars," said Razor. "Big ones, sounded like 120mm."

"Late in the game," said Murdock. "I'd rather it be never, but I can live with late."

"As long as they don't work the fire down the ridgeline once they get the range," said Razor.

"Wait a minute," said Murdock. He thought he heard something.

They were quiet, and during a gap in the explosions the faint sounds of helicopter rotors could be heard.

"Those aren't Gazelles," said Razor. "And they sure as shit ain't ours."

"Heavy rotors," said Murdock. "Russian Hips, sounds like about four. Twenty, thirty troops in each. Mortars are firing cover for a landing up north of the road. When the troops don't find anything they'll keep sweeping down. You know what that means."

"Yeah, our bet canceled out."

"That and it's time to get the hell out of here."

"I concur," said Razor.

Murdock deployed and aligned the antenna, then powered up the radio. The mortar bombs were exploding in a steady rhythm.

"Hope they don't put up flares," Razor murmured.

Murdock didn't like to think about bringing the pickup helicopters in under flare light. He tapped out a message on the keypad, dispensing with code words. He pushed the SEND button.

41

Saturday, November 11

1833 hours
Aboard the *U.S.S. George Washington*
Eastern Mediterranean Sea

"Sir, message," the communicator announced.

"God," Miguel Fernandez moaned. He'd been sitting in that room for more than eighteen hours straight. The CIA men and the Army aviators had only dropped in occasionally during the day to check the message traffic. They'd only filtered back into the room as dusk approached.

Fernandez had remained, as if his commitment would will a successful conclusion. The other SEALs had brought him food and drink. One of the communicators, accustomed to standing late watches, had helpfully informed him that Mountain Dew contained the highest percentage of caffeine of any soft drink. Fernandez had pounded down cans of it. He'd been stepping out to make quick calls at the nearby head ever since. His stomach felt as green as the beverage, and he was like a single pulsing nerve ending, only precariously contained. One of the SEALs suggested he take a break. No one made any suggestions to Fernandez after that.

Clean-cut young sailor types like the communicators and

intelligence specialists were intimidated by SEALs under the best of circumstances. Now Fernandez had them so freaked out they shied like ponies every time he shifted in his chair.

Everyone crowded around the terminal. The message read:

E70 STOP REQUEST IMMEDIATE EVAC STOP CONTACTS ALL DAY STOP CONTACT BROKEN FOR NOW STOP ONE WIA STATUS EMERGENCY STOP LZ ROCKY REQ LADDERS STOP LZ SECURE FOR NOW STOP ENEMY APPROACHING STOP LZ GRID 843591 END

One drawback to print transmission rather than voice was that it was difficult to convey a sense of urgency. Fernandez thought whoever had typed out the message, probably the lieutenant, had managed to do it just fine.

Fernandez rushed over to the map on the wall and plotted the grid coordinates. Damn, they were right on top of the mountain range. They'd covered one hell of a lot of ground. And "contacts all day." Knowing the SEAL habit of understatement, in official communications at least, Fernandez could easily imagine what it had been like. And emergency was the highest of the three evacuation categories. One of the boys was hurt bad.

Don Stroh immediately got on the satellite hookup to CIA headquarters to report the message. After the fiasco of that morning, he'd spent over an hour explaining to his superiors that the Army Blackhawk helicopters, with long-range tanks and flight-refueling probes removed, were indistinguishable at night from the carrier air group's Navy Seahawk helicopters. After wasting the better part of the morning, he'd finally convinced them. Just another in a long, dismal line of examples of people in power insisting on making military decisions even though they had next to no real understanding of weapons, tactics, or strategy. Except in their own minds, that is.

Even so, the *George Washington* had spent the entire day sailing back and forth across the eastern Mediterranean. Now they were charging toward the Lebanese coast, and would be in range to launch helicopters in fifteen minutes.

"Yes, sir," Stroh was saying into the handset. "Yes, sir, there may be enemy contact at the pickup. The fact that the Syrians are on alert and have presumably been pursuing the SEALs all day will most likely complicate the extraction. No, sir, I'm not being facetious, I'm simply stating fact. Yes, sir. Then we are clear to launch, sir? Thank you, sir. Yes, sir, I *will* keep you informed." He set the handset down. "We'll launch as soon as the ship is ready."

The Army major commanding the 160th task force slapped his palm down on the table. "Finally! You people were about to give me colitis or something." He picked up the phone to the ready room. "We'll be in range to launch in fifteen minutes, and I want to go as soon as possible after that. LZ grid is 843591. Rig the short caving ladders and a stretcher on the hoist of each bird. One friendly WIA, emergency. No, I'm not going to send a message asking the SEALs to clarify the enemy situation. Why make the poor bastards lie to us? Look, I'll be right there." The major slammed the phone down and stomped out of the compartment, grunting, "Finally!"

Miguel Fernandez thought that all the major needed was a cigar butt between his teeth. He picked up the phone, got the ready room again, and had them put Radioman First Class Ron Holt on the line. "Ron? Yeah. I want to go with me and Red on the lead bird, you and Scotty on the number-two. Right. SAWs for everyone. And trauma kits. One emergency, I don't know who. Have Red grab my gear and weapon, and I'll meet you down in the hangar deck ASAP. No, fuck that; we're going up the elevator with them. I don't want anyone screwing up and leaving us behind. Okay, I'll be right there."

Fernandez charged out of the compartment. When the door slammed behind him all the sailors, even the officers, let out an audible sigh of relief.

Don Stroh almost broke out laughing. He picked up his pen

and wrote quickly on a message pad. He ripped off the sheet and handed it to the communicator. "Send this now."

The hangar crew rolled the lead Blackhawk onto the starboard aft elevator. They set the second Blackhawk beside it. The horn sounded, the gate rose, and the elevator whirred up to the flight deck. Once it was there, two carts swooped in and hooked onto the helicopters' nose wheels, dragging them out on the deck.

The pilots boarded and started working through their checklists. They loaded the route and landing-zone coordinates into the navigation systems. There was an electrical whining as the main rotors unfolded and locked into flight position.

The two crewmen were checking out hydraulic lines and systems in the cabin. They were using the ANVIS-6 night-vision goggles attached to their helmets and infrared filters on their flashlights. Once in flight they would take up positions behind the two 7.62mm miniguns mounted in the port and starboard windows just behind the cockpit.

The two SEALs in each helicopter were dressed the same as the crew, in unmarked sage-green flight suits. But instead of helmets they wore intercom headsets. Gunners' belts were buckled around their waists, with the long webbing safety straps snapped onto tie-down rings on the cabin floor. The belts would keep them inside no matter what violent maneuvers the pilots put the aircraft through. The SEALs were all armed with the M249 Squad Automatic Weapon, as the Belgian Minimi light machine gun was called in U.S. service. It was chambered in 5.56mm, the same as the M-16, weighed fifteen pounds, and fired seven hundred to a thousand rounds per minute at the cyclic rate. A plastic box holding a two-hundred round belt clipped underneath the weapon. The SEALs were wearing night-vision goggles and had laser sights attached to the SAWs. They wore body armor and assault vests with two additional two-hundred-round belt boxes, grenades, and medical trauma packs attacked to the back.

The Blackhawks' turboshaft engines gasped, and then began to scream as they powered up. The rotors engaged, and then came up to speed. Light signals passed across the flight deck, and back and forth between the helicopters.

On the deck in front of the lead Blackhawk the light sticks came together vertically. The Blackhawk rose from the flight deck, and hovered momentarily. The light stick pointed the way, and the Blackhawk banked left over the sea. The second aircraft followed right behind.

Miguel Fernandez, listening to the crisp professional exchanges over the intercom, felt his gut smooth out slightly. At least they were doing something.

42

Saturday, November 11

1843 hours
North central Lebanese mountains

The keypad light blinked. Murdock almost didn't want to scroll the message. He did, of course, but mentally prepared himself for another kick in the nuts. Just in case.

The message read:

HELO LAUNCH IN 15 MIN STOP FREQ PER ORDER STOP WILL CONFIRM LAUNCH STOP HANG ON END

"That's a little more like it," Razor whispered in Murdock's ear.

"Right now it looks like the only problem is going to be hanging on," Murdock replied. "We know the Syrians are coming down the ridge at us from the north. For all we know they may be coming up from the south too, and we just didn't hear them over the mortar fire."

"Doc's got to stay with Higgins," said Razor. "Mister DeWitt might as well make it a threesome. Let's send Jaybird and Magic a couple hundred meters south. You and I go north. We'll slow down any Syrians who show up. Either way, when the helos come in we'll all collapse back onto this spot."

"Sounds like a winner," Murdock replied.

Razor brought everyone together around Higgins. Doc Ellsworth and Ed DeWitt kept two AKM magazines each and passed the rest of their ammunition and grenades to the others. Murdock had everyone turn on the MX-300 walkie-talkies. He wasn't concerned about alerting the Syrians now. They all made, tsk . . . tsk, sounds over the net to make sure all the sets were up and operating. Murdock rigged up his PRC-117 with the UHF antenna and voice handset so he could talk with the helicopters. The backup PRC-117 with satellite antenna and keypad was left with Doc, along with the sniper rifles.

While they were going over contingencies the keypad blinked and the carrier confirmed the launch of the helicopters. Murdock tapped out an acknowledgment and informed them he was switching both his sets over to UHF voice.

"Any questions?" Murdock asked his SEALs.

There were none.

"Okay," he said. "Razor and I'll meet you all back here."

43

Saturday, November 11

1903 hours
North central Lebanese mountains

Murdock and Razor crept slowly along the rocks. The mortar fire was still dropping up near the road, but at a much slower rate.

The wind was whipping; it was bitterly cold. Murdock guessed that the temperature was in the teens and dropping, with the wind chill making it much worse. Their pace wasn't fast enough to keep them warm. Murdock thought about sitting in the ocean at Coronado during Hell Week, the surf washing over him and the instructors saying that they couldn't come out until someone quit. He hadn't quit then. He told himself that it had been much colder then than now.

He and Razor reached the dome of rock that had been so much trouble to cross earlier. Then the mortar fire stopped suddenly, and all they could hear was the wind.

Murdock turned to look at Razor through his NVG. Razor nodded. The mortars had ceased fire because the Syrian commandos had reached the road.

The dome was a handy obstacle. The SEALs unscrewed the fuses from two Russian M75 frag grenades and replaced them with two push-pull instantaneous booby-trap fuses.

While no handyman worth his salt would ever be without duct tape, no SEAL would be caught dead without the military equivalent: olive-green ordnance tape, also known as hundred-mile-an-hour tape.

With Murdock holding onto him, Razor edged out onto the dome. When he came to the limit of Murdock's reach, he locked his legs, bent over, and taped a grenade to a smooth, dry portion of the rock surface.

Murdock pulled him in, and Razor taped the second grenade a little closer to the edge. As they backed away from the dome, Razor carefully unspooled the hundred-pound test fishing line he'd attached to the pull rings of the fuses. Murdock took one line, Razor the other.

They spread out among the rocks and settled down to wait.

44

Saturday, November 11

1908 hours
MH-60K Blackhawk
Over Lebanon

As they flew over the treetops, the Blackhawk crew and the SEALs heard a range of different chirping sounds in their headsets.

"We've got radars," the Blackhawk copilot announced somewhat redundantly. He consulted his display. "I'm reading Flat Face, Dog Ear, Gun Dish, and Spoon Rest. They're all over the place."

He'd given the NATO code name for a range of Russian radar systems. Flat Face was a surface-to-air missile or antiaircraft-gun acquisition system. Dog Ear was an early-warning radar associated with the SA-13 short-range missile system. Gun Dish was the radar atop the ZSU-23-4 self-propelled antiaircraft gun system. Spoon Rest was a surveillance radar, and the most dangerous because it could pick up low-altitude targets.

"Anything coming from the higher elevations?" the pilot asked.

"Two Gun Dish," the copilot replied.

"Shit," was all the pilot said.

Since they were skimming over the treetops, the radar would have to be higher and radiating down in order to pick them up. But the crew was somewhat comforted by the fact that most Russian radars weren't good at picking targets out of ground clutter.

But as the second Blackhawk, flying in trail of the first, swept over some trees, a string of green tracer bullets came floating up right in front of it.

The pilot turned away from the fire. It wasn't easy at such low altitude. Too hard a turn and they would be crashing into the trees. When they steadied out, the pilot realized how it had happened. Someone on the ground had fired at the lead helicopter, or at least the sound of the lead helicopter. But it was going so low and fast that it was already gone by the time he brought his weapon to bear. Unfortunately, the second Blackhawk was just in time to receive the fire. The pilot solved the problem by moving up in echelon with the lead Blackhawk.

The ZSU-23-4 was a small tracked vehicle with a rotating turret mounting four water-cooled 23mm rapid-firing cannons. Atop the turret the Gun Dish radar spun around, searching for targets. When it locked onto one, the Identification-Friend-or-Foe system electronically interrogated it. If the target was a foe, the gunner slaved the turret onto the radar track, the computer provided a solution, and the guns fired.

The Gun Dish radars on the early ZSU-23-4's had had trouble picking targets out of ground clutter at altitudes below six hundred feet. But in later models, notably the ZSU-23-4M, the Russians had introduced radar modifications to reduce that problem.

When the Syrians had put their forces in Lebanon on alert, several ZSU-23-4's had taken up station in the western foothills of the central mountain range. As it happened, one of those vehicles was high enough to be right on line with the Blackhawks' flight path as they came across the coastline and over the western plain. The dish antenna atop its turret stopped spinning and pointed west, wobbling slightly.

A continuous tone sounded in the crew headsets of the lead Blackhawk.

"Gun Dish lock," the copilot called out.

The pilot instantly swung into a gentle S-turn and thumbed a button on his stick. Chaff cartridges were ejected from tubes in the fuselage. The cartridges burst open and filled the air around the helicopter with distinct clouds of thin metallic strips.

The S-turn caused the Blackhawk to disappear within the chaff clouds that showed up on the Gun Dish radar as separate and distinct targets. The radar lock was broken. The Gun Dish tried to decide between the slowly dissipating chaff clouds, but couldn't. By then the terrain elevation had changed and the Blackhawks were safely back in ground clutter.

When the steady tone in their headsets stopped, Miguel Fernandez and Red Nicholson caught each other's eyes across the cabin and smiled weakly.

45

Saturday, November 11

1925 hours
North central Lebanese mountains

Murdock thought he heard movement on the other side of the rock dome. Yes, there it was again. All it took was one man to slip on a little loose rock, or one piece of equipment to swing free.

He could imagine the Syrians contemplating the dome. Would it stop them, or would they have the balls to try it in the dark?

Razor's voice came over the radio net. "This is Two, contact imminent."

Then Jaybird's voice. "You need help?"

"Negative," Razor ordered. "Stay put. And everyone keep off the net unless it's an emergency. We're going to need to talk over here."

A string of acknowledgments from the rest of the SEALs followed. The MX-300's were all set on low power, so with luck the transmissions weren't carrying past the mountain ridge. Not that the Syrians could be listening in on the encrypted messages. Murdock was worried about them getting a fix on the location of the transmissions. But it took a long time for any army to work that kind of information through its various levels of command.

Murdock heard metal knock against rock. The sound seemed to be coming from the side of the dome. So the Syrians were giving it a try. And they were doing a good job keeping quiet too. It wasn't easy moving over rock in the darkness. If they were a little less competent, he might be able to get an idea of the size of the force on the other side.

Then the sound of hammering started up at the dome. It culminated in a clear metallic ringing that carried far in the night air.

Razor's whispered voice came up on the net again. "If that wasn't a piton, then I'm not an E-7."

"Roger," Murdock replied. There was no mistaking that sound. A piton was a piece of mountaineering equipment, a metal wedge like a spike with a ring on the fat end. It came in various widths and sizes, and was designed to be hammered into cracks in rock in order to secure a climbing rope. The metallic ringing he'd heard was the sound a piton made when it was wedged solidly into a rock crack.

All the Syrians had to do was hammer in a line of pitons across the dome and rig a fixed rope to them. They could all just hook onto the rope and walk right across.

Murdock was also not pleased with the realization that he was dealing with specialty mountain troops experienced at moving over rock at night. They were not going to be easily dissuaded.

The hammering and ringing sounds gradually worked their way across the dome. Murdock kept his night goggle focused on the edge. The first booby trap was Razor's. It was his move.

Razor Roselli had the fishing line looped around his left hand. Even though he'd positioned the booby trap below any climber's line of sight, he didn't want to let a Syrian get too close to it. All they'd have to do to disarm the grenade was cut the fishing line.

It was time. He gathered up the line until it was taut in his hand, and then gave a hard yank.

The grenade explosion lit up his NVG and made his eyes hurt. There was a scream, and then sounds of thrashing and sliding. Then the screams were coming from lower on the dome, and went on and on.

The grenade had blown the climber off the rock, but the Syrian was tied to a rope hooked along the pitons he'd already put in. Whoever was belaying the other end of the rope had caught him, so now he was dangling from the rope a little lower on the dome. Just hanging there and bleeding and screaming. And he was going to keep on screaming until someone got him back and gave him some morphine. Or he died. Better him than me, Razor thought.

The screaming went on for five minutes by Murdock's watch. It stopped before more climbing sounds were heard on the dome. Then there was grunting as new climbers pulled the body up and passed it back.

Another piton was being hammered in. They were climbing again. But Murdock guessed that they were being a damn sight more careful. It wouldn't do them any good. He was able to see his grenade right at the edge of the dome, but no climbers would notice it until they'd already swung across.

Another piton rang out. The Syrians were getting closer. Murdock saw a man's hand come around the edge and feel around. But he wasn't checking low enough. Murdock took up the slack in his line.

The Syrian's body came around the edge. Murdock pulled on the line at the same time he ducked behind the rock.

The grenade blew, and Murdock thought he heard some of the fragments going past. There was no screaming this time. Murdock raised up his head. The Syrian wasn't there. The rocks had dark scorch marks on them from the explosion. At least Murdock thought they were scorch marks.

Someone shouted on the other side of the dome. Ah, thought Murdock, discipline was starting to break down. Maybe the next guy who'd been tapped to go across was a little hesitant.

So far the Syrians had no reason to believe that the booby traps were anything other than mines set to delay them. They might not even think there was anyone on the other side of the dome. That was just fine with Murdock.

The SEALs' AKMs were fitted with French SOPELEM PS 2 laser aiming lights. Just like the American PAQ-4, but not traceable back to the U.S. military. The small tube weighed only nine ounces and clamped to the AKM's barrel.

Murdock heard the climbing sounds start up again, and through his NVG he saw the dot from Razor's sighting unit blink on and settle on the edge of the dome.

"Okay, you've got the first shot," Murdock whispered into his microphone.

Razor responded by keying his mike.

In the green glow of his NVG, Murdock could see a Syrian's head peering around the dome.

Razor held his fire. The Syrian exposed himself some more. Razor settled the laser dot on the Syrian's chest and squeezed the trigger.

The Syrian must have unhooked himself from the rope. Razor could hear the body falling down the slope. Well, now they know we're here, he thought.

It didn't take the Syrians long to react. Murdock heard a series of hollow metallic pops on the other side of the dome. He forced himself not to duck for cover. He needed to watch to make sure the Syrians didn't come around the side of the dome. But he did hunker down a little lower in the rocks.

Five or six grenades exploded loudly behind the SEALs. BG-15's, Murdock thought. A Russian 40mm grenade launcher that mounted beneath the AK series of rifles much the same as the U.S. M203 attached to the M-16. Except the Russian grenade launcher was muzzle-loaded, lighter, and more compact and reliable.

The Syrians kept up a steady fire of grenades, but they were shooting blind and their range was too long; about a hundred yards past the SEALs.

Even so, Murdock was worried. Now they couldn't leave

even if they wanted to. Falling back meant having to pass through the grenade barrage.

Razor was his usual psychic self. "I guess we're stuck here for now," he said over the net.

A Syrian poked his AKM around the edge of the dome and hosed off an unaimed burst. Murdock and Razor treated that with the silent contempt it deserved.

The barrel came around again, and there was another wild burst. Then the Syrian stuck his head around the corner. Razor's aiming dot raced over. A single shot rang out, and the Syrian fell with a bullet in his head.

While Razor kept the Syrians pinned down, Murdock scanned the rest of the dome to forestall any nasty surprises.

He thought he saw the tiniest bit of movement near the very top of the dome. He kept his eyes on it and waited. The muzzle of a rifle barrel became visible. Murdock was impressed. It must have been a mother of a climb to get up there. The muzzle didn't look like a machine gun. Probably a sniper rifle with a starlight scope. The Syrian snipers had a good reputation. They used the excellent Austrian Steyr instead of the cruder Russian Dragunov.

"Sniper on top of the dome," Murdock reported into his microphone. "I've got him."

"Roger," Razor replied.

Murdock quickly weighed tossing a grenade. No, the way the dome was shaped the Syrian was going to have to lean farther out to get a shot. Murdock clicked on his laser light and placed the dot on the muzzle of the rifle above.

Laser sights were no panacea. If you failed to follow all the rules of good shooting, you could miss just as easily with a laser as a set of old-fashioned iron sights. Murdock had the AKM's stock locked into his shoulder. When the scope atop the Syrian's rifle appeared, he held his breath. When he could see the top of a head, he began his trigger squeeze.

He fired, and the rifle clattered over the top of the dome. Murdock kept watch, but there was no more movement up there.

The BG-15 gunners began to get the idea. They reduced their range with each barrage, and the grenades began falling closer to the SEALs.

"We've got to break contact," Murdock radioed. "One grenade each over the dome, at my command, then leapfrog. You first."

"Understood," Razor replied.

Murdock dug an M75 frag out of his pocket. He pulled the pin and kept the spoon pressed against his palm.

"Ready?" he asked.

"Hang on," said Razor. "I want to get rid of my PDM first."

Murdock saw their last Pursuit Deterrent Munition leave Razor's hand and drop in front of them. It would be in the Syrians' path once they made it around the dome.

"Ready," Razor said.

"Now!" Murdock released the spoon, let the fuse cook for two seconds, and lobbed the grenade high over the dome. He quickly picked up his AKM and got the laser dot back on the edge of the rock.

The grenades exploded. The BG-15's fell silent, but Murdock knew it would not be for long. Razor ran by him, and kept going past the spot where the grenades had been impacting. Murdock squeezed off a few rounds at the edge of the dome to keep the Syrians back.

The BG-15's began firing again, and the grenades began closing in on Murdock. He got out another M75.

"Ready?" he asked.

"Ready."

"Now." Murdock lobbed the grenade over the dome.

When the grenades exploded he turned tail and ran. But the BG-15's started up too soon. Murdock made a split-second decision not to take cover. If the grenades pinned him down he might never get out.

Murdock leaped from rock to rock. The grenades exploded all around him. Loud, very loud. A grenade went off right behind him and knocked him onto the ground.

46

Saturday, November 11

1952 hours
North central Lebanese mountains

Murdock pitched face-first onto the rocks. He knew he was hurt; it felt like hot needles sticking into him all the way down his legs. But sometimes blind terror was a help, not a hindrance. Murdock pushed himself up off the ground. If his legs worked he was going to move.

His legs worked. He got on his feet, but his ears were ringing and he was disoriented; he didn't know which way to run. Then he saw Razor's muzzle flash. More grenades exploded around him. They spurred Murdock into a loping, limping run across the rocks toward Razor.

"Razor!" Murdock spoke into his microphone. He got no reply. He kept running, but it didn't seem to him as if he was gaining much ground.

Suddenly rounds began cracking past him. Some Syrians must have finally made it around the dome.

Murdock threw himself over the rocks, almost into Razor Roselli's lap. Considering the expression on Razor's face, Murdock didn't think he was in such good shape. Razor was yelling into his radio. Murdock couldn't hear a thing in his own earpiece, and the ringing in his ears didn't allow him to hear Razor. In that kind of situation there was only one thing for a SEAL to do. Murdock leaned over the rocks and brought his weapon to bear. His NVG was smashed, so he ripped it off his face. The Russians had designed the AKM with handy luminous night dots on the front and rear sights. Murdock lined the dots up one on top of the other and began firing at the Syrian muzzle flashes in front of him.

Razor Roselli had to shout in his microphone to reach above the noise of the firefight. "Jaybird, you got anything going on down there?"

"Negative, Chief."

"Then you and Magic get your asses up here. The lieutenant's hit and we could use some help."

"On the way," said Jaybird.

"You need me?" Doc Ellsworth broke in.

"Negative, the lieutenant's still shooting," Razor said proudly. "I want you on the 117. You're the primary radio now. Stand by to bring those birds in."

"Roger," Doc replied.

There was an explosion among the Syrians in front of the dome. Razor knew it had to be his PDM. The Syrian fire slackened, so Razor stepped up his rate of fire. Between shots he kept sneaking glances over at Murdock. The lieutenant's face was bloody; it looked like blood down the back of his legs, but the game bastard was putting out rounds like he was back on the Chocolate Mountain range. Razor spoke to his Old Testament SEAL God like a chief—no sniveling. "Don't let me lose this one, sir, he's something special."

"Razor!" came a shout from behind them.

"Over here!" Roselli bellowed. "Come up!"

Jaybird and Magic crawled the last stretch on their bellies. The Syrian fire was getting hot.

"Put some rounds out!" Razor shouted.

Jaybird and Magic paused only for a second to look over at

Murdock, who was doggedly changing magazines. Then they began firing.

Razor had one grenade left. He crawled over to Jaybird and rummaged in his pouches. He found two frags and, holy shit, a smoke grenade! Just what the doctor ordered.

"I could kiss you, you sweet little shit," Razor shouted in Jaybird's ear.

Jaybird gave Razor a funny look and continued firing.

Razor took another frag off Magic. "Okay," he shouted over the sounds of the firing. "I'll throw two frags. Jaybird, you leapfrog back with the lieutenant. Two more frags and Magic and I'll go."

Everyone nodded. Razor whipped the grenades at the dome.

Jaybird went to put Murdock in a wounded-man carry, but was surprised to hear, "Stop grabbing at me. I can walk, goddammit!"

"Sorry, sir," was all Jaybird could think to say.

The grenades blew, and the incoming fire slowed again. Jaybird and Murdock set off. First they crawled, because they were still exposed to Syrian fire. Then they made the cover of a dip in the ground and got to their feet. Murdock's limp was more pronounced.

They ran until they reached the next bit of higher ground where they could get a good field of fire. A rising mound of rocks. Once safely behind it, they began putting down cover fire for Razor and Magic.

Razor pitched out two more frags, then dropped the white smoke grenade right in front of them.

The grenades exploded, the white smoke billowed up, and Razor and Magic were off to the races.

Razor heard rounds cracking past him as he ran. Then, just before they reached the rock mound, a stream of green tracers passed right across the gap between him and Magic.

An impact took Magic in the hip and spun him right around in the air. He fell forward over the mound.

Jaybird was on him instantly.

"Where am I hit?" Magic demanded. Nothing hurt. That was all right.

"A round hit the magazine pouch on your hip, you lucky fuck!" Jaybird shouted.

"Wish that'd happened to me," Murdock called from across the mound.

That reminded Razor Roselli that his lieutenant had been wounded, and now that they had a little cover and distance from the Syrians, he ought to be checking it out.

"Magic, if you ain't hurt get off your ass," Razor ordered. "You and Jaybird put out enough fire to keep 'em from charging us." He scrambled over to Murdock. "Hold on a second, Boss, I want to look you over."

Most of Murdock's hearing had returned. His legs felt stiff, but the burning was less if he didn't move. The pain wasn't that bad, but he had a headache and was sick to his stomach. "I'm okay, Chief, don't worry about it."

"No problem, Boss, just roll over on your stomach for me."

The lieutenant's radio pack looked like Swiss cheese. Razor cut the straps off his shoulders. There weren't any holes in the lieutenant's back. Small grenade fragment wounds were peppered across his ass and down the backs to his legs all the way to his boots. The holes were all oozing blood, but there was no serious bleeding going on. "Roll over on your back, Boss."

There were no wounds on Murdock's front. He had some shrapnel cuts on the face and forehead, but nothing near the eyes. "Boss, you got about a million little holes in your ass and legs. I'd like to wrap them up, but we ain't got enough battle dressings."

"Oh, fuck it," said Murdock. "Let 'em bleed."

Razor held up the radio pack. "This took most of the blast."

"I know you," said Murdock. "You're just trying to con me into carrying the radio from now on. You done?"

"You want a shot of morphine?"

"Hell, no. It doesn't hurt that bad, and I don't need to get any more slowed down."

"Then I'm done," said Razor.

Murdock felt the chest pocket of his jacket. "Would you believe I fell on my fucking Motorola? I was wondering why it wasn't working."

"I'll make sure you know what's going on," said Razor.

47

Saturday, November 11

2002 hours
North central Lebanese mountains

The Syrians kept up a heavy fire, but showed no signs of advancing. The four SEALs lay spread across the rock mound and wondered why they weren't being treated to a classic infantry assault. The Syrians could certainly tell that there were only four rifles shooting at them. Granted, the ridgeline wasn't wide enough to get more than ten to fifteen men on line abreast, but that ought to be more than enough to do the job.

The answer, Murdock thought, might be that in such a tight space it was easier for *him* to maneuver four men than the Syrian commander his much larger unit. Maybe the grenades they'd thrown over the dome had taken out some of the leadership.

Then the flashes and bangs started up again down in the valley. Murdock and Razor reached the identical conclusion at the exact same time.

"Run!" they shouted.

Each time they stopped, Murdock's legs got stiffer. And whenever they moved, the burning needles began jabbing him again. He tried twisting his back in order to throw his legs forward faster. Razor grabbed him under one armpit, Jaybird the other, in order to speed him along.

Murdock realized he'd forgotten to count. Damn.

The mortars landed, and the SEALs dove into the rocks.

The Syrians had fired without the benefit of a spotting round to try to catch their foes unaware. A good idea. The barrage of 120mm mortar bombs straddled the area where the SEALs had been. But the SEALs had had a good fifty-second head start to get out of the impact area. They had, but just barely.

The blasts were close enough to bounce them up and down on the ground like rubber balls. The shock waves pounded them, and the shrapnel screamed overhead and bounced off the rocks. The harsh high-explosive smoke made it hard to breathe.

"Don't nobody fire a round!" Razor screamed. "They'll adjust it onto us!"

None of the SEALs would have fired, even if they had been able to hear him over the din of the explosions.

In the midst of it all, Doc Ellsworth's voice came over the radio net. "Everybody still there?"

Razor only heard him because the earphone was stuck in his ear and his hands were clasped over his ears. "We're still here, Doc," he screamed.

"Great," said the Doc. "I've got the birds on the line."

The helicopters had announced themselves first. It was etiquette, done so the SEALs wouldn't have to keep calling on the radio and risk compromise while the helicopters were still out of range.

Doc Ellsworth had been sitting back against a rock, the PRC-117 handset up to his ear spitting out nothing but hissing static, when a human voice broke in and said clearly, "Echo Seven Oscar, this is Hammer-One inbound, over?"

The transmission was encrypted, so Doc didn't have to worry about tipping off the Syrians. "Hammer-One, this is Echo Seven Oscar, over."

"Roger, Seven Oscar, we are ten minutes out, standing by for zone brief, over."

There wasn't any fucking landing zone, but if the guy wanted to be humored, Doc was willing to oblige. "Hammer-One. LZ is a ridgeline, twenty meters wide at our position. LZ is covered with boulders, will require ladder. Wind is from the west, twenty knots. Recommend you approach from the southeast along the ridgeline, retire in the same direction. Enemy positions eastern valley, ridgeline northeast five hundred meters. LZ is not under fire at this time. Seven PAX for pickup. One emergency medevac, one priority ambulatory. Will mark LZ with IR strobe, over."

"Roger, Seven Oscar." The Blackhawk pilot repeated back what Doc had told him to make sure there were no errors. Then: "We have a stretcher on the hoist for your emergency, over."

"Roger," Doc replied. "Let me know when you want the lights on. Seven Oscar out." Doc raised the MX-300 microphone back up to his lips. "Birds are ten minutes out, got that?"

"Say again?" came the response.

Doc could clearly hear the explosions down the ridge. They were even louder coming over the radio. He enunciated each word this time. "Birds are ten minutes out, over."

Razor Roselli was still being slammed about by the mortar blasts. "Got it!" he screamed.

48

Saturday, November 11

2005 hours
North central Lebanese mountains

During BUD/S, Hell Week begins at 2100 hours on a Sunday night and continues nearly nonstop until Friday evening. Most of Thursday is spent in the demolition pit. The pit is one hundred feet long and twenty-five feet deep, surrounded by barbed wire and filled with mud. Two heavy ropes stretch across. Completely exhausted by constant physical exertion and lack of sleep, the SEAL trainees spend the day crawling under the barbed wire, over the ropes, and through the slimy mud while explosives are detonated all around them. Anyone inclined to crack under the strain of prolonged loud noise and explosive concussion does so in the pit, not on an operation.

The mortar fire ended. The tubes in the valley fell silent. Less than a minute later the last bombs fell on the ridge.

It took Razor Roselli a few seconds to get used to the quiet. He was still hearing explosions in his head. "Sound off," he whispered into his microphone.

"Jaybird."

"Magic."

Lieutenant Murdock was beside him without a radio. "Sit

tight," said Razor. The oldest trick in the book was for artillery or mortars to fire a mission, then, just when you were brushing the dirt off your uniform and congratulating yourself on your survival, resume firing.

It didn't happen.

Murdock leaned over and whispered in Razor's ear. "Let's get out of here before the smoke clears and the Syrians show up to take inventory."

"Right," Razor whispered back. "Okay, we're moving. Magic, you're on rear security. Jaybird, take the point. I'll help the lieutenant. Doc?"

"I'm listening," Doc Ellsworth replied over the net.

"We're coming in. Try not to shoot us."

"Never happen," Doc replied. "At least not as long as Jaybird owes me money."

Jaybird quickly got out in front. Murdock slung an arm over Razor's shoulder and limped along. Every time he put his foot down, the pain was like an electric shock. The blood had soaked into his trousers. Now it stuck to his skin and the wounds whenever he moved. It hurt. Bad. Especially when climbing rocks. He was seriously regretting his decision on the morphine. He'd talk to Doc once they got back to the LZ.

Behind them, a great many automatic weapons opened fire with a loud roar.

"They're finally making their assault," Murdock whispered to Razor.

"Chicken-shit sons of bitches had to sit down and call in a mortar prep before they went after four guys."

"Take it as a compliment," said Murdock.

The SEALs were well beyond where the Syrians were assaulting, but that didn't mean they were out of danger. It was like being beyond the target line on a rifle range. You could still get shot even if they weren't aiming at you.

Green tracers skipped off the rocks and made bright trails in the night sky. Rounds that had gone long were hitting the ground all around the SEALs. They couldn't stop. All they could do was hurry along and let fate throw the dice.

But that didn't keep them from flinching every time a close one went by.

"I hate this," Razor muttered quietly. "At least when you're shooting back you've got something else to think about. With this shit you just have to walk along and wait to catch one."

Murdock was well into that stage that every SEAL experiences first-hand during Hell Week. Normally, when the body hurt, the brain reacted to the pain. But whoever hung on to become a SEAL discovered that you could tear the brain loose from the body and just keep going. That's all you had to do—just keep going. The brain eventually got tired of you not paying attention to all those signals to stop and take it easy. After a while it gave up and came along for the ride.

Jaybird was waiting for them in the rocks. "Doc's right over there," he said, pointing.

Murdock and Razor shuffled by him. Jaybird waited for Magic. You always counted your people off as you walked into a position. One or two bad guys might attach themselves to the back of your file and try to walk right in with you. SEALs had been known to pull that trick on others, so they were very careful not to fall for it themselves.

Razor positioned everyone in an all-around security perimeter. But he weighted most of his firepower to the northeast, where he expected the Syrians to be coming down the ridge very soon. Ed DeWitt and Doc covered the southern axis of the ridge, just in case some Syrians had been quietly moving up while all the shooting was going on. DeWitt was there because he could only shoot one-handed, Doc to protect the only remaining PRC-117.

Razor briefed everyone on how he wanted the LZ evacuated. SEALs worked it systematically; they didn't just haul ass for the helicopters. Everyone knew their sectors of fire and order of withdrawal.

"Echo Seven Oscar, this is Hammer-One, over?" said the voice in Doc's handset.

"This is Seven Oscar, go," Doc replied.

"Hammer-One is two minutes out, over."

"Roger," said Doc. He, like the rest of the SEALs, could hear the Syrians moving down the ridgeline. "The LZ isn't hot now, but it's going to be when you come in. So hurry it up if you can, and heads up. Over."

"Roger," the pilot replied coolly. There wasn't much to say after that. "Hammer-One, out."

Doc spoke into his MX-300 microphone. "Two minutes."

"Pull your tape," Razor told them over the net. The SEALs had sewn strips of thermal tape onto the front, back, and sleeves of their Syrian camouflage jackets. The tape would show up in the helicopter door gunners' night-vision goggles and make it easy for them to pick out friend from foe if the extraction got messy. Until now the thermal strips had been concealed by green ordnance tape. The SEALs ripped it off.

"I'll initiate fire," Razor informed them. "I want to hold them as far back as we can. Take it easy and make your rounds count, we ain't many left. I don't want to be down to throwing rocks before the birds come in."

49

Saturday, November 11

2013 hours
North central Lebanese Mountains

Blake Murdock had spent his whole career expecting to find himself in his present situation. But at this point in all the scenarios he'd fought out in his head, he was supposed to be directing FA-18's, helicopter gunships, AC-130's, or naval gunfire against the enemy while the helicopters rushed in to pick them up.

Now that it was finally for real, he didn't have any of that. What he had was seven SEALs, only six and a half capable of shooting and all of them sucking wind, AKs with only a magazine or so of ammo left, and maybe a couple of grenades. Murdock knew Doc would be angry at him for not thinking positively, but it didn't look good. Damn, he'd forgotten about the morphine. Well, too late now.

Without an operational set of NVGs, Murdock planned to hold his fire until he could see something. Maybe his rounds would come in handy while they were boarding the helos. Now he knew how Ed DeWitt felt. Not worth a shit.

Through his goggles Razor could see the Syrians bobbing among the rocks in the distance. It was a difficult call. He had to let them get close enough so they wouldn't be able to call for mortar fire without getting hit themselves, yet keep them far enough away so they couldn't easily overrun the LZ. It looked just about right. He settled the laser dot on the Syrian point man and fired.

The rest of the SEALs followed his signal and opened fire also. Slowly, carefully, a single shot only when they had a clear target.

The Syrians had to transition from a movement formation to a skirmish line while under fire. It took them a while. The SEALs could tell. The Syrians only fired their AKMs on automatic. First there were two firing, then six. Then eight. They finally worked up to around ten or twelve, which must have been all the men they could fit across the width of the ridgeline.

With only four SEALs calmly firing single-shot, it was a wonder the Syrians didn't quickly gain fire superiority. But if the bullets weren't hitting or coming close enough to make you take cover and stop shooting, it didn't matter how heavy the fire was. The Syrians were what the SEALs scornfully called sprayers and prayers, hoping to make up for lack of accuracy with sheer number of rounds. It didn't work.

Every time a Syrian rose to advance, a SEAL cut him down. But the Syrians learned quickly. Several began crawling forward using the cover of the rocks. That would work, but it would take time. The question was whose side time was on.

Jaybird was anchoring the SEALs' far right. His magazine ran out and he slid his last one into the AKM. Thirty rounds left. The Syrians were getting better. Every time he fired, a couple of them would concentrate their own fire on his muzzle flash. It was getting hairy. He had to keep moving from rock to rock.

A BG-15 fired, and the grenade exploded with a shower of sparks in rocks right in front of him. Jaybird would have pissed his pants if he hadn't been so dehydrated.

Something had to be done about that grenade launcher.

Jaybird couldn't let the Syrian get the range on him. He only had two M75 frags left. Jaybird pulled the pin on one and palmed it, waiting. The BG-15 flashed again, and Jaybird's grenade was in the air. The 40mm grenade exploded off to his side. Jaybird saw his grenade go off. He waited, but the BG-15 didn't fire again. It seemed that the Syrians were getting closer. The shit was getting serious now. Where the fuck was the helicopter?

Magic Brown was experiencing a sniper's frustration. It wasn't that an AKM in his hands was like a surgeon operating with a linoleum cutter. It was that he was racking up a score but it wasn't making any difference. He would take a man down only to have the Syrians quickly replace him in the firing line. Faithfully counting his rounds, he knew that he was a third down on his last magazine.

The Syrians fired a hand-held flare. The parachute popped over the SEALs' heads, and the harsh yellow glow fell over them. But the swirling mountain wind quickly pushed the parachute back down the ridge toward the Syrians. The SEALs flipped up their goggles and had a few sounds of good shooting until the flare fizzled out. The Syrians didn't fire any more flares. The SEALs went back to their NVGs.

The flare had given Murdock the opportunity to finally fire some rounds. Now he could only watch the firefight. They weren't getting many BG-15's; he'd been most afraid of that. The Syrians had probably used up most of their basic ammo load at the dome. Murdock sensed that the Syrians were slowly building up their fire for an assault. He remembered some Marine officers telling him once that a light infantry defense—a continuous series of ambushes and withdrawals—was the most difficult and infuriating thing to fight against. The Syrians must have taken a lot of casualties in the previous ambushes. If they got the idea that their adversaries were finally pinned down, they wouldn't let up.

Doc Ellsworth spoke into the PRC-117 handset. "Hammer,

this is Seven Oscar. The LZ is now under fire. Enemy fifty meters northeast along ridgeline, over."

"Roger," the Blackhawk pilot replied calmly. "Mark the zone."

Doc pressed the rubber button on the bottom of his strobe light. He heard the electric *zing . . . zing* sound when the blinking began. The strobe had an infrared cap on the lens and a plastic sleeve that directed the light straight out. Doc heard the beating of rotor blades. He aimed the strobe at the sound.

2015 hours
MH-60K Blackhawk Hammer-One

Miguel Fernandez and Red Nicholson cocked their Squad Automatic Weapons. The door gunners were crouched behind their miniguns.

"I'm going to come up along the ridgeline," the pilot informed the crew over the intercom. "Otherwise we'll never see that strobe. When we hit the LZ I'll turn and point the nose east. That way the hoist will be on the side away from the enemy. Jimmy," he said, talking to one of the door gunners. "Your side will be clear, you'll work the hoist. Stan, the enemy will be on your side so you'll be gunning. You SEALs handle the ladder."

The pilot pressed the mike button on his stick. "Hammer-Two, Hammer-One, over."

"Hammer-Two," the second Blackhawk replied.

"Hammer-Two, when we go in I want you to hold back a half klick down the ridge. I'll call you if I need you. When we come off the zone I'll form up behind and follow you out, over."

"Affirmative," the second pilot replied. "Hammer-Two, out."

The lead Blackhawk came up the side of the ridge and then made a hard left turn. Now he was skimming low over the top of the ridge, following it up.

Fernandez and Nicholson opened the sliding cabin doors. The freezing wind blasted through the cabin.

The copilot was working the forward-looking infrared turret. "I've got tracers in the air farther up," he reported. "There's the firefight."

The pilot was flying on night-vision goggles. "I see it. Okay, there's the strobe in the rocks."

"I've got it too," said the copilot.

The pilot keyed the microphone button. "Seven Oscar, Hammer-One. I have your strobe."

"Roger," Doc Ellsworth replied. "Hurry up, we're down to our last rounds here."

The Blackhawk tore up the ridge. With the FLIR the copilot could easily pick out the hot human bodies among the cold rocks. He identified the SEALs in their small perimeter around the strobe by the thermal tape on their clothing.

"Jesus Christ!" the copilot exclaimed. "The bad guys are right on top of them."

The pilot rose up over the strobe and turned the helicopter sideways. As soon as his side was unmasked, the door gunner opened up. The minigun gave off a high-pitched whine as the six Gatling gun barrels fired at two thousand rounds per minute. That much 7.62mm coming in that fast would turn solid rock into gravel. Anything that got in the path of a minigun's bullet stream had a tendency to go away. The door gunner worked his fire right across the Syrian front line.

The other door gunner pushed the stretcher out the opposite door and lowered the hoist cable.

Fernandez and Nicholson kicked the caving ladder out the other side.

Pinging sounds reverberated inside the helicopter.

"We're taking rounds," the copilot shouted.

Fernandez and Nicholson threw themselves onto the cabin floor and opened fire with their SAWs.

2015 hours
North central Lebanese mountains

As the Blackhawk reached the zone, the SEALs on the ground tossed the last of their grenades to put the Syrians' heads down.

The Blackhawk turned and dropped until it was only seven feet or so above the ground. The wheels were almost touching the rocks. That took some flying.

When the metal-frame Stokes stretcher came down the hoist, Doc Ellsworth grabbed one end of Higgins's stretcher and Ed DeWitt the other with his good hand. They slid Higgins into the Stokes, and Doc cinched the webbing straps tight. Doc waved and the stretcher rose. It spun around as it went up. The door gunner grabbed the stretcher, worked the control to give the cabin some slack, and yanked the stretcher into the cabin.

DeWitt raced around to the other side of the helicopter where the caving ladder was flapping back and forth in the rotor wash. He made a running leap at it, trying to hit as high up as he could. He climbed one-handed, almost falling as the helicopter shook, but made it high enough for Fernandez and Nicholson to reach down and grab him. As they dragged him roughly into the cabin, DeWitt screamed from the pain in his broken arm. But once in, he still got up on his knees and emptied his last AKM magazine out the door.

After DeWitt went up, all the SEALs fell back toward the ladder.

A Syrian with a PKM machine gun rose up in front of Jaybird Sterling and fired at the Blackhawk. Jaybird cut him down with his last few rounds rapid-fire. When the magazine ran out, he threw the AKM in the direction of the Syrians. He pulled out his Makarov pistol and sprinted for the helicopter.

Murdock saw the caving ladder flapping free. He knew that if it got blown up into the rotors their ride was going to come crashing down. He made a diving grab for the ladder and hooked an arm around one rung. He put his weight on it and brought the AKM up to his shoulder. The minigun was screaming just above his head.

Jaybird came running up.

"Go, go, go!" Murdock shouted.

Jaybird hesitated a brief instant, then went up the ladder.

2015 hours
Blackhawk Hammer-One

The belt on Miguel Fernandez's SAW ran out just as he saw a Syrian stand up from the rocks with an RPG-7 launcher on his shoulder.

Fernandez screamed at Red, but couldn't be heard above all the noise. He forced himself to take his eyes off the RPG gunner and tear off the old belt box, get a fresh one out of his vest, and snap it in. Too slow, too slow. The feed cover was open—he laid the new belt over the feed tray.

The RPG rocket came out of the launcher with a tremendous flash. Fernandez saw it heading straight for him.

The rocket passed right over the top of the rotors. Fernandez hammered the feed cover down.

The Syrian stood staring at the helicopter as if he couldn't believe he'd missed. Fernandez let fly with a continuous fifty-round burst that left the SAW barrel smoking. The Syrian fell back into the rocks. Unlike Jaybird, Fernandez wasn't dehydrated, and he did piss his pants.

Warning lights were blinking in the cockpit. The pilot held the Blackhawk steady. They weren't going anywhere.

2015 hours
North central Lebanese mountains

Magic Brown shot another Syrian soldier as he backed toward the helicopter. The Syrians were pushing forward. Magic had just reached the ladder when two Syrians appeared near the tail of the helicopter. Magic dropped one of them, then the hammer clicked on an empty chamber as the second Syrian reared back to throw a grenade. Rounds cracked past Magic's shoulder. The Syrian fell, and lost his grip on the grenade. Magic ducked. The grenade exploded beside the Syrian.

Murdock had fired from the base of the ladder. He gestured frantically for Magic to get up. Magic did.

Razor Roselli killed a Syrian who'd made it all the way up to the perimeter, only to hesitate fatally when confronted with someone wearing the same uniform. Razor bolted for the Blackhawk.

A round hit him in the ankle and took him off his feet. Razor tried to get up off the ground, but couldn't.

Murdock released the ladder. He got over to Razor and dropped to his knees. Razor threw his arms around Murdock's neck. Murdock strained to his feet with Razor hanging onto his back. The pain was blinding.

Murdock staggered over to the ladder. He dropped his AKM and grabbed the rungs. He pulled himself up one step, and it seemed like lights were flashing before his eyes.

Six 120mm mortar illumination rounds popped in the air above the helicopter. The effect was like being on the field of a football stadium during a night game.

Murdock made it up another rung, and then couldn't make his legs move any more.

Then Razor's weight suddenly came off his shoulders.

2016 hours
MH-60K Blackhawk Hammer-One

When the flares popped, the Blackhawk crew flipped up their now-useless night-vision goggles. It was an incredibly dangerous transition to make while flying.

When they saw the lieutenant stop moving on the ladder, Jaybird and Magic scrambled back down. They snatched Razor off Murdock's back and passed him up into the cabin. Then they took hold of Murdock's wrists and lifted him up. The others grabbed him and pulled him into the cabin. Jaybird and Magic clambered up the ladder.

"Go!" the SEALs in the cabin screamed. "Go, go, go!"

The pilot swung the Blackhawk down the ridge while the SEALs were still pulling up the caving ladder. A few seconds later the ridge masked the Syrian fire. Then the Blackhawk was out from under the light of the flares, and the crew went back on the NVGs.

There was no cheering or exultation in the back of the Blackhawk. There were hurt SEALs who needed to be attended to. Fernandez and Nicholson slammed the cabin doors shut.

The metal floor was slick with blood, and the empty cartridge casings rolled around underfoot like ball bearings. Doc Ellsworth slipped twice trying to get across the cabin. One of the door gunners handed Doc his infrared flashlight.

Magic had already tied a battle dressing onto Razor's ankle. The bone was broken, so Doc slipped on a splint, gave him a shot of morphine, and started an IV with a bag from Fernandez's trauma kit.

Murdock sat slumped against the back wall of the cabin. Doc was busy, and enough was enough. He took out one of his own morphine syrettes, jabbed it into his thigh, and squeezed the tube dry. What was that sensation? It couldn't be the morphine yet. Ah, that was it. It was warm in the cabin. He hadn't felt that way in a long time.

The Blackhawk sped down the mountain ridge. The crew saw the thermal strips of the circling backup bird and formed up behind it. Far too many warning lights were still lit up on the console. The copilot ran through the systems.

"FLIR is down," he reported. "So is the radar."

With no forward-looking infrared or terrain-following-and-avoidance radar, the pilot was going to have to ride the treetops with no aids other than his Mark-1 eyeballs looking through night-vision goggles. Well, that was how the first Nightstalkers had done it. So could he. The stick was feeling heavy. He didn't want to put the Blackhawk through any sudden maneuvers. Something might break.

"Do we have the nav?" he asked the copilot.

"Nothing but GPS, and that keeps going down and coming up. Radar warning is down too."

At least they didn't have to sit and worry about being shot at, the pilot thought. They wouldn't know until they were already hit. He keyed his mike button. "Hammer-Two, Hammer-One, over?"

"Hammer-Two."

At least the radio worked. "Hammer-Two, we don't have a lot of systems left. We'll follow you all the way. Keep an eye on us in case we lose our radio, over."

"Roger."

The Blackhawks turned off the top of the ridge and headed west down the slope. They followed a different route from the one they'd taken in.

If the injured Blackhawk could no longer stay in the air it would put down, hopefully without crashing, and everyone inside would transfer to the second ship. No one looked forward to doing that in the middle of Lebanon at night. Of course, if anything happened to a helicopter at that altitude, there wouldn't be much time to react.

The turbines were screaming too loud for casual conversation. Jaybird got the attention of the door gunners and pantomimed drinking. One of them tapped his hand to his forehead as if to say he was sorry for not thinking of it. They passed around all the crew canteens and water bottles.

Murdock refused a canteen until all his men had something to drink. He finally accepted one, and the flat tepid water tasted delicious. The morphine was providing a wonderful soothing warmth.

The port turbine engine started to give off a knocking sound. Jaybird waved his hand, as if signaling for a waiter, to get the door gunners' attention again.

Ed DeWitt was sitting near the front of the cabin. He tapped a gunner on the leg and pointed to the back.

Jaybird aimed his thumb up at the engine. The gunner picked his way through the crowded cabin until he was right below the engine. He lifted up the bottom of his helmet so he could hear clearly. Then he began talking rapidly into his microphone.

"If it goes we'll shut it down," the pilot replied, still unruffled. "But we've got too much weight and not enough altitude to shut it down now and still keep flying."

The knocking continued. At least it was rhythmic, Murdock thought. He couldn't fly a helicopter, and he tried not to get agitated about things he had no control over.

The two Blackhawks crossed the coastline between Byblos and Batroûn.

"Feet wet," the pilot reported.

Murdock motioned for Fernandez and Nicholson to open the cabin doors. If the helicopter died there was no possibility of landing now, only a crash into the sea. And when helicopters hit the water, even gently, they sank. And because the heavy engines and rotors were above the cabin, helicopters flipped upside down when they sank. If that happened, everyone inside would need to get out fast.

"Screw it," the pilot said. "We're outside the territorial limits, I'm getting some altitude." He pulled back on the cyclic and began a very slow, very gentle climb.

The engine knocking became faster. Murdock could see the reflection of the moon on the water below. He really didn't feel like ending the evening with a swim. This was about the time Razor would say: "Don't worry, Boss, we probably won't survive the initial crash anyway." But Razor wouldn't be saying much until the drugs wore off.

One of the door gunners was pointing to the front of the helicopter. Those SEALs who could raised themselves off the floor to be able to see out the windscreen. And there was the *George Washington* glowing in the moonlight.

The lead Blackhawk peeled off to allow the damaged one to land first. The carrier was sailing into the wind, which was how the helicopter would land.

As the Blackhawk dropped, Murdock's view out the cabin door changed from dark ocean waves to flat black no-skid flight deck.

As soon as the wheels touched down, the copilot instantly shut the engines down. They were finished taking chances for the night.

There was minimal crew on the flight deck, and they had been instructed to forget everything they saw. Or else.

White-shirted and red-crossed medical corpsmen were waiting with stretchers. The SEALs passed Higgins out first, then Razor. DeWitt walked to sick bay, as did Murdock with the aid of the morphine.

The SEALs didn't kiss the flight deck. But now that his officers and chief were gone, Jaybird Sterling leaned between the cockpit seats and planted a firm wet kiss on the cheek of the pilot. The warrant officer jumped, startled, and then broke into a huge grin. He knew SEALs, and was probably glad he hadn't been French-kissed. Then Jaybird gave him the traditional, heartfelt, but very unofficial Special Forces crowning tribute. "You sweet motherfucker, don't you *never* die!"

50

Saturday, November 11

2145 hours
Aboard the *U.S.S. George Washington*
Eastern Mediterranean Sea

Blake Murdock would have loved to catch a little shut-eye. But he was lying naked, on his stomach, atop an examination table in the sick bay. And a doctor was giving him the facts of life.

"No, I wouldn't even think of putting you under," the doctor said, shaking his head. He was a lieutenant, wearing nice clean khakis. "Not in your present condition." He pinched the skin of Murdock's forearm. When he released it the skin stood right up. "See how dehydrated you are? No, we'll just give you a local and probe for fragments. The big ones, that is. The little ones will work their way out on their own, eventually."

"Great," Murdock said dryly. He handed the beaker to one of the corpsmen. "How about another water, Doc?"

"That's your third one," the corpsman said in amazement. It was a liter beaker. "Are you sure you don't have to go?"

"You'll be the first to know," Murdock assured him.

Doc Ellsworth entered the compartment, freshly showered and dressed in a clean unmarked flight suit. He cast a professional eye over Murdock's backside. "Hey, Lieutenant, we're going to have to get you a laminated chit for when you go through airports. You'll never make it through a metal detector after this."

"What's the word?" said Murdock.

The Doc turned serious. "The Professor is still in surgery. He's critical. Razor's in surgery too. I saw his X-rays, the ankle's pretty well shattered. They'll just clean things up in there. When we get to CONUS they'll open up the leg again and screw everything back together."

"Is he looking at a medical?" Murdock asked. Meaning a medical discharge or loss of SEAL qualification.

Doc shrugged. "Time will tell. Mister DeWitt's fracture didn't get any worse. He's in plaster now. He may have bruised some internal organs; we'll be keeping an eye on him. As far as everyone else, you're talking first- and second-degree burns, bruises, sprains, ripped and pulled muscles. I'll be handing out Motrin for quite a while."

"You did a hell of a job, Doc." Murdock smiled. "Shit, just the positive thinking alone."

Doc grinned back. "I kept telling you, sir, but I guess you had to experience it for yourself. Now you see that it works, you'll be thinking extra positive next time and you won't get hurt at all."

"You must have converted Jaybird. I don't think he got a scratch."

"It's his aura," Doc explained. "Son of a bitch has an aura so bright you could read by it."

From the puzzled looks they were getting, no one else in the compartment had the slightest idea what they were talking about.

"Get some sleep, Doc. I'll see you tomorrow."

Doc Ellsworth took another look at Murdock's situation and shook his head sadly. "I'd tell you to have fun, Lieutenant, but you aren't going to."

They had to stab him so many times to administer the local

anesthetic that Murdock started to wonder if he shouldn't just self-administer another syrette and let them go ahead and probe.

Don Stroh walked in. Evidently, Murdock thought, he'd flipped a coin with Kohler and lost.

"Blake, what can I say except that I'm sorry for everything."

Murdock made no reply.

Stroh went on. "The word from the overhead imagery is that the warehouse was absolutely flattened. Communications and signals intercepts indicate that you took out close to five hundred Syrians and Hezbollah, both at the warehouse and afterward."

Murdock thought that went a long way toward evening the score for the Beirut bombing. But what he said was, "I lost a good man, and I didn't have to. My men are wounded, and there was no need for them to get hurt."

"Blake, I . . ."

"Look, Don, I know it wasn't your call not to launch. But you can tell those assholes back at Langley that they better pray we don't take some leave when we get back and go spook hunting. Fuck!" Murdock looked over his shoulder. "Jeez, Doc, what are you using, a bayonet?"

"I'll talk to you later, Blake."

"Sure, Don."

Stroh left, and a whole platoon of SEALs came thundering in.

The doctor looked up from Murdock's ass and said in outrage, "Get all these people out of here!"

The corpsmen looked at the burly SEALs, then at each other, as if to say: "Who, us?"

"It's okay, Doc," Murdock said. "They're family."

"Hi, sir!" said Jaybird Sterling, as usual the spokesman. "We just talked with Doc Ellsworth. He said your ass was a sight to behold, so we had to come in and check it out for ourselves."

Murdock could hear the doctor grumbling behind him. "It's

okay, Doc. We'll be lucky if they don't head right for the mess deck and sell tickets to the crew." He turned to his SEALs. "I'm glad you're here. I wanted to tell you how proud I am of every one of you."

SEALs had the balls to do just about anything except accept a compliment without screwing around like a bunch of hyperactive schoolboys. They grinned, shuffled their feet, hung their heads, punched each other on the shoulders, and made remarks like, "We know you're just saying that 'cause your ass is hanging out, sir."

"Okay," said Murdock, "I showed you my ass, now get the hell out of here. Jaybird, you and Magic hold on for a second."

The rest of them left. Jaybird said, "The helicopter guys are taking pictures of our bird down in the hangar deck. They think it's probably the record for the most hits taken by a Blackhawk that still kept flying."

"They said another few minutes and that engine would have caught fire," said Magic.

"Thanks for getting me up that ladder, you two," said Murdock. "I ran out of gas."

"No problem, sir," said Magic.

"You try carrying around a moose like Razor and that'll happen," said Jaybird.

"What I really wanted to talk to you about," said Murdock, "is my choice for who's going to pinch-hit for Razor as platoon chief."

"Don't worry about a thing, sir," Jaybird said earnestly. "We may get a little crazy every now and then, but while you're laid up we'll back the guy one hundred percent."

Murdock began to shake with suppressed laughter, so much that the doctor, by now highly annoyed, had to halt work behind him.

"I'm glad to hear that," said Murdock, straining to hold it in. "Because you're the new platoon chief."

Jaybird's jaw dropped all the way to the deck. He stood thunderstruck. "No way, sir."

The laughter burst out of Murdock. "Way," he insisted between guffaws.

Magic Brown fell to the deck laughing.

"You're kidding, right, sir?" Jaybird said hopefully.

Murdock had to hold onto the table to support himself. He shook his head and managed to squeeze out, "Date of rank. You're the senior first class. Can't do anything about it. Hey, Magic," he called down to Magic Brown, who was still writhing on the deck. "Guess what? You're the new leading petty officer."

"Whatever you say, sir," Magic gasped, holding onto his belly. Every time he looked up at the expression on Jaybird's face, he went hysterical again.

Murdock wiped the tears from his eyes. "You're going to love the prestige. I've heard you say it before. The chief just dicks off and orders people around."

Jaybird opened his mouth to protest.

"No, no, that's okay," said Murdock. "I want you to consider this a reward for a job well done. You can start with the equipment. Make sure everything we brought aboard is cleaned, accounted for, and packed for disembarkation. Get Razor's inventory list out of his quarters. We left a lot of gear behind in Lebanon, including some very expensive sniper rifles. Prepare a list with serial numbers so we can start work on the paperwork to write it off as lost in combat. While you're doing that, start putting together a chronology of events and statements from everyone, including Miguel and Red, for the after-action report."

Jaybird's mouth was still hanging open.

"Get some chow first," Murdock said benevolently. "And a good night's sleep. You can get cracking on everything tomorrow morning. Then come and see me in the afternoon and I'll give you the rest of the things to do."

"The rest?" Jaybird asked faintly.

"The rest," Murdock said definitely. "And I want you to know that I've got every confidence in you. Now get out of here and quit distracting the doctor before he sews my butt cheeks together."

Magic, still giggling, led a dazed Jaybird Sterling from the compartment.

Murdock allowed himself another good laugh. He felt fifty pounds lighter. "Sorry about that, Doc. You can go back to work." He glanced over at the corpsman. "I think you need to hand over that urinal and help me roll over. Now I've really got to go."

"Quite a group you have there," the doctor mumbled from behind.

"Oh, they'll break your dishes and piss on your floor," said Murdock. "But they're worth the trouble."

51

Tuesday, November 14—Wednesday, November 15

In transit

Murdock made sure Razor was still pretty well doped up when he told him who was standing in for him. Murdock didn't want him to have an embolism or anything.

Razor's evil smile was a little dreamier, but still a sight to behold. "Jaybird'll get me back on the job if he has to take charge of my rehab himself," he predicted.

Murdock spent the next three days limping around with his own evil smile well hidden as the responsibility, rather than the authority, worked its magic on Jaybird Sterling. Just as it had on Razor Roselli. And George MacKenzie before him.

Jaybird organized, cajoled, persuaded, and occasionally threatened. The gear was cleaned, inventoried, and packed. The paperwork was started. The platoon was ready to go.

They flew off the ship on the 14th. The platoon was on one of the Chinooks, with Razor and Higgins strapped to stretchers and a Navy medical team attending. The other Chinook carried the Army maintenance people, with the wounded Blackhawk slung beneath it. The surviving Blackhawk flew off under its own power.

They landed at Sigonella after dark. C-5's were waiting to take the helicopters back to Fort Campbell, Kentucky.

The SEALs and the medical team went from helicopters right onto an Air Force C-9 Nightingale. This was a McDonnell Douglas DC-9 airliner specially fitted out as an aeromedical evacuation aircraft to transport casualties between theaters of operation. The Navy medical team disembarked and left Higgins and Razor in the care of the Nightingale medical crew.

The Nightingale lifted off immediately and flew from Sigonella to Rhein Main airport in Frankfurt, Germany. Higgins was taken off to the hospital there for more surgery. He was still unconscious, and for security reasons the platoon couldn't accompany him off the aircraft. But a SEAL lieutenant commander and senior chief from Special Operations Command Europe were there to take care of one of their own.

At Rhein Main the SEALs dragged Razor Roselli and their equipment off the C-9 and onto a C-141 transport. That too took off immediately.

The C-141 stopped in Shannon to refuel. The SEALs ate foil-wrapped TV dinners and stared longingly out the windows in the direction of the duty-free shop.

From Ireland they stopped in Newfoundland to refuel. The SEALs were not allowed off the aircraft. The C-141 hopped across the U.S., finally touching down at North Island Naval Air Station.

Razor Roselli was taken off in an ambulance to San Diego Naval Hospital, and the rest of the very exhausted and jet-lagged 3rd Platoon boarded trucks for the short drive to Coronado.

52
Epilogue

Third Platoon received a very respectful reception back at SEAL Team Seven headquarters. No one knew the details of the operation, or would, but word had gotten around that 3rd Platoon had really counted coup.

In his will Kos Kosciuszko named Blake Murdock the executor of his estate. There wasn't much for Murdock to do. Kos's parents were dead. As Kos said in a letter attached to the will, "My other relatives never cared about me, and the feeling is mutual." He'd been married once; a SEAL divorce and no children. The Navy was his home and the teams his life.

"Don't any of you feel sorry for me," he said in the letter. "I loved every minute of it."

Kos left most of his money to Navy Relief. Treasured possessions, souvenirs from his travels, and his beloved gun collection were earmarked to specific SEALs.

Blake Murdock got a Remington 12-gauge autoloader because he'd never managed to outscore Kos when they'd shot skeet. Razor Roselli got a lovingly customized Colt .45 because: "He's always getting himself into trouble and ought to have something to get him out."

Magic Brown received a pre-1964 30–06 Model 70 Winchester with a beautiful walnut stock. The first time Murdock ever saw Magic cry was when he gave him the rifle.

Jaybird Sterling got a mahogany sculpture of some long-forgotten pagan fertility god with fantastically outsized genitalia. For a long time after that Jaybird walked around with a faraway look of remembrance in his eyes.

The other SEALs of the platoon all got something. The rest of Kos's possessions, never more than would fit in a self-storage locker during deployments, went to Goodwill.

Contrary to what Murdock had thought, there was to be no burial of an empty coffin with full military honors. Kos had been to too many of those, the letter said. He'd always hated them.

In an eerie piece of prophecy that raised the hairs on the back of Murdock's neck, Kos wrote that if he had fallen in battle, he hoped that no one would get hurt or go out of their way on his behalf. "Once you're done with it, the body is just an empty container. It's stupid to concern yourself with the container, only what's inside it."

But if it wasn't too much trouble, Kos wanted to be cremated and his ashes scattered at sea. He didn't want the service for burial at sea to be read "by any pencil-neck Navy chaplain. I'm definite on that, sir. It has got to be a SEAL Master Chief. If George MacKenzie isn't around, anyone you can dig up will do. And no eulogies or speeches. I hate the idea of you all lying about what a great guy I was. Just keep it to yourselves."

There were so many SEALs and chiefs from Special Boat Squadron One who wanted to go that they ended up on a large and elderly LCU landing craft. It was a gray and overcast day, with heavy chop. The SEALs wore their blues. Razor Roselli was in a cast that ran all the way up to his crotch, supported on either side by Jaybird and Magic.

The members of 3rd Platoon had made up a package with letters, mementos, and Budweiser badges. George MacKenzie read the centuries-old service for those lost at sea. The package slid over the side. SEALs from the other teams tossed wreaths. The LCU headed back to shore.

Kos had left money for an open bar at his favorite drinking establishment. A place where the proprietor didn't mind a ring of solemn SEALs each tossing a shot of Bacardi 151 onto the bar and setting the liquid ablaze. It was a SEAL tradition—their version of the Viking funeral. Then they all got loudly shit-faced and told Kos Kosciuszko stories long into the night.

George MacKenzie's drinking days were long over. When the glass fell out of Blake Murdock's hand while he was in the process of swallowing, Mac thought it was time to take the lieutenant home. Before he did he picked the pockets of all the SEALs in the platoon and removed their car keys. He left cab fare for them with the bartender, along with an unveiled threat that it had better be used for cab fare.

"Let's get out of here," he said to Murdock.

"Okay," Murdock replied. He was well into the zombie mode. If someone had said set yourself on fire, he would have replied, "Okay." He got off the bar stool.

Mac caught him before he hit the deck. He got Murdock out to his pickup, positioning his head carefully so that any vomiting would take place out the window. Mac wasn't a Master Chief for nothing.

"I did it, George," Murdock mumbled drunkenly as they drove along.

"Sure you did," said Mac. Always humor the drunk.

"I killed him."

"That you did."

"I killed Kos."

"What the hell are you talking about?"

"I killed him. Walked right into the ambush."

MacKenzie had heard the story from Razor Roselli. He brought Murdock back to his apartment, threw a blanket over him, and positioned a wastebasket next to his head within easy reach.

He waited until afternoon the next day to give Murdock a call and invite him over for dinner.

Murdock showed up on time, still looking a little shaky. Mac's SEAL wife and SEAL kids had left for the evening. He threw steaks on the grill and offered Murdock a beer.

Murdock shook his head. "I'm on the wagon."

They ate, and then stretched out on the lawn chairs listening to the bug-zapper.

"You think you're responsible for getting Kos killed," said MacKenzie. "You're full of shit."

Murdock glared at him.

"If you're responsible for Kos being dead, then you're responsible for the other six being alive."

"Sure," said Murdock. "For Higgins being in the hospital for the next six months. For Razor maybe never being able to parachute or even run on that ankle again."

"Saint Murdock," MacKenzie said scornfully.

"You trying to piss me off, George?"

"You piss *me* off. You've lost SEALs before. We've lost SEALs before. So what is this bullshit?"

Murdock got up to leave.

"Is it because Kos died and you loved the guy more than you loved the others? Or is it because your dad's a scumbag politician so you have to be the white knight who carries every decision he makes like a two-ton cross? Sit down, I'm not done yet."

Murdock was livid. But he stopped, and leaned against the grape arbor.

"I read your after-action report," said Mac. "Quite a barn-dance card."

Murdock looked up at him

"You think that report is going to be your revenge against the CIA for leaving you out there. Nail their hides to the wall. Kos died before they left you hanging, so that's your fault. And everyone else who got hurt is theirs." MacKenzie snorted in derision. "You're a real fucking Boy Scout, you know that?"

"George," Murdock said angrily, "I'm telling you—"

"You know who that report goes to?" MacKenzie shouted. "The admiral, who is going to question your judgment for writing it up that way. And then it goes to the fucking CIA! And they're going to take that report and classify it Top Secret You're-an-Asshole-Lieutenant-Murdock. And they're going to make sure that the only person cleared for it is the Director of the CIA, and then they're going to forget to tell him about it. He's got too much to read already. They're laughing about it right now!

"Let me tell you something," said Mac. "And I'm only doing it because you're a hell of a fine officer and I'd hate to see the community either lose you or get rid of you. Generals and admirals hate Special Forces because they hate covert operations. Politicians love Special Forces because they love covert operations. You're dreaming if you think a sixteen-man SEAL platoon is ever going to be master of its fate. We are going to get used, occasionally stupidly. And the same stupidity is going to get some of us used *up* every now and then. Let me clue you in. We are professional warriors. We take the King's shilling and we fight the King's war. When you, me, Higgins, Razor, and Kos pinned on that Budweiser, we signed a contract of unlimited liability. Kos knew that. You read his letter. You just didn't understand it."

"I understood it."

"All bullshit aside, you do this job because you like to fight. So do I. You've got the real license to kill, but you don't get to pick—they do. Now, those are the facts of life. You've got a choice. I made it, so did Razor, and so did Admiral Raymond. You either do the job or you pick up your hat and you go."

"I can't," Murdock said desperately. "You're right, I love it. I hate the part you talked about, but I love the job."

"You can't separate the parts. We tell you to take care of your men, love them like your own children. We tell you to accomplish the mission. But if you or your men have to die to accomplish the mission, then we expect you to die. Why do you think there are so few SEALs? And there aren't even that many of them who can talk the talk *and* walk the walk."

"I guess I have to live with it, then."

"I'm glad to hear you say that. You've got to live with Kos too, because a man can't take back anything that's happened in his life. Now, I want you to hang that Boy Scout uniform back up in the closet while I give you some real world. You did the CIA's work. They're happy, and they're going to pay you off. I've seen the citations. Navy Cross for you and a posthumous one for Kos. Silver Stars for the rest. DFCs for the helo crews. Bronze Stars with Combat V's for Miguel and Red. Should do your careers some good. And if you walk into Admiral Raymond's office and talk to him about it before he forgets all about you, you'll probably get that posting to the Kampfschwimmers."

"So that's how you do it."

"No, you can be Saint Murdock and get burned at the stake with the rest of the holy men. And while you're doing that, some political ass-kisser is going to end up being our admiral instead of you."

Murdock let his breath out hard. "Have dinner with the Master Chief and you'll never need a psychiatrist. You should be the admiral, George."

"Now you're talking like an officer. An admiral can fuck up every hour and it makes no difference. Without Master Chiefs the whole Navy shuts right down. So what are you going to do?"

"I guess I'm going to call Inga tonight, and go see the admiral on Monday."

"Now that sounds like a plan," said MacKenzie. Sometimes it took a Master Chief to wrap things up.